Introductions seem to be in order . . .

Even as Rory was jumping up from the couch, she was taking aim at the man in the chair. In spite of her trembling hands, she managed to keep him firmly in her sights. How could the shadowy product of her imagination actually exist in the harsh glare of the lamp? The bogeyman was never in the closet when you finally built up the courage to look. And the monster was never really under the bed, even if you were sure you could hear it breathing. So why hadn't this shadow simply evaporated in the light, leaving her to laugh at her own foolishness? But there he was in her crosshairs, and what made it even worse, he seemed perfectly relaxed and comfortable in spite of her obvious advantage over him. In fact, she thought she detected a bit of a smile on his lips as if he were just fine with the way things were going.

Rory felt anger quickly overtaking shock. "Who the hell are you?" she demanded, her voice strong and steady even though her insides were quivering.

"Ezekiel Drummond," he said, in a drawl that was a mixture of southern and something else she couldn't immediately place. "Pleased to make your acquaintance, ma'am."

"A police artist matches wits with the ghost of an Old West marshal as they work together to solve a double homicide, but it's the chemistry between this modern woman and crusty cowboy that will draw readers in to *Sketch Me If You Can*. A spirited debut!"
—Cle

Sketch Me
If You Can

Sharon Pape

BERKLEY PRIME CRIME, NEW YORK

THE BERKLEY PUBLISHING GROUP
Published by the Penguin Group
Penguin Group (USA) Inc.
375 Hudson Street, New York, New York 10014, USA
Penguin Group (Canada), 90 Eglinton Avenue East, Suite 700, Toronto, Ontario M4P 2Y3, Canada
(a division of Pearson Penguin Canada Inc.)
Penguin Books Ltd., 80 Strand, London WC2R 0RL, England
Penguin Group Ireland, 25 St. Stephen's Green, Dublin 2, Ireland (a division of Penguin Books Ltd.)
Penguin Group (Australia), 250 Camberwell Road, Camberwell, Victoria 3124, Australia
(a division of Pearson Australia Group Pty. Ltd.)
Penguin Books India Pvt. Ltd., 11 Community Centre, Panchsheel Park, New Delhi—110 017, India
Penguin Group (NZ), 67 Apollo Drive, Rosedale, North Shore 0632, New Zealand
(a division of Pearson New Zealand Ltd.)
Penguin Books (South Africa) (Pty.) Ltd., 24 Sturdee Avenue, Rosebank, Johannesburg 2196,
South Africa

Penguin Books Ltd., Registered Offices: 80 Strand, London WC2R 0RL, England

This is a work of fiction. Names, characters, places, and incidents either are the product of the author's imagination or are used fictitiously, and any resemblance to actual persons, living or dead, business establishments, events, or locales is entirely coincidental. The publisher does not have any control over and does not assume any responsibility for author or third-party websites or their content.

SKETCH ME IF YOU CAN

A Berkley Prime Crime Book / published by arrangement with the author

PRINTING HISTORY
Berkley Prime Crime mass-market edition / August 2010

Copyright © 2010 by Sharon Pape.
Cover illustration by Dan Craig.
Interior text design by Laura K. Corless.

ISBN: 978-0-425-23604-8

BERKLEY® PRIME CRIME
Berkley Prime Crime Books are published by The Berkley Publishing Group,
a division of Penguin Group (USA) Inc.,
375 Hudson Street, New York, New York 10014.
BERKLEY® PRIME CRIME and the PRIME CRIME logo are trademarks of Penguin Group
(USA) Inc.

PRINTED IN THE UNITED STATES OF AMERICA

10 9 8 7 6 5 4 3 2 1

For Jason and Lauren,
children of my heart and soul,
this child of my mind.

Acknowledgments

A loving thank-you to my family for their help brainstorming plot issues.

Special thanks go to Vivian Sanzeri, dearest of friends. Your advice is always invaluable, your instincts always dead-on.

I'd also like to thank Suffolk County Detective John S. Majoribanks (Ret.) for kindly fielding my questions.

Any inaccuracies in the depiction of police procedure should be attributed solely to the author.

Prologue

It was over in less than three minutes. The intruders went about their work with the spare efficiency of professionals. The taller man held the flashlight at exactly the right angle while his shorter companion applied the cloth steeped in chloroform to the victim's nose and mouth. He held it there just long enough to prevent the man from awakening and resisting their ministrations. Then he placed the cloth in a zippered plastic bag and withdrew a hypodermic needle. The taller man refocused the flashlight, synchronizing it to his partner's needs as if they worked with one mind. No high-wire act was more practiced, more seamless in its performance.

To ensure that the puncture mark would be virtually undetectable, the shorter man dispensed the contents of the needle into the underside of the victim's tongue. Then he placed all the evidence of their visit back into the small duffel bag on the floor between them. The taller man turned off the flashlight and picked up the duffel.

As the two drew back from the bed, the clock radio on the nightstand crashed to the floor, startling them. After a hurried discussion they decided that one of them must have stepped on the wire, pulling the radio down. They continued on to the bedroom door where they planned to watch the results of their handiwork. But as they waited for the next act to unfold, the security alarm started wailing. Both men had the same thought—the system had not been engaged when they'd picked the lock and entered the premises. Of course, it didn't matter how the alarm had become activated. All that mattered was that they would have to leave before seeing the grand finale.

They were already making their way down the stairs when their victim bolted upright in bed. His breathing was shallow and labored, his eyes wide with terror. He clutched at his chest with one hand and with the other grabbed frantically for the telephone on the nightstand. He managed to punch in 911 before losing consciousness. In the darkness of the room, he never saw the darker shape standing at the foot of the bed.

Chapter 1

It was six o'clock by the time Rory finished with the elderly couple who'd come into Suffolk County Police Headquarters to report the theft of the woman's purse. Rory should have been able to produce a reasonable likeness of the thief in fifteen minutes, tops. Unfortunately, though, they weren't able to agree on any of the details, from the length of the man's hair, to the shape of his eyes, to the pattern of his shirt and endlessly on down to the type of shoes he was wearing. By the time she'd ushered them out the door, almost two hours had passed.

She made a few final adjustments to the sketch and dropped it off with Detective Leah Russell, who agreed to distribute it in-house and fax it to the other precincts. Then Rory dug her purse out of the deep lower drawer of her desk and grabbed her linen blazer off the back of her chair. On her way out, she took a minute to stop in the ladies' room and freshen up for her meeting with Lou Friedlander, Mac's attorney.

When she checked her image in the mirror, she was grateful that her hairdresser had talked her into going short so that her auburn hair framed her face and required little effort to maintain. There was no need to fix her makeup since she didn't wear any. The hazel eyes that peered back at her were wide and canted up ever so slightly at the outer edges, a narrow, black line ringing the irises like the outlines in a child's coloring book. At twenty-eight the only distinguishing mark on her face was the single dimple that notched into one side of her mouth when she smiled. The asymmetry gave her a disarmingly unfinished look, as if she'd been snatched away a moment too soon from the gifted artist who had created her. In Rory's opinion, it just made her smile appear lopsided.

She splashed some cold water onto her cheeks, blotted it off with a piece of paper towel from the dispenser and headed for the door. If rush-hour traffic wasn't too bad on the Long Island Expressway and no eighteen-wheelers had jackknifed from going seventy miles an hour two feet from the car ahead of them, she might still make the six thirty appointment.

The one benefit of having spent the last two hours trying to wrest a description from the elderly couple was that Rory hadn't been able to dwell on the reason why she was going to see the attorney. Her uncle Mac's death a week ago had been so sudden that even now it didn't seem entirely real. One moment life was clicking along at its normal, often tedious pace, and the next, without any warning, the world dropped out of its orbit and started freefalling through space. How could a heart just stop? Shouldn't there be a pain, an ache, a skipped beat necessitating tests, worried phone calls between family members, conferences with specialists, anxious decisions about the best course of action to take? Shouldn't there be time for prayers? Time to say good-bye? A heart pumps for fifty-two years as reliably as the sun rises and sets, and then one day it just stops?

Uncle Mac had been so much more than her father's brother and her favorite uncle. He'd been her friend, her mentor, her ice skating buddy, her sand-castle-building engineer, her partner in crime who would come to babysit and take her out to have a banana split at ten o'clock at night. He'd always seemed so much younger than her parents, although there were only five years between him and her dad. Somehow he lived bigger, acted younger.

Once, after she and Mac had been busted returning home too late from one of their ice cream forays, her parents banned him from babysitting for a month. Mac had suffered his punishment with quiet equanimity, promising Rory that he'd plan a special day for their reunion. But for six-year-old Rory, it was the longest month of her life.

Lost in her memories, Rory missed the entrance into the parking lot of the brick colonial building on Commack Road. Surprised to find herself there already, she made a quick U-turn at the next light and backtracked. As she pulled into a parking spot, the digital clock on the dashboard of the Honda indicated that she had two minutes to spare.

She locked the car and drew in a deep breath to steady herself as she marched into the building. Her stomach was clenched with the kind of tension that reminded her of trips to the dentist when she was a child. She'd already postponed this meeting twice, pleading first a migraine and then job-related issues. Friedlander had rescheduled without complaint, simply reiterating that he needed only fifteen minutes of her time. He had no idea just how much she was dreading those fifteen minutes.

She found Jacobs, Milo and Friedlander listed in the directory in the lobby and took the elevator up to the second floor of the three-story building. At forty-eight, Lou Friedlander was the youngest of the three partners in the small firm, which was not to say that he was young by Rory's standards.

When she entered the office suite, there was no one at the reception desk. She was about to show herself down the carpeted hallway to the left in search of Friedlander when a man emerged from one of the half dozen doors that marked its length. He was short and stocky with a manicured mustache and goatee that Rory figured was an attempt to compensate for his receding hairline. He had his suit jacket on, but his shirt collar was open with no tie, a concession to either the warm weather or the lateness of the hour. Not that the informality bothered Rory, who considered most of society's rules outdated and often as ridiculous as the pillory and stockades. It was just an observation, a noting of details. She supposed it was the artist in her that subconsciously processed every angle and nuance, every hue and shadow.

When she'd been struggling to select her college major, Mac had pointed out that her attention to detail would serve her well if she chose to follow in his footsteps as a private detective. But while Mac's work intrigued Rory, she'd wanted to incorporate art into her career. She'd finally settled on a major in criminology, with a minor in portrait art. For the first few years after college she'd been happy enough working as a sketch artist for the Suffolk County Police Department, but lately she was finding it harder and harder to muster up the enthusiasm to crawl out of bed in the morning.

"Lou Freidlander," the man said, extending his hand as he came up to her. "You must be Aurora McCain. I would have known you anywhere." His voice was appropriately solemn, but his lips curved up in a small, sympathetic smile within the framework of his beard. "I'm so very sorry for your loss." His hand squeezed hers for emphasis before he let it go.

She nodded her thanks. "Please call me Rory."

"Yes, of course," Friedlander said as he ushered her into his office. "I should have remembered that."

A large oak desk was the centerpiece of the office, its surface awash in paper, a computer monitor rising out of the chaos like a lighthouse rising above a stormy sea. There was a contoured, leather chair behind the desk and two smaller chairs in front of it. A credenza, also in oak, ran the length of the window, and several wooden filing cabinets occupied the far side of the room.

"Please, have a seat," he said. "Can I get you some coffee? I can make it iced if you like."

"No thanks, I'm fine," Rory said, sitting on the edge of the closest chair. The last thing she wanted was to prolong her time there.

"If you change your mind, it'll only take a minute."

She forced a smile, wondering if her desperation to leave was that clearly written on her face.

"We've actually met before, you know," Friedlander said as he took his seat behind the desk. "At

a housewarming Mac had years ago when he bought
his first house, that little Cape Cod. You couldn't have
been more than seven or eight at the time. Of course, I
don't expect that you'd remember me. I was just another
grownup in a house full of them. But even back then you
made it clear to everyone that you hated being called
Aurora."

Rory had refused to answer to "Aurora" by the time
she was enrolled in nursery school. "Rory" suited her
just fine. That, and of course "L'il Mac," which her
parents had dubbed her because she was always trying
to emulate her uncle whom they'd long referred to as
"Big Mac." Not only was he three inches taller than his
brother, but he also had a serious addiction to fast food,
the greasier the better.

"In fact," Friedlander was saying, "looking at you
now, I can still see that fiery little redhead with the
freckled nose pocketing a handful of cookies after her
mom said she couldn't have anymore."

"I actually remember that party." Rory felt her face
relax into a smile at the memory. "Those peanut but-
ter chocolate chip cookies were my favorite. That's why
Uncle Mac ordered them."

"He was crazy about you," Friedlander said with a
little sigh. "I'm sure you know that he thought of you
more like a daughter than a niece."

Her smile faded. "It was mutual," she murmured.
She looked down at her watch. She didn't need to be
anywhere else, but she needed to leave this office before
she dissolved into a sobbing mess.

Friedlander noted her discomfort. "I'm sorry," he
said in his back-to-business voice. "I know I promised
to have you out of here in fifteen minutes and I will."

Rory nodded her thanks, not trusting herself to speak around the knot still lodged in her throat.

The attorney sifted through the piles of documents on his desk until he found the one he was looking for. He pulled it out, creating a small avalanche in the process. "As I told you over the phone, Mac's will is very simple. He didn't leave a huge estate, but what he had he left to you. He also named you executor. Are your folks likely to contest it?"

"No, no, they're just pleased for me."

"Good. Mac was sure that it wouldn't be a problem, but I had to ask. You understand. There's really no need for me to read the will to you. This is a copy that you can have for your records." He leaned across the desk to hand Rory the two pages that constituted Mac's "Last Will and Testament." The words were formal and final, devoid of emotion. Rory wasn't sure what she had expected. Maybe something more colorful and Mac-like: "Laugh, love, enjoy life. Hope this helps."

Rory realized that the attorney was still speaking. She forced herself to focus on what he was saying.

". . . the house on Brandywine Lane is yours free and clear along with everything in it, all furnishings, artwork, et cetera. The mortgage was paid off last year, so if you want to hold on to it, all you'll have to do is keep up with the taxes. Mac's car is also yours free and clear."

"Safe, yet sexy," Mac had proclaimed when he'd stopped by three years ago to show the family the bright red Volvo convertible he'd just driven off the lot. They'd all piled in for a ride, Rory's folks reminiscing about the convertibles of their youth. Her mom didn't even complain that the wind was wrecking her hair.

"Of course you'll have to change the title, registration and insurance. You also inherit Mac's detective agency. In the beginning it wasn't worth much, but then it took off suddenly about five years ago. That's how he was able to renovate the house and all. I imagine you'll want to sell the business name and client list. You'll probably see a good profit from it.

"Mac's only other assets were two bank accounts. There's a checking account with three thousand dollars left in it after I paid the outstanding bills, as he'd instructed, and a savings account with another ten grand and change. Mac wasn't a great believer in saving for the future."

"I know," Rory said. "Mac was all about the here and now." By the time she was eleven, she pretty much understood why. Mac had lost the love of his life in a car crash two blocks from their home. They'd been married for less than a year.

Friedlander opened one of his desk drawers and withdrew a large manila envelope. "Mac's checkbook and savings passbook are in here, along with the contents of his safety deposit box. He'd given me a key and made me a cosignatory on the box years ago when he first rented it. He never kept cash or valuables in it, just important papers relating to the house, the business and the car. In any case, in his will he requested that I empty the box and turn the contents over to you. I found one additional item in the box, a letter in a sealed envelope with your name on it. I have no idea what the letter contains, but he did leave a note to me asking that I encourage, no, the word he used was *urge* you to read it as soon as you can."

Rory nodded, adding that bit of information to all the

other bits that were already swirling around in her head like snowflakes in a crystal globe.

"I've put half a dozen copies of the death certificate in here as well," Friedlander said, leaning across the desk to hand Rory the envelope. "You'll need them for things like closing out the accounts and changing the titles. The keys to the house, the office and the car are also in there. I've labeled them for you and noted the security codes and passwords for each. I think it would be prudent to change the locks on the house and the security—" He interrupted himself with a sheepish grin. "Sorry, I forget—you're with the police department."

Rory managed a smile. "That's okay, I appreciate the concern."

"So, that's all of it. Do you have any questions?"

Rory shook her head. She had a lot of questions, but none that the attorney could answer. "Thank you." She slid the will into the envelope with the other documents and stood up to leave.

Friedlander rose and came around his desk to take her hand again. "If there's ever anything I can do for you, please don't hesitate to call on me. Mac wasn't only my client, he was my friend."

Rory thanked him again and assured him that she would.

Once she was back in her car she exhaled a deep, shaky sigh. She laid the envelope with the remains of Mac's life on the passenger seat along with her pocketbook and turned on the air conditioner. "Get a grip," she scolded herself. "Mac would never approve." She did some deep breathing as the cool air washed over her, and after five minutes she felt better, steady enough to make the trip home. In this case "home" meant back to her parents' house in Woodbury. Like so many other college grads who couldn't find affordable housing on Long Island, Rory had moved back into the family nest. Although she got along well enough with her folks, who were only too happy to have their only child back under their roof, it was still awkward. She couldn't very well entertain dates in her room, and telling her mom and dad not to worry if she didn't come home on a Saturday night would never be a comfortable alternative.

Rush hour had wound down while Rory was in Friedlander's office, and traffic was moving along Jericho Turnpike well above the posted speed limit of forty. She stayed in the right lane, too preoccupied to trust herself in the Indie 500 that was barreling past her on the left. Although she had intended to go straight home, when she reached the turnoff that would take her to Mac's house, she changed her mind.

As she made the left into the West Hills section of Huntington, it occurred to her that the place of her own that she'd longed for but despaired of ever having was now hers. Along with the thought, a tidal wave of guilt broke over her. She knew that if Mac were there he would be laughing at her reaction, pointing out that since she hadn't actually shot, knifed or poisoned him; hadn't planned, abetted in or hoped for his demise, she had no right to the guilt she was feeling. Yet there it lay like a heavy, wet overcoat dragging at her shoulders and soaking into her.

She turned onto Brandywine Lane, following the graceful curve of the road past houses that had been built as long ago as 1798 or as recently as the previous year. Given the many inconveniences of older homes, buyers had three options. They could either raze the existing structure and start from scratch; save the shell but gut it to create a more modern, open floor plan; or just update the kitchen and bathrooms and restore the rest of the house to its original condition. Rory had been glad that Mac had chosen the latter route.

She pulled to the curb in front of Mac's home, her home now. She wondered how long it would take until she thought of it as hers. Built in 1870, the three-story frame Victorian sat well back from the road on an acre and a half of gently rolling land. The area was zoned for horses, two per acre, and the neighbors on either side had small, neat stables with rings and paddocks surrounded by whitewashed fences. On most days horses could be seen grazing in the paddocks or being put through their paces in the rings.

Rory turned off the engine and left the cool oasis of the car, pleasantly surprised to find that the air temperature had dropped a few degrees during her drive. A light breeze riffled through the leaves of the old oaks and maples that lined the street. The sun at her back, she leaned against her car and stared at the house as if she were seeing it for the first time. It didn't have too much of the fussy gingerbread detail often associated with Victorian architecture, which was why Mac had liked it. It was graceful yet strong, a man's Victorian. For Rory the best part was the deep, welcoming porch that embraced the front and sides of the house and invited you to come and relax on a warm summer's day.

As she stood there, the sun dipped below the tops of the trees, casting dappled shadows across the lawns and houses, then winking at them through the wind-stirred leaves. In the shifting light, Rory saw something move past the center window in Mac's bedroom. Her heart

tripped into double-time. She forced herself to shut her
eyes and take a deep breath. This would never do. The
past week had been such an awful roller coaster ride,
one soul-despairing drop after another, that it was no
wonder she was seeing things that were nothing more
than the tricks of light and shadow.

She waited until her pulse had slowed to something
approaching normal before opening her eyes again.
Across the lawn, the house sat quietly within its beds of
azaleas, spirea and yews, Mac's large bedroom window
as clear and featureless as all the others.

Chapter 2

Rory sat on the floor with her legs curled under her in the larger of the two rooms that had been her uncle's office suite in the old port town of Huntington. The rooms, like the squat brick building that housed them, were completely lacking in character or grace. The dull white walls were punctuated by Mac's diploma from the State University of New York at Stony Brook, his police academy certificate and his private investigator's license, all framed in wood, and three large posters from *Star Wars* episodes IV, V and VI framed in silver. It occurred to Rory that the strange juxtaposition of professional certificates and sci-fi posters was an uncanny mirror of Mac's personality, the serious businessman one minute, lighthearted child the next.

Faux wood miniblinds hung at the two large windows that overlooked West Carver Street, half a block from its intersection with Main Street. Two trailing ivy plants in blue and yellow ceramic pots crowded the top of a filing cabinet where they basked in the sunlight streaming through the partially opened slats. The plants had been gifts from Rory's parents when Mac opened the office. To him they were proof that miracles still happened, given that he rarely remembered to water them.

Rory shifted her weight, trying to find a more comfortable position. The tightly woven gray carpeting had clearly been designed to last for the lifetime of the building or until the next ice age, whichever came first. It would never win any prizes for comfort. It rasped against her bare legs like sandpaper, and she found herself wishing that she'd worn pants instead of the narrow pencil skirt that kept riding up her thighs. While she'd known she'd be leaving work early to begin tying up all the loose ends of Mac's business, she'd had no reason to suspect that she'd be spending the afternoon sitting on the floor. After all, Mac did have a desk. But it had quickly proven inadequate for the job of separating the files of ongoing investigations from those that had been completed or referred to other detective agencies, and those that were paid in full from those that had outstanding accounts. Apparently filing had not been one of Mac's priorities. For that matter neither was the alphabet. He seemed to have had his own unique system, and Rory had yet to crack the code.

Mac had hired a secretary when he first opened the agency. Rory vaguely remembered a petite blonde with a dazzling white smile who'd once worked for the dentist across the hall. By the end of the second month she was gone. Now Rory wondered if she and Mac had argued over the best way to organize files. In any case, Mac had never looked for a replacement. The unused desk in the anteroom had quickly become the repository for cases that needed refiling, telephone books that needed recycling and the random article of clothing that Mac had forgotten to take home.

Although Rory had anticipated the controlled chaos associated with Mac's work space, she was surprised at the extent of the disorder. It looked as if he'd spent his last days searching for a file that even he couldn't find.

Still, it was easy to forgive Mac his lack of organizational skills, since he more than made up for them in intelligence, fairness and hard work. It had proven to be a successful combination. He never needed to advertise; satisfied clients begat new clients with the alacrity of rabbits. His reputation was impeccable.

After the funeral, with its attendant commotion, Rory had made her uncle a silent promise. Before she tackled any of the other details left unfinished by his sudden death, she would do right by his clients. She would contact them, refund their retainers and suggest other reputable detectives to handle their cases. She wouldn't sell the business name and client list as his attorney had suggested. The extra money would have been nice, but there was no way to ensure that the buyer would be as ethical as Mac had been, no sure way to protect his good name.

By seven o'clock, Rory had compiled a list of eleven open cases. Grateful to finally be off the floor, she sank down in Mac's scarred leather chair. She set the eleven files and her list to one side and pulled the telephone closer. The first call she placed was to order two slices of pizza, a tossed salad and a Diet Coke. She hadn't eaten since the carrot muffin at work that morning and she was ravenous.

While she waited for her dinner to be delivered, she checked the names of the clients on the active list against the names of callers who'd left messages on Mac's answering machine. No point in calling the same people twice. She'd spent the first twenty minutes when she arrived that afternoon just listening to all the messages and jotting down names and numbers. She hadn't bothered to note the reasons for each call. They were all academic now.

Only three callers were not on the active list. That would cut down considerably on her phone time. She started dialing. The first two went directly to voice mail, and she left brief messages requesting a call back. She couldn't quite bring herself to say that Mac McCain had passed away, not to such an impersonal piece of equipment.

The next three clients were home. Rory introduced herself and explained the reason for the call. In all three cases there was a moment of hesitation while the client made the connection between her and the private investigator they'd hired. Then there was stunned silence, followed by the inevitable "Oh my God!" and "What happened?" Rory tried to keep the answers short and to the point. "He had a heart attack. It was very sudden. No, no warning signs at all." Then she told them that their retainers would be refunded in full and asked if they wanted her to recommend another detective.

When the delivery boy knocked on the outer door of the suite, she was glad to put the telephone aside. The calls had been more painful than she'd anticipated, like the deep, sharp pain of a paper cut you could barely see on the outside. She bit into the first slice of pizza with a little groan of pleasure. Crisp and oozing with melted cheese, pizza had always been her perfect comfort food. Well, that and ice cream.

"And brownies of course," Mac would have added had he been there.

While she ate, she thought again about the shadow she'd seen moving across Mac's bedroom window earlier in the week. She knew that at best it had been only a trick of light, at worst a hallucination conjured up by her overwrought mind. Before leaving, she'd walked the perimeter of the house checking for signs of forced entry, although that was highly unlikely now that the security system was engaged. She hadn't told anyone, since in the end there was really nothing to tell. But neither had she gone back to the house. She told herself that she'd stayed away in order to focus on putting Mac's business affairs in order. Once things in his office were properly squared away, she'd devote herself to the house. Her mother had offered to tackle it with her.

Everything had been left exactly as it was when Mac went to bed his last night on earth. He'd apparently been awakened around one twenty in the morning by a searing pain in his chest and had realized immediately that it wasn't just indigestion from the fried chicken he'd picked up for dinner. He'd managed to pull the phone from its cradle on the nightstand and dial 911 before he lost consciousness. The emergency operator traced the call, and the paramedics pulled to a screeching stop in the driveway eleven minutes later. When they found Mac, his upper body was hanging over the side of the bed, his legs still tangled in the sheets, the phone on the floor near his outstretched hand. There was no pulse. They worked on him for half an hour anyway, in constant communication with the emergency room resident at Huntington Hospital. Rory's parents were contacted just before three a.m.

They'd gone into the house just once since then, to clean out the fridge, dispose of the garbage and select the suit that Mac would be dressed in for his funeral. They set the alarm before they left. When Mac was home he never bothered with the alarm, contending that he invariably set the damn thing off every morning when he went outside to get the newspaper. Besides, he had a gun and he knew how to use it.

Rory was surprised to hear another knock on the outer door of the suite. Maybe the delivery boy had forgotten to give her a garlic knot that came with her meal. Almost anything that derailed her current train of thought would be welcome.

"Come in," she called, and was immediately sorry that she had. Although it was not yet fully dark, the rest of the tenants in the building were probably long gone to a home-cooked meal and some quality time with their families or the television. She should have locked the door. Before the thought was fully formed, her hand slid to the Glock that was clipped onto her belt. The pistol had become such a normal part of her attire that she hadn't thought of removing it when she shed her blazer and settled down to work. Just as well. You could never be too careful these days. Suburbia was not the safe, insulated world it had been in her parents' youth, as her mother was always quick to point out.

Even so, Rory had been surprised to find that as a sketch artist for the police department she would have to become a detective and carry a firearm. To her further amazement and Mac's delight, she turned out to be an excellent marksman. But she was equally pleased that she'd never had to draw her gun on anyone. She had a hard enough time killing a moth that was on its way to a rendezvous with her sweaters.

Just beyond her line of sight, the door opened tentatively on its squeaky hinges. If a burglar or rapist was coming in, he wasn't very self-assured.

"Hello? Uh . . . excuse me?" But apparently he was very polite.

"In here," Rory called, her gun hand beginning to relax.

A moment later her visitor came into view. He was in his late twenties, average height, slender, with light brown hair that fell onto his forehead. He was wearing trousers from a suit and a dress shirt, the sleeves rolled up to the elbows, no jewelry other than a silver watch. As he came closer, she could see that he had brown eyes and an interesting cleft in his chin. No other distinguishing marks, no facial hair. She'd been drawing suspects for so long that she automatically drew a mental sketch whenever she met someone new. She'd make a great eyewitness.

"Hi, I'm Jeremy Logan," the man said, weaving his way toward her around the stacks of folders that were still on the floor. "I was looking for Mac McCain." He glanced around the office as if he expected to find Mac hidden somewhere in the corner.

Rory recognized the name. Jeremy was one of the two people she'd left messages for earlier. She rose from her seat and extended her hand across the desk. "I'm Rory McCain, Mac's niece."

Jeremy leaned closer to shake her hand. "Nice to meet you. Sorry if I interrupted your work, or your dinner." He nodded to the desktop where the detritus of her pizza sat along with the file folders and the list.

"No problem," she said forcing a smile. "I actually tried to call you a little while ago."

His eyebrows drew together in wary curiosity. "Is everything okay?"

Rory sighed. "Not really, I'm afraid." She steeled herself for the shocked look, the tumble of questions, the awkward condolences. "Mac passed away last week."

Jeremy surprised her. He didn't say anything, just shook his head and sank into one of the two small armchairs in front of the desk. "I knew something was wrong," he said finally. "Something major. Mac always calls me back the same day."

Rory took her seat again. Neither of them spoke for a minute. She could tell that Jeremy was trying to absorb what he'd been told.

"Mac was one of the good guys," he murmured, looking down at his hands. "Honest. Conscientious. He played by the rules." He lifted his eyes to meet Rory's. "I hope he didn't suffer."

"It was a massive coronary."

He nodded. "This world's worse off without him. But I'm sure you know that."

"I do," she said, struggling to keep her emotions from running wild. If she was going to make it through this little meeting, she was going to have to stick to the business at hand.

"I know he'd want me to do right by his clients. That's why I'm here, trying to tie things up properly." Rory opened the top center drawer of the desk and withdrew Mac's business checkbook that she'd stowed there. "I'd like to refund your retainer." She glanced at the list where she'd jotted down the amount due each of the clients along with the corresponding name and phone number. "Does three hundred sound right?"

"I'd prefer to have you keep it and take over the case."

"I'm sorry," Rory said, caught off guard. "But that's just not possible." The thought had never even crossed her mind. She could draw a suspect's likeness with the best of them, and she might be called Detective McCain, but she had no real experience doing detective work. She would hardly know where to begin.

"Well, there I'd have to disagree with you," Jeremy said. "Almost anything is possible. And though your lips are saying 'no way,' that gun you're wearing says you must be involved in some kind of police or security work."

Rory had to suppress a smile. "I can recommend half a dozen experienced private investigators who would be glad to help you. I already have a nine-to-five."

Jeremy wasn't smiling. "Before I was lucky enough to meet your uncle, I'd been to those other guys and they weren't interested in taking the case."

Private eyes who weren't interested in a paying client? Rory hadn't taken the time to read through all of the files she was organizing, but like Mac she was a sucker for a good mystery. She knew she shouldn't ask, but she couldn't resist.

"Exactly what does this case involve?"

Jeremy didn't answer immediately, and Rory wondered what Pandora's box she'd just pried open.

When he spoke, his voice was calm but strained, like a seasoned pilot asking for clearance to land when all of his engines have flamed out. "The murder of Gail Oberlin, my sister."

Rory found herself stumbling over the same words and condolences of which she'd lately been the recipient, and she found it wasn't any more comfortable on this side of the conversation.

"Aren't the police investigating it as a homicide?"

Jeremy shook his head. "Not since the ME ruled her death an accident."

"Obviously you don't think it was. But if there was any indication that it was murder, the police would still be on the case."

"Hunches and instincts don't hold much sway with the police department. But I know what I know. There are dozens of ways to make murder appear to be an accident. And there are enough people who would have liked to see Gail dead."

"Listen, I would help you if I could," Rory said. "I'm sorry if the gun gave you the wrong impression, but I'm just a police sketch artist. Believe me, you'd do better investigating this yourself.

Jeremy leaned forward in his seat, his eyes locked on hers. "I'm a high school English teacher. Compared to me, you're Nancy Drew and Matlock rolled into one. I know you understand how I feel. You've just lost someone dear to you. There's a huge hole ripped out of your heart. But at least you know how Mac died."

Yes, she did. For some reason she found no consolation in that thought. A massive coronary at the age of fifty-two was still incomprehensible to Rory. She may have understood all the medical jargon about *how* Mac had died, but she still didn't understand the more basic question of *why*. Her parents were satisfied with the doctor's assertion that his diet had been his downfall, but somehow Rory couldn't quite wrap her mind around the concept that Mac had been felled by one too many fried chicken wings.

Yet wasn't that the only explanation that made sense? Especially in light of the police report that said there were no signs of forced entry, no signs of a struggle, nothing out of place except for a clock radio they'd found a couple of yards away from the bed, the glass on the LED display smashed. When Rory had questioned that finding, the lead detective on the case had offered up a possible scenario in which Mac had knocked the unit off the nightstand in his effort to grab for the phone and the paramedics had kicked it across the floor as they tried to reach him. That had been enough for her father, Mac's next of kin. He'd chosen not to desecrate his brother's body with an autopsy. Mac's doctor had concurred. Given Mac's roller coaster blood pressure and cholesterol-laden diet, along with his failure to take his medications with any kind of regularity, the doctor agreed that a heart attack was not an unreasonable outcome. And yet for Rory it still was.

"Jeremy," she said, "the bottom line is that when someone dies alone, there are always questions left unanswered."

"Maybe so, but just imagine how you'd feel if you were sure someone was responsible for Mac's death." Jeremy took a shaky breath before continuing. "It eats away at you. It consumes you. There's no peace."

Rory saw the pain and exhaustion in his eyes and she knew that he was right. She wouldn't be able to sleep or eat or work if she suspected that Mac had been murdered. She would be obsessed with finding the murderer, and if she did, she wasn't sure she could wait for the courts to mete out justice. She'd seen the system fail too often. She might very well be tempted to take matters into her own hands.

"Coroners are only human," he said, "and in my book that means they're not infallible."

"Everything you've said may be true, and believe me, my heart goes out to you, but even if I wanted to take this on, I'm not allowed to moonlight. I could lose my job."

Jeremy slumped back in his chair, head down. He seemed worn out, defeated. "Of course. Sorry." His voice was hardly more than a whisper. "I should never have tried to put you on the spot like that. I don't know what I was thinking."

"It's understandable. There's no need to apologize."

Jeremy drew himself to his feet. "Thank you. You've really been very kind."

Rory opened the checkbook and started to write.

"No, please. Keep the money. Mac was already working on the case when he . . . when he passed away."

She started to protest.

"Please. I insist."

She put the pen down and came around to the front of the desk. "I'll read through Mac's notes and type them up for you. That's the least I can do."

"I'd appreciate that. Thank you."

"And I'll ask around at the precinct. Maybe someone can suggest a PI you haven't tried."

Jeremy nodded, then turned and once again made his way around the file folders and into the anteroom. Rory followed him.

"I hope you find your answers," she said at the door of the suite. She watched him as he headed toward the single elevator that served the building. His shoulders were slumped as if the burden he carried had physical weight and mass.

Rory closed the door and locked it. She went back to the desk and threw away the remainder of her dinner. She wasn't as hungry as she'd thought. She tried to focus on the list of clients she still had to call, but all she could think about was Jeremy and his certainty that his sister had been killed. Relatives sometimes had a sixth sense about such things. She remembered Mac telling her that. Maybe that was why he had taken the case when the police had closed the file and other investigators had declined to help. What did it matter? There was nothing she could do about it anyway.

With Jeremy's words still ricocheting around in her mind, she dialed the next client on the list but hung up before the call went through. She couldn't imagine telling one more person tonight that Mac had passed away. The rest of the calls would have to wait.

She started cleaning up the piles of folders and placing them in the large cardboard boxes she'd brought along. For now she would store them in Mac's basement. She put the active files in a separate box. These she would send to the clients in the hope that they would find them useful in pursuing their investigations.

When she came to Jeremy's file, she put it aside with the intention of taking it home to type up the notes immediately. But before she'd finished packing the remaining files, curiosity got the better of her. She picked up Jeremy's file and sat down at the desk again.

Mac's notes were carefully dated and well detailed, but they were handwritten and therefore required some patience to decipher. He may have surfed the Internet and shot off e-mails like one born to it, but he'd insisted on using pen and paper for his notes.

Most of the file proved to be background information that Mac had gleaned from Jeremy and then checked out for himself. That was Mac's style. It had nothing to do with how much he believed or trusted his client; he knew that everything processed through the human brain wound up slanted and colored to one degree or another. After her first week as a police sketch artist, Rory had come to the same conclusion.

When she finished reading the notes on Gail's case, she knew that in spite of everything she'd said, she couldn't just let this case go. She picked up the telephone and dialed Jeremy's number.

Chapter 3

Jeremy answered the phone on the third ring.

"Hi," Rory said and reintroduced herself. "I'm glad I caught you."

"Good timing, I just got in."

"I haven't been able to stop thinking about you and your sister, so I started reading over the case file. Now, like I told you, I can't moonlight, but I guess there's nothing wrong with me checking out some things for a 'friend.'"

"Hey, that's terrific," Jeremy said, more animated than she'd heard him previously. "Just name your price."

"No, that would mean I was working for you and I can't do that. Besides, 'friends' don't charge each other for little favors. And that's all this can be."

"Right, sorry. You just took me by surprise, but I understand completely and I'm so grateful, you have no idea. Do you mind if I ask what made you change your mind?

"I'm not really sure I know. Maybe it was your absolute belief that there was more to Gail's death than what the medical examiner saw. I mean—what if she was just one more case at the end of a long day? You know, work her up and get home in time to tuck in the kids with a bedtime story? Maybe it's because Mac believed there was merit to your concerns. Or maybe you just got to me when you said I wouldn't be able to rest either if I didn't know how Mac had died. But I don't want you to have unreasonable expectations about what I can find out for you."

Rory didn't mention that the small piece of cellophane the medical examiner had found tangled in Gail's hair had piqued Mac's interest. He'd even scribbled a note about it in the margin of the report. Most people might have simply accepted the ME's conclusion that the stray bit of trash had come to rest in Gail's hair courtesy of an innocent gust of wind, but Mac had solved a number of his cases in the past few years on the basis of just such an unlikely clue. In any event, Rory wasn't Mac, and coming up with anything new remained a long shot, so there was no point in pumping up Jeremy's already soaring hopes.

"Okay," Jeremy said, sounding almost lighthearted. "What's the next step?"

"I'll have to read through Mac's notes again and decide where to start. Of course, I welcome any input from you along the way."

"Sounds like a plan."

After they'd said good-bye, Rory put down the receiver and sat there for several more minutes second-guessing her decision to help. It had seemed like the right thing to do, but it wouldn't be the first time her impulsiveness had led her into trouble.

"Mom!" Rory called in a voice that sounded a lot like the "quick, come kill the spider" voice of her childhood.

Arlene McCain jerked her head up from the armoire drawer that she'd been emptying of Mac's shirts. "What's wrong?"

Rory was across the room from her mother, sitting on the floor near the open closet. She was holding a pair of Mac's old sneakers and frowning over her shoulder at the empty doorway to the bedroom. "Did you see that?"

Arlene followed Rory's gaze to the doorway. "I didn't see anything," she said. "What are you talking about?"

"I thought I . . ." Rory shook her head as if to clear it. "Never mind, it's nothing. Probably just a floater in my eye."

"What did you think you saw?"

"Something, a shadow. I don't know. It was gone so fast I'm not sure."

"If it's a floater it may just go away by itself," her mother said, turning her attention back to the drawer of shirts. "But if it doesn't, you should probably see an ophthalmologist."

"I suppose," Rory murmured as she dropped the sneakers into a carton marked "garbage." Or maybe a psychiatrist, she added to herself. Twice now she'd seen something that apparently wasn't there. And both times it had been at this house. In spite of what she'd said, she was pretty sure they weren't floaters. She just didn't want to alarm her mother. It was bad enough that it was beginning to rattle *her*, and she wasn't a person who rattled easily. Though she had to admit, the very prospect of going back into Mac's house had been daunting. Walking into that deep emptiness conjured up images of wading into the cold waves of the Atlantic too early in the season. It would have to be done in stages, preferably with someone beside her. Her reluctance had nothing to do with fear. Fear was the bogeyman hiding in the closet when she was five. Or being lost for hours when she wandered away from the family picnic when she was eight. Fear was a child of the unknown. She knew what awaited her in Mac's house—memories, so many memories that she might drown in them. She'd been grateful for her mother's offer to help.

On their first visit, they'd stayed only long enough to stow the cartons of Mac's old business files in the unfinished basement. The second day they spent several hours going through the mail and newspapers, feeling uncomfortably like trespassers. They didn't venture upstairs until their third visit, that Saturday morning. They came in separate cars in case Rory decided to stay overnight. There had to be a first night alone in this house, she'd told herself sternly, and it might as well be sooner than later. Accept that the first night would be uncomfortable and just get it over with. On a rational level she knew that each subsequent night would be easier than the night before. Slowly, but inevitably, she would come to feel that the house was hers and the aching memories of Mac that now filled every corner would take up peaceful residence in her heart.

Rory had stopped at a local deli to pick up sandwiches for their lunch, turkey with lettuce, tomato and honey mustard on whole wheat. She would have preferred the rare roast beef that was beckoning from the deli case, but in light of Big Mac's heart attack, she figured it might be a good idea to start paying better attention to what she ate.

When she'd pulled into the driveway, her mother's sedan was already there, and Rory was glad to see that she was waiting in the car. Apparently she hadn't wanted to go inside alone either.

They'd unlocked the door and turned off the alarm. After putting the sandwiches into the empty refrigerator, they'd grimly marched up the creaky, old stairs. In unspoken agreement, they'd started with the two smaller bedrooms. The one that had served as a guest room was spare and neat, the closet bare except for a dozen assorted hangers. The other Mac had used as a study. Bookcases lined three of the walls, all crammed with books in no particular order or design. Rory would go through them at her leisure once she was moved in.

They'd spent some time going through the papers on the desk to make sure that no bills had been overlooked. Then they'd turned stoically to Mac's bedroom to tackle his clothing and other personal items. The plan was to give the best of the clothing to charity and dispose of the rest.

As Rory worked she kept checking the doorway, but whatever she had seen, or thought she'd seen, refused to show itself again. She couldn't decide if she was pleased about that or not.

The hours passed. They worked right through lunch

without feeling hungry. Finally the closet and drawers were emptied. The boxes destined for charity were taped closed and loaded into her mother's trunk to be taken over to her church's thrift shop. The boxes of discarded items were stacked near the front door to be brought down to the curb on Monday for garbage pickup.

"Well done." Her mother sighed. She was standing at the front door, pocketbook and car keys in hand. "So, what do you think? Are you staying here tonight or coming home?"

Rory was tempted to say that she would go back to her parents' home for at least one more night. Or maybe until her new mattress was delivered. But she knew that she was just looking for excuses, and she refused to cut herself any more slack on the issue. Tonight would be it. Tonight she would stay here in this house, *her* house. And if she couldn't bear to sleep in the bed that Mac had died in, well, she could sleep in the guest room or on the couch in the living room.

She drew her mouth into a halfhearted smile. It was the best she could manage. "I'm going to stay here tonight," she said firmly.

Her mother didn't try to talk her out of it. "I'll speak to you tomorrow then," she said brightly. Rory nodded, grateful that she didn't have to justify her decision to stay.

As soon as the sedan pulled out of the driveway, Rory prodded herself into action. She had to keep busy. No time for brooding, or for wallowing in memories. No time for her imagination to create things that weren't there.

She went into the kitchen and picked up Jeremy's file

from the kitchen counter where she'd left it along with her purse that morning. She took the pad of paper and pen that Mac kept near the telephone. Then she settled herself on the tan leather couch in the living room. Although Mac loved Victorian houses, he'd found he couldn't quite talk himself into the fussy, overwrought furnishings of that era. So the interior décor often came as a shock to first-time visitors. After the details and embellishments of the Victorian façade, they were momentarily stunned by the spare, uncluttered lines of the contemporary interior with its emphasis on glass, chrome and leather. Most newcomers stood in the small foyer, mouths agape like travelers who'd just crossed into the twilight zone.

Rory figured she'd find some comfortable middle ground that wasn't quite as disorienting to the senses. But any redecorating would have to wait until she had more time and money. Right now she had more important matters to address.

She opened the folder and started reading through Mac's notes again, jotting down questions as they occurred to her. She was once again struck by the fact that Jeremy might have been the only person in his sister's life who *didn't* want to murder her either literally or figuratively. Certainly none of the people Mac interviewed had shed any tears when Gail Oberlin died at the age of thirty-five.

At the time of her death, Gail was estranged from David Oberlin, to whom she'd been married for six years. The divorce filings mentioned a woman by the name of Casey Landis. Gail had been a successful interior designer in hot demand by the upwardly mobile on Long

Island. Two years earlier she'd left her position under Elaine Stein at Elite Interiors to open her own design firm. The new business skyrocketed into the seven-figure stratosphere the year it was launched and came close to doubling its revenues the following year. It was generally accepted knowledge in the industry that Gail had taken her entire client list with her, which although unethical, was hardly unusual. But what stood out more glaringly was that Gail had also managed to lure a dozen of her boss's most affluent clients to her new firm by undercutting Stein's prices and by waging a subtle yet powerful campaign of lies against her. Gail might have become a pariah to her peers, but success and money bought her their grudging, if wary respect. No one wanted to cross her and find themselves the next target of her venom.

While Rory was reading, the daylight had slowly withdrawn from the room as if the sun in its retreat toward the horizon had recalled all of its minions. As she reached up to turn on the arced floor lamp behind the couch, her stomach grumbled loudly. She hadn't paid much attention to the time all day, so when she glanced at her watch she was surprised to find that it was already past eight o'clock. She was glad that she still had her sandwich in the refrigerator. If she'd had to go out for food now, coming back into the lonely house would have been a tough sell.

She went into the kitchen and started munching on her sandwich while she made herself a cup of chamomile tea. She generally didn't care much for the dull flavor of chamomile, but it was supposed to be a good sleep aid, and tonight she was probably going to need all the help she could get in that department.

Before leaving the kitchen, she went to her pocket-book and withdrew the small pistol she carried when she was off duty. She wasn't sure why she suddenly felt the need for protection. This was as safe a neighborhood as any. But if it made her more comfortable to have the weapon nearby, then where was the harm and who would ever have to know? That was one of the perks of living alone. She didn't have to explain herself to anyone.

She set the gun on the glass cocktail table in front of the couch and sat down again with her tea and sandwich to finish going through Mac's notes. Most of what remained concerned the people he intended to interview, along with some of the questions he wanted to ask them. By the time Rory closed the folder, her eyelids were beginning to droop from fatigue and chamomile. She put her mug and plate on the cocktail table beside the pistol, turned off the lamp and stretched out on the couch. She made a deal with herself that if she couldn't get comfortable, she'd go upstairs to sleep in the guest room.

When Rory opened her eyes again, the room was completely dark, except for a pale slip of moonlight filtering through the front window. She sat up with a start, heart pounding, momentarily disoriented. As her eyes adjusted to the darkness, she exhaled a shaky sigh of relief. She was in Mac's house. On the couch in Mac's house. Mac's house that was in the process of becoming her house. She felt an embarrassed giggle shimmy up her throat. But before it could reach her mouth, her heart slammed against her rib cage again. Someone was sitting in the curved easy chair diagonally across from the couch.

Shadows she told herself. Just shadows. She'd locked the doors and set the alarm after her mother left. But the longer she stared at the chair, the more certain she became that the shadows there were deeper, denser, like a black hole in the darkness of space.

Yet if it was an intruder, why would he be sitting there just watching her sleep? A burglar would have been ransacking the house, a rapist would have attacked her by now and a murderer would surely have made better use of the fact that she'd been sound asleep. And if for some unfathomable reason he'd been waiting for her to wake up, why was he still not saying or doing anything? In his strange vigil, had he also fallen asleep?

Logically Rory knew that even her questions made no sense and that the shadows occupying the chair could only be shadows, but viscerally she was certain that she was not alone in that room.

Even as these thoughts ricocheted wildly around in her head, she was reaching for the gun on the cocktail table. Her hand knocked against the mug she'd set there, toppling it loudly onto the glass table and spilling the remnants of the tea onto her hand. If an intruder had in fact fallen asleep, the noise she'd just made would surely have awakened him, but no other movement, no other sound disturbed the silence.

Afraid to take her eyes off the suspicious darkness for even a moment, she continued to grope around frantically until her fingers finally closed around the grip of the pistol. A small quiver of relief rippled through her. She flipped off the safety and aimed the gun at whatever might be occupying the chair. Then she reached up and switched on the floor lamp. Her breath caught in her throat. In spite of her near certainty that an intruder was sitting there, she was not at all prepared to see that she was right.

Chapter 4

Even as Rory was jumping up from the couch, she was taking aim at the man in the chair. In spite of her trembling hands, she managed to keep him firmly in her sights. How could the shadowy product of her imagination actually exist in the harsh glare of the lamp? The bogeyman was never in the closet when you finally built up the courage to look. And the monster was never really under the bed, even if you were sure you could hear it breathing. So why hadn't this shadow simply evaporated in the light, leaving her to laugh at her own foolishness? But there he was in her crosshairs, and what made it even worse, he seemed perfectly relaxed and comfortable in spite of her obvious advantage over him. In fact, she thought she detected a bit of a smile on his lips as if he were just fine with the way things were going.

Rory felt anger quickly overtaking shock. "Who the

hell are you?" she demanded, her voice strong and steady even though her insides were quivering.

"Ezekiel Drummond," he said, in a drawl that was a mixture of southern and something else she couldn't immediately place. "Pleased to make your acquaintance, ma'am." He dipped his head as if he were introducing himself at a polite social function.

"You can drop the phony act, Mr. Drummond. Just tell me how you got in here and why you've been sitting there watching me."

"Phony?" he said, affecting a stricken look. "And here I was doin' my best to be charmin'."

Rory was in no mood to engage in witty banter with a potential rapist or murderer. "Just answer the questions."

"Well, you were sleepin' so peaceful, it didn't seem right to wake you."

"But the breaking and entering—that part seemed all right to you?"

"Now hold on a minute there," he said, "or we're goin' get off on the wrong—"

"Too late," Rory interrupted. "So this is how we're going to fix that. You're going to get up very slowly and take that gun out of your holster and drop it on the floor. Then you're going to kick it over to me and put your hands on your head. Don't even *think* about trying anything funny."

"Yes, ma'am," he said as he stood and followed her instructions. He was tall, an inch or so over six feet, with rough-hewn features, deep-set blue eyes, an unruly thatch of dark hair and a thick moustache. What really caught Rory's attention was that he appeared to be dressed for a party with a Wild West theme. But the clothes hadn't come from any costume shop; they were well worn and not recently laundered. He had on brown pants and scuffed boots, a long-sleeved white shirt that was on its way to yellowing at the collar and cuffs, and a vest with the tin star of a lawman. Even the gun in his holster looked like an authentic Colt single-action. He could have walked straight out of any number of old TV or movie westerns.

He drew the gun slowly out of the holster and let it drop to the floor. It landed on the hardwood without making a sound. Rory assumed that in her current state of mind and with the racket that her heart was making in her chest, she simply hadn't heard it. But when she glanced down to see where it had fallen, it was nowhere in sight.

"What did you do with the gun?" she snapped, cocking her own weapon.

"It's gone. Seemed like the best thing to do under the circumstances."

"Gone? What the hell does that mean?"

"For a pretty little lady, you sure like to use that word 'hell' a lot."

"I'm not finding this the least bit amusing, Mr. Drummond. And in case you've forgotten, I'm the one holding the gun. So unless you want to test my patience or my accuracy, I suggest you start answering my questions."

"Okay, okay, no need to go gettin' yourself all in a lather."

In a lather? Rory tried to remember the location of the nearest psychiatric hospital, because it was becoming more obvious by the moment that Ezekiel here, if that was in fact his name, had taken an unauthorized leave of absence from a well-padded cell where he spent his days rounding up cattle rustlers and heading up posses. But that still didn't explain what had become of the gun or how he had managed to break into the house to begin with.

"The gun wasn't real," Ezekiel said with a shrug of his shoulders. "I made it up."

"You can't just make up a gun or think one away for that matter." Unless . . . "Was it some kind of hologram?" That seemed like the only plausible explanation, but holograms required equipment and she was fairly certain there was no equipment of that nature in the house.

"Hollow gram?" Ezekiel said, rolling the word around in his mouth as if he were trying it out for the first time. "No, ma'am, can't say as how I know what that is."

If he wasn't crazy, he was sure one damned good actor. Maybe somebody put him up to this, she thought, seizing on the possibility with relief. She worked with a few young detectives who loved practical jokes. She didn't know why she hadn't thought of that sooner. But even as she was warming to the theory, she realized that not even the most socially inept among them would have orchestrated a prank like this so soon after her uncle's passing.

She was back to where she had started. Her arms were tiring and starting to shake with the weight of the gun. She wished she'd taken handcuffs with her, but she'd left them behind in her other purse, since she couldn't imagine any use for them while she was cleaning out Mac's place.

She had to put more distance between herself and her uninvited guest. She ordered him to sit down in the chair again, and she back stepped carefully until she could perch on the arm of the couch and rest her gun hand on her knee.

She knew she should call 911 or her own precinct house. She should have done it right away for that matter, but she'd wanted to have some kind of handle on the situation before she made the call. She didn't want to sound unhinged, even if she was feeling like Alice in a free fall down the rabbit hole. She'd try one more time to get a sensible answer out of him. Then, whether or not she succeeded, she'd call for help.

"I'm still waiting to hear how you got in here, Mr. Drummond," she said, temporarily putting aside the matter of the vanishing gun.

"Well now, the truth is that I never actually left."

"All right, then, *when* did you gain entrance to this house?" Was it possible that he'd been here since yesterday? Was he the shadow she'd thought she'd seen in the bedroom doorway? The shape she'd seen in the window last week? A chill leapt up her spine, and she steeled herself to keep from shuddering. It wouldn't be wise to show vulnerability.

"You really expect me to believe that you don't know?" Ezekiel no longer sounded amused. "Mac said he'd make sure you knew. And one thing about Mac—he always kept his word." His tone was accusatory, and Rory actually felt herself squirm under his suddenly baleful gaze.

"What exactly am I supposed to know?" she replied sharply, determined not to be put on the defensive. Her unwelcome guest knew Mac? Had talked to him about her? It didn't seem possible that this encounter could become any stranger.

Ezekiel ignored the question, a frown working over his eyes. "He said he'd put it all down on paper so that there'd be no misunderstandin'," he muttered as if he were trying to make sense of this apparent lapse on Mac's part.

Rory realized that he could still be playing her. He might have seen the notice of Mac's death in the obituary column. Her dad had listed his brother's full name along with the nickname that most people knew him by. But even if this assumption were true, she still had no idea what the intruder's motivation could possibly be, which brought her right back to the question of his sanity.

Okay, time was up. From her perch, she grabbed the portable phone from its base on the side table adjacent to the couch and dialed 911. *Oh my Lord, the letter!* Before anyone could pick up, she clicked off and set the phone down again. How on earth could she have forgotten the letter? The one Friedlander had given her, the one that Mac wanted her to read as soon as possible. She'd put it into the manila envelope with the rest of the papers. Although she'd already closed out Mac's bank accounts and transferred the title documents to a safe deposit box at the bank, the few remaining papers, including the letter, were still in the envelope on the passenger seat of her car. It was hard to imagine any explanation that would make sense at this point, but she had to give Ezekiel the benefit of the doubt before turning him over to authorities. For all she knew, Mac had given the man a key to the house, which would at least answer one of her questions.

"Mr. Drummond," Rory said, rising. "I have to get something that I left in my car. With any luck, we should have this whole thing sorted out very soon." She wasn't ready to admit that she might be at fault in this encounter. "But I have to make sure that you stay put for the next few minutes."

The only door in the house that could not be opened from the inside was the coat closet that was tucked beneath the staircase. Rory marched her unwelcome guest across the room to it with the gun at his back. He walked with a peculiar gait that was jerky and poorly coordinated, as if he suffered from some neurological problem.

She opened the closet door and switched on the low-wattage bulb that illuminated the cramped space, and Ezekiel, although still clearly disgruntled, stepped inside without argument, which in retrospect should have set off some alarms in her head.

She retrieved the envelope from the car and took it back inside with her. But before she sat down to read the letter, she went back to the closet to assure her prisoner that she would soon be letting him out.

"Mr. Drummond, are you okay? It will just be a couple more minutes."

There was no response.

"Mr. Drummond?"

Nothing. He couldn't have used up the oxygen in the closet that quickly. But if he were claustrophobic, he might have fainted. Rory drew the gun out of her pocket where she'd temporarily stowed it and cautiously unlocked the closet door. It was a shallow closet, and without clothes hanging from the single pole, it was immediately clear that Ezekiel was no longer in there.

She spent the next twenty minutes going through the house in search of him. She had no idea how he had managed his escape, but it was just one more unanswerable question to add to the growing list of them. Once she was certain that she'd checked every conceivable place in which a man over six feet tall might hide, she decided that he must have slipped out of the house while she was retrieving the letter.

She locked all the doors and windows and reset the alarm, and when the house was as secure as she could make it, she sat down on the couch with her gun beside her and opened Mac's letter.

Chapter 5

My Dear Li'l Mac,

As they say in those hammy old B movies, "If you're reading this letter, I guess I'm dead." That was the easy part. I'm not exactly sure how to tell you this next part, which is probably why I didn't tell you up until now. I kept meaning to, but I was afraid it might change our relationship, that you might think differently of me. Hell, I even think differently of me. So hold on, here goes:

I don't know how much you remember about the early years of my detective agency. Suffice it to say that it paid my bills, most of the time anyway. When I bought the house, I could barely hang on to it. In fact your folks bailed me out a few times when I couldn't manage the mortgage payments. But then pretty suddenly the business turned around.

Everyone said that I'd finally found my groove, my inspiration, my sixth sense. They all had different names for it, but technically none of them were right. And I never tried to correct their misconceptions. I couldn't. By the time you've finished reading this letter, I hope you'll understand. And I hope that you'll forgive me for having been less than honest in this one regard.

Anyway, as I got better and faster at closing each case, word of mouth spread and it wasn't too long before I had the luxury of choosing the ones I wanted to pursue. My clients were happy, and the money was finally rolling in. Which brings us to the big "reveal," as they say on those reality shows. I didn't do it alone; I had help. A federal marshal by the name of Ezekiel Drummond. This guy can out think Colombo. He's the one who's inspired, intuitive, in the groove, whatever you want to call it. But that's not the whole story. Zeke came east from Arizona on the trail of the man who'd kidnapped and strangled several young girls. Even after their files had been relegated to cold case limbo, Zeke refused to give up, made it his life's work to find the son of a bitch right up until the day he was shot in the back in the living room of what is now your house. That was on October 16 in 1878 and he's been there ever since.

Okay, L'il Mac, about now I imagine that you need to take a deep breath. Maybe a couple of them. Don't worry, your uncle has not come unhinged, though I imagine that explanation might be easier for you to live with.

Now you have every right to choose never to enter the house again. You can put it on the market

*today and never have to deal with Marshal Drum-
mond. I would never hold it against you. But I've
known you all your life and I've never seen you run
away from anything. I'm betting that given a little
time to process what I've just dumped on you, you
won't run from this either. There's a lot you can
learn from my friend Zeke.*

*As always, you have my love, sweet girl. I'm not
quite sure how things work where I'm headed, but if
I can pull some strings, I'm determined to spend the
first part of eternity watching over you.*

The letter was signed: *With love, Your Big Mac.*

Rory put the letter down on the cocktail table, away
from where the spilled tea had dried to a pale brown
circle. Tears had risen in her eyes as she came to the end
of the letter, but her mind was in chaos. All she could
think to do was grab her gun, get her purse from the
kitchen and leave the house as fast as possible.

The sun had just scaled the horizon when she jumped
into Mac's Volvo. She started driving with no destina-
tion in mind, because her mind was too preoccupied
to come up with one. She stopped at traffic lights and
stop signs. She signaled before turning. She maintained
something close to the speed limit. Yet when she finally
bothered to look around, she found herself on Jericho
Turnpike two towns away in Syosset, with no real sense
of how she'd gotten there. She needed someplace where
she could stop and think before she found herself in
Ohio.

It was too early to go back to her parents' home,
especially if she didn't want to explain why she was,
quite literally, up at the crack of dawn. Then she spotted

one of the ubiquitous Starbucks signs up ahead. Low on options and craving caffeine, she pulled into the lot.

Given that it was a Sunday and most decent folks hadn't even awakened to go to church yet, she was the only patron in the coffee shop. The middle-aged man behind the counter gave her a broad grin, pleased to have a customer to wait on. She ordered a mocha frappachino with extra whipped cream. If he thought it was a strange beverage for that time of day, he didn't say so.

Rory settled herself at a table in a back corner. She sipped the creamy confection that was only loosely related to plain old coffee, and tried to bring some order to the anarchy raging in her head.

She wondered if her reaction would have been different if she'd read the letter immediately, as Mac had asked her to do. She decided that under the circumstances, it wouldn't have mattered very much, except that she might have questioned her uncle's state of mind as she now questioned her own. In the absence of a family gene for a highly specific hallucination, she would have to accept that Ezekiel Drummond was real, or at least that he had been. Since Mac had never mentioned a belief in ghosts during any of their long talks over the years, he must have gone through a hectic period of adjustment himself before he was able to accept his unexpected housemate. On the plus side, if Mac's letter were to be believed in its entirety, Drummond had been a good man, the best kind of man, one who went to his grave trying to find justice for those young girls and their families. Of course, the downside was that if she wanted to keep the house, she was going to have to learn to live with a ghost.

Rory sighed and took a big, icy swallow of her

frappachino. How she would love to crawl beneath the covers of her childhood bed where she had once dreamt of things fearful and fantastic but had been able to leave them all behind her when she awoke.

She had long since finished her drink when the tables around her started to fill up with the usual complement of drowsy, caffeine-starved Sunday patrons. She tossed her empty cup away and went back to her car. She'd had no epiphanies and the only conclusion she had reached was that it was going to take more than a couple of hours and a sugar-caffeine high to come to terms with this new world order. Although it might prove to be impossible, she needed to put it on a back burner of her mind and try to go on about the normal business of her life. With any luck, her mind would acclimate in its own good time. Any decision she made regarding the house would have to wait until then.

Since the normal business of her life now included Jeremy Logan's case, she'd planned to drive out to Mount Sinai for a firsthand look at the house where his sister died. According to Jeremy, the place was up for sale again and there was an open house scheduled for today. The owners had apparently decided that they didn't want to live in a house where someone had died. After the past twenty-four hours, Rory couldn't say that she blamed them. In any case, their decision came at a fortuitous time, since she'd had no idea how she would have gotten inside to look around if the owners had been living there. She couldn't very well have told them that she'd taken it upon herself to reopen the investigation into the death of their interior decorator, at least not if she wanted to keep her day job. Now she could just say that she was house hunting.

But before that, she needed a shower and a change of clothing. It was seven thirty by the clock on the dashboard, which would put her at her parents' house a little before eight. She hoped that was a reasonable enough hour to deflect any suspicions about how her first night in Mac's house had gone.

When she arrived she found her parents in the kitchen drinking coffee. Since they seemed a bit surprised to see her there so early, she admitted that it had been a little weird to spend the night alone in Mac's house. There, close enough to the truth that it didn't feel like lying. Her father gave her a hug and said that it had been a little weird to spend the night without her, too, and her mother was so pleased to see her that she whipped up a batch of pancakes.

Rory found The Woodlands of Mount Sinai without a problem. Construction had almost been completed on the thirty-acre subdivision. She passed streets aptly named for woodland creatures, where families were already settled in their new homes, busily pursuing the American dream. Children rode bicycles and skateboards, played catch and threw Frisbees. Fathers mowed their lawns and washed their cars. Mothers pushed baby carriages or stood in small groups chatting. Dogs barked from behind fences. The scene was so idyllic that it was hard to believe that just around the corner Gail Oberlin had either fallen or been pushed to her death.

Rory made a right turn onto Pheasant Lane where some of the houses were occupied, while others still awaited roofs and landscaping. According to Jeremy, the owners of 16 Pheasant Lane had been waiting for his sister to finish decorating the interior of their new home before they moved in. Gail had been out at the house almost daily during the previous month, supervising all the details. When the carpenter arrived on May 10 to finish the crown molding, he'd found her sprawled at the base of the circular staircase, a dark halo of blood around her head and her legs bent in ways that human limbs were never meant to bend.

Rory found number 16 in the middle of the block. It was a stately brick colonial with oversized windows and double doors of highly polished mahogany. There was a "For Sale" sign hanging from a post near the curb with the listing agent's name. A placard announcing the open house from noon until three was suspended on hooks beneath it. There was a white Mercedes sports car in the driveway and an old Chevy parked at the curb. Rory tucked the Volvo behind the Chevy, walked up to the front door and rang the bell. When no one responded, she tried the door and found it unlocked. Having gone to a number of open houses with Mac, she knew that open-house etiquette allowed for visitors to let themselves in, since the agent was often busy showing the house to another party.

Rory walked into a large entry with a breathtaking cathedral ceiling that would have done any church proud. To the left, a wide stairway with a hand-turned oak banister led to the second story where a balcony with matching railing overlooked the entry below. The formal dining room was to her right and the living room to her left, past the stairway. Neither of the rooms was furnished. The hallway that stretched in front of her presumably led to the kitchen, family room and any other rooms that might be in the rear.

The house was very still. "Hello," Rory called out, her voice echoing through the empty rooms without answer. She stood there for another minute before deciding to show herself around. Since she was unaccompanied and didn't need to feign an interest in the whole house, she went straight to the staircase.

There was no evidence of Gail's blood on the beige and white marble floor. Not that Rory had expected to find any. The kind of people who could afford a house like this would have replaced the entire floor if so much as a speck of a stain had remained.

She started up the stairs, her shoes sinking into plush beige carpeting. Even though the scene had been processed by the CSI team, she'd promised Jeremy that she would go over everything herself, so she stopped on each step to check the wall for blood residue or other evidence that a life had ended there, but the ecru silk wallpaper was pristine. She checked the banister and the railings as well, with the same results.

As she made her way up the steps in this halting fashion, she saw a young man coming toward her along the upper hallway. His head was down, and he had a knapsack slung over his arm. He was moving fast, as if he wanted to get out of there and the sooner the better. He didn't even seem to notice her until he was brushing by her on the stairs. Then his head came up, and for an instant his eyes met hers. There was something troubling about his expression. The furtiveness of guilt? She couldn't quite put her finger on it. She wondered what he was doing at the open house. Unless he was a successful rock star or one of the new dot-com millionaires, he wasn't likely to be a prospective buyer. In fact, the odds were that he was the owner of the old Chevy parked outside.

By the time she reached the upper hallway and turned to look back down the staircase, the young man was out of sight. She made a mental note to talk to the real estate agent about him, just in case anything went missing. Then she turned her thoughts back to Gail and the ME's report. She'd more or less memorized it after the third reading. In the absence of any evidence that Gail had been struck with a heavy object, and given the cushioning effect of the carpeting, he'd concluded that the injury to Gail's head had come from landing on the unforgiving stone floor. So far Rory agreed with his assessment. She was still standing there, thinking that this view from the top of the stairway was the last thing Gail Oberlin ever saw, when someone grabbed her shoulder.

Chapter 6

When Rory felt the hand closing on her shoulder, she instinctively jerked away. She realized too late that she'd compromised her balance. Her left foot skimmed the edge of the top step without finding purchase. Panicked, she grabbed for the banister but only managed to rake her nails across the polished wood before losing contact with it completely. An image of herself, like Gail, lying broken on the marble floor below, shot through her mind in the frantic moment before she was pulled back from the edge.

"Hey, honey, take it easy; you looking to break your neck?"

Rory couldn't manage a reply. The adrenalin that had surged through her body at the prospect of death was now sluicing out of her; she was left gasping for air as if she'd just been rescued from drowning. Her legs were wobbly and making no promises to keep her upright.

She leaned back against the wall, thankful for the solid feel of it.

"Are you all right?" her rescuer asked, eyeing her warily, as if she might have suicide on her mind.

He was only a few inches taller than she was, but broad shouldered and lean muscled, with intense blue eyes and the sun-streaked hair of someone who spent a lot of time outdoors. He was wearing a gray polo shirt tucked into faded jeans and Docksiders without socks. He looked more like a surfer than a real estate agent, Rory thought, taking stock of him. She didn't know whether she should be angry with him for sneaking up behind her or grateful to him for saving her life. Anger won out.

"What the hell were you thinking?" she demanded once her heart had stopped pounding in her ears. "You should never sneak up on someone like that, especially at the top of a staircase."

"I wasn't trying to sneak up on you at all," he replied, clearly bewildered by her rage.

"But you did a remarkably good job of it anyway," she snapped. He could have at least said "hi there" or "hello" as he approached her. Even a polite cough or throat clearing would have helped.

"I was on the phone in the study down the hall when you got here. As soon as the conversation was over, I came out to welcome you. To be honest, when I saw you there at the edge of the stairs, you looked like you were going to do a half gainer. I was afraid to speak or do anything that might startle you."

"Yeah, well that worked out well," she said dryly.

"Point taken. I apologize."

"Apology accepted." Rory took a few tentative

steps away from the wall. Okay, her legs were under her control again. She held out her hand to him. "Rory McCain."

"Vince Conti," he said, covering her hand in his larger one.

"I take it you're the real estate agent?"

"For today I am. Are you a prospective buyer?"

"I suppose I am," she said, since she didn't want to say she was investigating Gail's death.

Conti nodded, and Rory saw him glance at her left hand. "As you can see, it's a magnificent house, but maybe too much house for a single woman?"

"You shouldn't make assumptions, Mr. Conti. For all you know, I'm married with four kids, a mother-in-law and two dogs."

"Okay then," he said, laughing, "let me show you around."

It was a charming laugh that was easy on the ears, and Rory couldn't help but smile back at him. She wasn't sure that he was buying her story, but he seemed willing enough to play along for now.

"So, Mr. Conti, what are you when you're not a real estate agent?" she asked as they walked down the hall.

"It's Vince, please. And to answer your question, I'm the builder of the development. This is the last house for sale here. Tomorrow I start work on a new subdivision. So when my real estate agent had an emergency, I decided to run the open house myself. I like to have things tied up before I move on, if possible."

He showed her into the first bedroom. It was elegant but understated, in navy and ecru; silk draperies framed the windows and puddled richly on the floor.

"There are five bedrooms total," he said as Rory

walked around the room, "including a maid's quarters off the kitchen. Each bedroom has its own bath, and there's also a powder room on the main floor."

"It's beautifully decorated," Rory murmured, admiring the way the different patterns worked so well together. If she had tried to pull that off, the room would have looked like a huge patchwork quilt. She was beginning to understand why Gail was so sought after.

"The owners were planning to use this as a guest room," Vince said.

"Owners? But I thought you said that it hadn't been sold." Rory waited to see if he was going to be upfront about what had happened here.

He shrugged. "The people who bought it changed their minds before they even moved in. You know the type, so much money that losing a hundred grand is like losing cab fare to them. So I bought it back, made a little profit and got some furniture in the bargain."

They walked down the hallway to the next bedroom, which had clearly been decorated for a little girl. It was all lilac and white with French provincial furniture, yards of sheer, billowy curtains, and an elaborate dolls' tea party set up in one corner.

"So you don't think their decision to sell had anything to do with that woman who died here?" Rory had seen her colleagues conduct enough interviews to know that sometimes taking the direct approach worked best at catching people off guard.

"You know about that, huh?" Vince smiled sheepishly.

Rory gave him credit for having the decency to be embarrassed over the deliberate omission.

"Yeah, I'm sure it figured into their decision," he said. "But if you think about it, there must be an enormous number of houses where people have died. Cancers, heart attacks, strokes, accidents, you name it. This one just got a little more press."

"In other words, it's been tough to sell."

"You could say that." Vince stopped outside the next room and turned to face her. "You're not really interested in buying this place, are you?"

"Well I might be, if I could afford it," she said, aware that she'd played the game to its end.

"So you're here because . . . ?"

"Curiosity I guess."

"Fair enough. There's a lot to be said for honesty. Apparently anything else can just come back to bite you in the ass."

"Thanks for the graphics," Rory said wryly. If Vince was right about that, she was going to have a very sore posterior.

"Sorry. I guess I should be more careful what I say when I'm wearing the real estate agent's hat. Look, since you're here anyway, would you like to see the rest of the house?"

"If you don't mind."

"It would be my pleasure. But may I ask if there really is a husband, mother-in-law and two dogs?"

"None of the above, but I'd love to have two dogs some day."

"Touché." Vince laughed, shaking his head.

"I almost forgot," Rory said as they left the girl's room. "I saw a young man bolting down the stairs when I was coming up. Did you see him?"

"You must mean Andy. Knapsack, skittish looking?"

"Yeah, he was in such a hurry I thought he might have stolen something."

Vince shook his head. "No, Andy's a good kid, just a little slow and socially inept. He's my real estate agent's son. He didn't know his dad was off today."

"Oh, I'm sorry," Rory said. "I feel terrible for having even mentioned it."

"Don't be silly; you had no way of knowing. And it's a legitimate concern with open houses. I've had things stolen in the past."

Rory knew he was trying to make her feel better, but she wasn't about to absolve herself so easily. She shouldn't make snap judgments about people like that.

Vince showed her through the rest of the second floor, including the study he'd mentioned earlier and a large master suite. Then he took her down the back stairs that led into the kitchen by way of a butler's pantry. He was a pleasant enough tour guide, but Rory needed to tour the house by herself. She couldn't really inspect the rooms for potential clues with him at her side. She would have to make another visit, preferably at night and alone. Of course, that would require picking the lock, and probably dealing with an alarm system. There was sure to be all sorts of unpleasantness if she were caught. She'd have to come up with something less likely to lead to a jail sentence.

"Did you have a chance to sign the visitor's log when you came in?" Vince asked as they returned to the entry. He motioned to a parson's table that stood against one of the entry walls. A small leather-clad book lay open on it.

"No, I didn't know I was expected to," she said.

"If you wouldn't mind. It's just your name, address and phone number. You never know, I might just decide to drop the price on the property, or I might find myself in need of a charming dinner date."

"Well, in that case," Rory said, "how can I refuse?"

She walked over to the table and picked up the pen that lay along the inner binding of the book. The date had been written at the top of the left-hand page, and beneath it two other visitors had printed their information. She added hers, then rejoined Vince at the door and thanked him for the house tour.

"No problem. It's not like potential buyers are knocking each other over to get in here today. Just promise me one thing," he said as he opened the door for her.

"Sure, name it."

"When you win the lottery you'll come back and make me an offer."

"You've got it. Of course it might take some time, since I never actually play the lottery."

On the drive back to Woodbury, Rory thought about her conversation with Vince. One thing in particular had stuck in her mind. Although she'd never really thought about it before, he was right. Houses had always been the theaters in which both the tragedies and joys of life played out, where some lives began and others ended. The number of houses that had borne silent witness to all manner of death throughout the centuries must be mind boggling. In that context, Zeke Drummond was just one of the unfortunates souls, unwilling or unable to let go. Somehow, thinking of it in that way made the prospect of sharing Mac's house with the marshal easier to accept. But when her mind tiptoed over to the "g" word, her logic mainframe once again threatened to crash. She reminded herself that Mac had

lived peacefully with Drummond for years and that he
believed she could benefit from the experience as well.
How could she give up without even trying? Especially
since Mac had always talked about keeping the house
in the family. He'd invested so much of himself in the
restoration, working right alongside the contractors. No
detail had been too small for his attention. He'd spent
days picking out the finest faucets, the perfect door-
knobs, the most ergonomic light switches.

Okay, that was it! She slammed her palm on the
steering wheel. No more fence sitting! She was going
to move into the house. With one caveat—Drummond
would have to agree to some ground rules. And if it
didn't work out, she could always play her trump card
and put the house up for sale.

With the decision made, Rory spent the rest of the
trip home writing a mental list of what she needed to
do next. She wanted to look at the title search that Lou
Friedlander had given her along with the rest of the
papers concerning the house. That should name all the
people who had owned the property prior to Mac, as
well as the amount of time they'd owned it. She wasn't
entirely sure why she felt the need for that information, but she suspected that it might prove helpful in her
negotiations with Drummond.

Then she was going to confront Marshal Drummond with her list of nonnegotiable terms. Of course,
she wasn't sure how to go about summoning him. It
occurred to her with an unpleasant jolt that she might
not even know if he were standing right next to her. Too
bad Mac hadn't left her some kind of handbook. She
was fairly certain that the local bookstores didn't stock

guides like *Living with Ghosts for Dummies* or *Chicken Soup for the Haunted House Owner*. At any other time she might have found that thought amusing, but now it only served as an unsettling reminder that she was about to set sail on a vast, uncharted sea.

Chapter 7

The title search proved interesting. In the hundred and thirty-nine years since Winston Samuels took title to the house that had been built for him, it had known over thirty other owners before Mac. What's more, many of the owners had chosen to default to the bank that held their mortgages rather than stay in the house until they could sell it, certainly not a prudent fiscal decision. In many instances the banks held on to the property for years before they were even able to sell it at auction. Apparently gossip had always traveled quickly along the suburban grapevine.

Rory also found it noteworthy that Samuels had lived in the house until 1878, the same year that Drummond was shot to death there, according to Mac's letter. Of the subsequent owners, none stayed longer than two years and most were gone in a matter of months. At five years, Mac had actually been there longer than anyone except

Samuels himself. And all of it made perfect sense if you factored in Ezekiel Drummond.

On one hand Rory was pleased with this reassurance that she and Mac were not suffering from some *folie a deux*, but on the other hand, she wondered just how Drummond had managed to scare away the other thirty-three people. Had Mac simply proven unscareable? Or had Drummond finally found a kindred soul in him, someone with whom he was willing to share his purloined residence?

It did briefly occur to her that Drummond might have caused Mac's heart attack, but she quickly dismissed the idea. After all, what could he have done to scare Mac to death after they'd been living together for five years? In any case, since title searches don't provide information on the health or well-being of the people who sell their homes or default on their mortgages, she added that question to the growing list of questions she intended to put to the marshal.

W alking into the squad room Monday morning, Rory nearly collided with Leah, who was busy punching a number into her cell phone as she sprinted for the door. Her curly brown hair was pulling loose from its clip as she ran, the square line of her jaw clenched with purpose.

"It can't be lunchtime yet," Rory said, laughing and doing a quick dodge to the side just in time. Leah was always the first one out the door at lunch, although no one had ever actually caught her eating anything. She spent the time running the continuous loop of errands that came with being a wife and mother. When she and

Rory wanted to spend some girl time together, Rory had to eat whatever she could grab on the run as she tagged along to the cleaners, the supermarket, the pharmacy, the post office or whatever destinations would satisfy the needs of the Russell family on that particular day.

"Good, you're here," Leah said over her shoulder as she dashed by. "Grab your laptop and meet me outside."

"What's going on?"

Leah, who was already halfway down the hall, just gave her a "hurry up" wave.

"Three alarms in Riverhead," another detective said, pausing in his own rush to the door. "Arson. At least one confirmed dead. They're a bunch of eyewitnesses who saw it go down. We need you there to put a face on this bastard."

Rory pulled the laptop out of her desk drawer, adrenalin pumping through her veins with a stronger kick than a double shot of espresso. This could be the break they'd been waiting for—an identity for the arsonist who'd set half a dozen fires across Suffolk County in the past six months. The casualty count now stood at five, including one young fireman who'd died when the roof of a Lloyd Harbor mansion collapsed on him. There had never been any witnesses before. And the fires had always been at night. The arsonist was getting sloppy. Or craving more attention. Rory intended to see that he got just that.

Outside Leah was waiting at the curb in an unmarked car. Rory slid into the passenger seat, trying hard to tamp down the feeling of buoyancy that this unexpected break from her routine was producing. Arson and homicide should never elicit the same response as having a substitute teacher did when she was a child. Yet, truth be told, it did feel a tiny bit the same.

As soon as Rory pulled the door closed, they were off and running. They made the trip to Riverhead in less than fifteen minutes, courtesy of the bubble light and siren on the roof and Leah's heavy foot on the accelerator. Since they weren't driving an ambulance and the Riverhead police were already swarming all over the area, Rory didn't think the situation required such reckless speed on their part. But not wishing to distract Leah, she kept her thoughts to herself, relying instead on a few silent prayers as they zipped around the other cars on the expressway.

Before they reached their exit, they could see the gray-white smoke hanging over the treetops like poorly laundered clouds set out to dry. Leah grudgingly eased off the gas as they made their way through the suburban streets between the exit and the house. As soon as she turned onto the block where the fire was raging, she was forced to stop. Two police cruisers were turned sideways to create an outer perimeter that would stop any nonessential vehicles from getting closer to the fire. A uniformed cop was sitting behind the wheel of one of them. A second cop came up to Leah's side of the car. She opened her window and held her shield out to him. Satisfied that she was a comrade in arms, he gave his partner a thumbs-up to let them through.

The police had evacuated the residents from the houses in closest proximity to the fire and were keeping them and their neighbors behind a second perimeter of yellow tape, well back from the dozen or so fire trucks, emergency vehicles and police cars that crowded the street. The residents stood in knots on lawns and sidewalks, watching the drama unfold, exchanging theories about what had happened and shaking their heads as bits of news and rumors trickled down the line. They had their cats in carriers at their feet, their dogs on tight leashes and their children under watchful eyes.

Leah moved forward at a crawl, worried that at any moment someone might step out into the street without looking and add to the casualty toll. Ten minutes and barely fifty yards later, she and Rory gave up and abandoned the car. They made their way by foot through the deepening pall of smoke. Without the car as a buffer around them, the crackling of the fire was loud, almost gleeful, as it sank its sharp teeth into the wooden bones of the house. The air was gritty and foul with the odor of melting plastics and other synthetics, and Rory found herself thinking that fires must have smelled better back in simpler times.

Shields in hand, they ducked under the crime-scene tape and were directed to the ranking police officer, a captain by the name of Joe Flagg. Flagg had a long face topped off by a gray military buzz cut and narrow lips that were pinched into a grim line. If he was pleased to see them, he did an admirable job of hiding it.

"Good," he grunted when Rory introduced herself as the sketch artist. He motioned for her to follow him and led her to a lawn several houses down on the far side of the fire.

"We assembled all the witnesses over here so you wouldn't have to waste time looking for them," he said, yelling in order to be heard above the roar of the fire and machinery. "You need anything, I'll be back there where you found me."

He turned away before Rory could tell him that he

hadn't done her any favors by corralling the four eye-witnesses where they'd no doubt been comparing what they thought they'd seen. Over time she'd discovered that most people had fairly unreliable memories, especially when they were in crisis mode. Instead of fielding several different perspectives from the group, she was probably going to wind up with one homogenized description, and it would be a happy coincidence if her rendering actually turned out to resemble the suspected arsonist.

When she introduced herself, the three women and one man all started talking at once, adding to the general commotion. To restore some order, Rory assigned each of them a number and took them one by one onto a nearby porch, where she could sit on a rattan bench and have an actual lap on which to perch her laptop. She was just finishing with the first witness when the woman she'd dubbed witness number three rushed up the steps to them.

"That's him. Over there," the woman said, gasping with excitement and gesturing madly across the street at a short, heavyset man in his thirties. He was staring at the fire, as transfixed as a teenybopper watching a rock star.

"Are you sure?" Rory asked.

"That's him. I'd know him anywhere."

The other witnesses had joined them on the porch. Three of them were in agreement. The fourth dissented. Based on her first sketch, Rory wasn't entirely sold. Then the suspect saw them pointing in his direction and he bolted, a picture far more telling than any thousand words.

Rory set the laptop aside and ran down the porch

steps. None of the Riverhead police nor the detectives from her own precinct were nearby or looking in her direction. She couldn't just let him get away.

"Go get help," she shouted to the group on the porch as she raced on down the walkway and into the street. Her progress was slowed by the thick fire hoses that were writhing through the street and the crazy quilt of emergency vehicles she was forced to circumvent.

The suspect was out of sight by the time she reached the lawn where he'd been spotted. Assuming he'd disappeared around the back of the house, she kept going in that direction. There was no sign of him there or in the adjoining yards. Fences of various heights and styles prevented her from seeing any farther. She supposed that he might have fled into one of the closest houses through an open back door. There was a good chance that the residents, routed by the police or by the general excitement, hadn't bothered to lock up. But it would take too long for her to check each house, and there were too many places in them where he could be lying in wait to ambush her. If that's where he'd taken refuge, her colleagues would find him eventually. For now her priority was to make sure he hadn't left the area.

The best option for an arsonist on the run was probably to cut through one of the unfenced backyards to the next street. If he'd planned ahead, he might even have left his car there. Rory's hand went to the gun holstered at her waist. Reassured by the weight of it, she charged on, slowing only to pass between the arbor vitae that separated this house from the one behind it. Still no sign of him. When she reached the next block, she saw him scuttling across the street toward a small, dark blue car with a dented back door that had seen its best days back in the eighties. He didn't appear to have a weapon in his hands, and since the weather was warm, he wasn't wearing a jacket that might have concealed one.

Still, Rory would have liked to hear the pounding of other police racing to the scene, but the only pounding was her own heartbeat echoing in her ears. Since she couldn't very well ask the suspect to hang out a while and wait for her reinforcements to arrive, she stopped and drew her gun, steadying it with both hands.

"Stop, police!" she shouted. "Stop or we'll shoot." No harm in letting him think there were several guns ready to take him down. With any luck there would be, and hopefully soon.

The suspect slowed and glanced back over his shoulder. He was out of shape and breathing hard, his eyes skittering back and forth as he tried to decide on the odds of making it to his car without being shot.

"Forget it," Rory said with conviction, "I always hit what I aim for." The suspect didn't need to know that she'd never had to shoot a real person before.

"Okay, okay." He turned to face her, arms raised in surrender. "But you got the wrong guy."

Rory kept him in her gun sites as she moved toward him. "It's amazing how often that happens," she said wryly. Where the hell was the cavalry? "I need you facedown on the ground, now!"

"I'm in the middle of the street. What if a car comes?"

"I guess you'd better start praying that doesn't happen." Of course, he did have a point. It probably wouldn't sit well with the brass or the media if she let him get run over without benefit of a trial. But she couldn't let on that she was such a novice that she hadn't thought of that herself.

"I got rights," he was sputtering. "Hey, tell her. Tell her she can't treat me like this."

Who was he talking to? She resisted the urge to look behind her in case it was a ruse.

A moment later Leah was standing beside her as two uniformed cops ran past them to take the suspect into custody. Rory thought he looked as relieved to see them as she was.

"What the hell were you thinking?" Leah asked her. They were alone, walking back toward the tumult of the fire.

Rory stopped short, frowning at her as if she'd suddenly sprouted a second head. "You're kidding, right? I was thinking we had to catch the guy before he got away and killed someone else."

"*You* could have been the 'someone else'!"

"Or it could have been you," Rory replied, more sharply than she'd intended. "Or the captain, or anyone else who tried to bring him in." She knew she was overreacting, but damn it, she deserved some credit for getting that creep off the street and maybe keeping future victims out of the morgue.

"Stop it, Rory, you know what I mean."

"That I'm an artist and I don't have the street experience to go after guys like that on my own?"

"Well, do you?" Leah asked.

"I graduated from the same academy you did, and I carry the same weapon."

"When was the last time you used it outside the firing range?"

"That's not my fault."

"When you're lying dead in some alley somewhere, whose fault will it be then? Look"—Leah took a deep breath and her tone softened—"you scare me, because you're me twelve years ago." She put her hand on Rory's arm, needing her to feel the connection between them. "You're not immortal, my friend, and you're not expendable."

Something inside Rory relaxed. Leah wasn't the enemy. Her only crime was perhaps caring too much for her friend. She nodded, and they walked back to the scene of the fire without any further need for words.

Captain Flagg was supervising the loading of the suspect into one of the police cars. As soon as he spotted Rory, he marched over to her.

"Well done, Detective," he said, a salute in his tone. "You've done the job proud. I'm going to make sure your captain knows what you did today. There could be a commendation in it for you."

"Thank you, sir ," Rory replied. Just behind her, she heard Leah groan.

Chapter 8

At half past five on Monday evening Rory arrived at the house on Brandywine Lane. She'd decided to think of the house in those generic terms until she was ready to call it her own. Fortunately her shift had ended on time, which wasn't always the case, since criminals weren't any more interested in abiding by police schedules than they were in abiding by the laws themselves.

As she rolled two suitcases up the flagstone walk to the front door, she was glad that it was June and that the sun was still hours away from setting. There was definitely no need for the additional drama that night always brought to all things strange and eerie.

She didn't have to turn off the alarm. She hadn't bothered to set it when she'd fled the house the previous morning.

Leaving the luggage in the entryway, she went from

room to room looking for Drummond and wondering just what a ghost did to while away the hours.

There was no sign of him anywhere, but then she never actually expected to find him playing solitaire at the computer, watching television, taking a shower or fixing dinner. In fact, if it hadn't been for Mac's letter, she might now be questioning whether her first encounter with him had been a strange dream and nothing more.

She stood in the middle of the living room, a vantage point from which she could see parts of the dining room and kitchen as well as the lower portion of the staircase. She was about to draw the gun that was holstered on her belt when she realized that even if she were packing an Uzi and a missile launcher, there was no way to threaten or kill someone who was already dead. Besides, it probably wouldn't set the right tone for their conversation.

"Marshal Drummond?" she called out. "Ezekiel Drummond?"

"Right here, ma'am. Were you thinkin' there might be more than one Drummond in residence?"

Although Rory had summoned him, she jumped at the sound of his voice behind her. She spun around to find him leaning against the back of the couch, wearing the same outfit he'd worn the day before.

"Nice to see ya," Zeke said casually, as if it were perfectly normal to suddenly appear out of the ether. "I take it Mac's letter vouched for me or you wouldn't be back here with those suitcases."

"Yes, it did. But let me assure you, Marshal, I have no intention of letting you or anyone else take Mac's house away from me without a fight."

"That was never my plan." Lines like cat's whiskers

crinkled the leathery skin around his eyes, and his moustache hitched up a notch with the makings of a smile.

"Good," Rory said, hoping that it wasn't the smile of the cat just before it swallowed the canary. "Now, if we're going to be sharing this house, I have some questions that need answers and there are some things we need to clear up between us." Her voice sounded spunkier than she felt, which in turn bolstered her confidence.

"I'm listenin'."

Rory walked past him and sat in the chair he'd occupied the other night. Zeke sat on the couch, but she never actually saw him walk around to the front of the couch and sit down. One moment he was leaning against the back of the couch and the next he was sitting on it.

"This house had more than thirty owners before my uncle. That's a lot of owners even for a house as old as this one. So it's pretty clear that you must have scared them all off. I'm just not sure why."

"For a police detective you've gone and gotten your facts all jumbled. I never tried to scare anyone away. Except maybe the old lady whose dog howled nonstop from the day they moved in till the day they left. She didn' mind the howlin' cause she was pretty much stone deaf. But he used to follow me around all the time, and I gotta tell ya, it was annoyin' as hell."

Rory had to suppress a smile at the image of the beleaguered marshal being tormented by the dog. "Okay, but if you didn't try to scare the others away, why did they leave?"

"A little of this an' a little of that, I suppose. I might've moved things around, flipped some switches, made some noises. . . . You try livin' in the same place for over a hundred years. It's borin' as all get out." He paused for a moment and when he continued, his voice was low and weary. "But mostly they left because I went and tried to make their acquaintance."

"So why was it different with my uncle?"

"It wasn't in the beginning. We didn't hit it off straight away. No, ma'am. But he dug his heels in. How'd he put it? Oh yeah, 'Nothin' short of a damned atom bomb' was gonna make him leave this place. Now I'm not familiar with atom bombs, but since I'm stuck here myself, we had to work it out between us. And mostly, we did."

"But if you died in 1878, why *are* you still here? Isn't there some kind of light you're supposed to go toward when you die?"

"Don't *you* go talkin' to me about the light," Zeke growled. "I already heard it all from Mac, and I'm not followin' any light 'til I find out who the coward was that shot me in the back."

"Whoever he was, he's dead by now, so how could it possibly matter?"

"It matters." Zeke started pacing around the living room in the same peculiar, halting fashion that he'd exhibited the other night. And Rory was certain that she hadn't even seen him get up. Apparently he wasn't any better with transitions than he was with walking. She felt as if she were watching a poorly edited movie.

"Just how do you plan to find out who it was?"

Zeke winked out of sight midstride and reappeared instantly leaning against the fieldstone fireplace. "Mac was tryin' to help me with that, but he never did make much progress. Not that I blame him. I know the trail's gone cold."

Cold? Rory thought. Glacial was more like it. But she had no idea how to convince a ghost with a stubborn streak that the odds were against him in pursuing a case over a century old. Ezekiel Drummond didn't seem to care that justice would never be served even if the truth were somehow deduced.

"Okay, Marshal, since it seems that we're going to be sharing this house, we need to have some ground rules."

"Mac and I never needed any rules." Zeke frowned, his thick brows inching together as if they'd been pulled by a tailor's thread. It created a sinister effect, one that was no doubt useful in his line of work, but for Rory it was more like a call to arms.

"As you may have noticed," she replied tightly, "I am not Mac."

"Don't go gettin' snippy on me." Zeke's tone matched hers. "I may be dead, but I ain't blind."

Under any other circumstances Rory would have found that statement amusing. Now it just caused a tangle of muscle and nerve to start pulsating over her left eye. She drew in a deep breath. Her voice was even, if not conciliatory, when she said, "I'm going to need some privacy. I assume that you're an honorable man, a man of your word. I need your promise that you won't enter my bedroom or bathroom without asking for permission."

Zeke's mouth twisted into a wry smile. "You got no worry on that score. As willing as the spirit may be, the flesh is long gone."

"That's not the point," she said, refusing to be cajoled. "I'm not at all interested in what you can or cannot do. The rule is for my comfort level, not yours. Now, do I have your word?"

"Do I have a choice?"

"Yes, of course you do. You can rattle around alone in this place for another century, waiting for someone else who's willing to stay here with you."

"That's a fine rule then, Miss Aurora. You have my word as a federal marshal and as a gentleman that I will not trespass on your privacy"

She studied his face, looking for any sign that he was dissembling. He returned her gaze evenly. Nothing about his body language indicated that he was lying, but she'd never dealt with a ghost before. Trusting that Mac would never steer her wrong, she decided to take Zeke at his word, at least for now. Okay," she said, "but before we go any further, how did you know my full name?"

"Mac talked about you a lot and, as I recall, he mentioned how dead set you are against your given name."

"Then you ought to know better than to address me by it," she said with a defiant thrust of her chin.

"Yes, ma'am." Zeke's voice was conciliatory, but there was mischief in his eyes.

Rory refused to rise to the bait. "Rule number two."

"Hold on a minute there," Zeke said. "I thought the Aurora thing was number two."

"Mocking me is not going to win you any points, you know."

"I wasn't mockin', I was just countin'." Zeke managed to sound genuinely confused, even though Rory was sure she could still see laughter dancing in his eyes.

"Have it your way. Rule number three: I'd appreciate it if you would find a way to let me know when you're nearby, so that you don't keep startling me."

Zeke nodded. "Fair enough."

"Rule number four—"

"Just how many rules are there?"

"Four for now. But I reserve the right to add more as I see fit."

Zeke crossed his arms and adopted a weary expression.

"If I have visitors, you'll stay out of sight and refrain from any mischief that might raise questions."

He wagged his head. "You put me in mind of an old school teacher I had. I swear that woman did not own a smile."

He looked so discouraged that Rory laughed in spite of herself. "Okay, I guess I had that coming."

"Well, would you look at that—we agree on somethin' after all. Is there anythin' else?"

With the ground rules out of the way, Rory debated asking the question that had been uppermost in her mind since she'd read Mac's letter. While she wasn't at all sure that she was ready to hear the answer, she knew that if she didn't ask, the question would continue to nag at her.

"There is something I've been wondering about," she said, turning to face Zeke, who had resumed his position on the couch, "something maybe you can answer for me."

"I'll do my best."

"I've been told that my uncle's heart attack was sudden, massive. I'd just like to know for sure that he didn't suffer. You were here; you saw it happen, right?"

Zeke was silent for a minute and when he spoke again, there was a strange undercurrent in his tone that Rory couldn't immediately name. It was sad, defensive and a little surly all at once.

"You don't get how it is," he said. "It takes a heap of energy and focus to manifest like this. From time to time I need to recharge, so I ain't always payin' attention to what's goin' on in your world. Anyway, to answer your question, Mac was unconscious before I even took notice. I'm not real good with time anymore, mind you, but I'm thinkin' he went mighty fast."

Rory had hoped for a more specific answer, but she knew there was no point in giving Zeke the third degree. She tried a different tack. "I'm not sure how to say this; what I mean is . . . did Mac . . . did you see Mac pass through where you are?"

"Yes, ma'am," he said, sounding more relaxed now that he was the bearer of good news. "He sure did. But he never stopped, never hesitated for a second. And he never looked back. It was like he knew exactly where he was goin' and he was in a fierce hurry to get there."

"I'm glad to hear that." Rory sighed, comforted for the first time since Mac died. "After he lost Claire, I had the feeling that he was only marking time here."

"Could be if I had someone waitin' for me on the other side, I'd be more amenable to movin' on too," Zeke murmured, staring past her into a distance that she couldn't begin to fathom.

Rory was surprised to find herself moved by the loneliness and regret that she heard in his voice. She didn't know what to say to him, what words might bring comfort to a soul still tethered to a world in which he didn't belong.

The silence grew until it occupied all the empty spaces in the room and the air became heavy with its weight. Then Zeke seemed to jolt himself straight out of his reverie.

"For now, there's things here that need tendin' to," he said, meeting her eyes again as if there hadn't been any lag in the conversation.

"The people you're talking about, Zeke, the events you're talking about, don't exist anymore," Rory said as gently as she could. "There's no shame in letting go of a pursuit that ended so many years ago. No shame—."

Zeke was on his feet, glaring down at her, red-hot rage burning in his eyes. His reaction was so volatile, so unexpected, that she had to fight the urge to shrink back from him.

"Don't you try tellin' me what's shameful and what's not," he seethed.

Rory rose and stood toe to toe with him. "You need to back away from me and calm down," she said in the steely, measured tone she rarely needed to use in her capacity as a police sketch artist.

Zeke didn't move. "I'm thinkin' I need some ground rules of my own," he said, anger still flashing like heat lightning in his eyes. "For starters, don't you go meddlin' in things that don't concern you, *Aurora*. And don't you ever talk down to me like I was your dotty old grandpappy."

Before Rory could open her mouth to respond, he was gone.

"Disappearing is a great way to win an argument!" she shouted into the empty room. "And stop calling me Aurora!"

1878

The Arizona Territory

Five men drew their horses up short beneath an outcropping of rock that provided a small oasis from the withering glare of the Sonoran sun. The horses were blowing hard, lather rising on their flanks and sides like foam rising on a beach at high tide. Around them an army of saguaro cacti stretched across the desert scrub to the horizon, their limbed shadows too narrow to provide shade for all but the smallest creatures. The riders clothes stuck to their bodies in puddles of sweat, and their deep brimmed hats, broken and stained from past labors, slouched on their heads as if deflated by the heat. A tin star, dulled by layers of grit and dust, marked the only lawman in the group.

"There's a creek a couple miles west," the marshal said, plucking the bandana from around his neck and using it to mop the sweat from his forehead. "The horses won't get much farther without water."

"What makes you think that creek ain't dried up like the rest of 'em?" one of the other men grunted.

Before the marshal could answer, the smallest man in the group stood up in his stirrups. The proprietor of Jensen's Mercantile sat a horse as well as any of them, but he never seemed as comfortable in the saddle as he did behind the counter of his store.

"I still say Drummond here's got us headed in the wrong direction," he said, a tight desperation in his voice and eyes. "I'd bet my life Trask's taken her to Goose Flats. It's the kind of place that suits a man like him. Silver fever, guns and whores. The kind of place where people won't pay him no mind." He looked around at the other men. "I'm heading back that way. Who's coming with me?"

"Hold on, Frank, just hold on," the marshal said. "You all saw the tracks headed this way. You never saw any doublin' back, did you?"

There was a moment of silence as they all chewed on that thought. "Those tracks played out more than an hour ago," Jensen came back. "Ground around here's so dry, it just won't hang on to tracks for long." This met with a chorus of grumbled agreement.

"I'm going to Goose Flats," he added with finality. "The rest of you can come with me or not." He wheeled his horse around and dug in his spurs. One by one the others turned to follow him, leaving Ezekiel Drummond alone in the shade. Muttering about fools and idiots, he retied the bandana around his neck and continued westward alone.

It was late afternoon by the time he reached the creek. An hour earlier, he'd given his horse the last of the water from his canteen, even though he knew the chestnut would slop more of it out of his cupped hand than he swallowed. So when he saw that the creek still carried a few inches of spring runoff, he closed his eyes for a moment and said a quick "thank you" to whatever angel was watching over them.

Once he and the horse had quenched their thirst, he filled up his two canteens and they set out again. They'd gone only a few yards when he pulled the chestnut up sharply and jumped down. A scrap of blue and white gingham was impaled on the needle of a barrel cactus off to his right. He tugged the fabric off, and clasping it in his fist, mounted the horse again. Eight-year-old Betsy Jensen had been wearing a blue and white gingham dress when she was abducted. His instincts hadn't failed him. Somewhat heartened, he pressed on.

As darkness crowded daylight from the sky, he stopped at another small spring. His eleven-year-tenure as federal marshal for the southern Arizona Territory had etched in his head a pretty fine map of the region and it was serving him well this day.

Under any other circumstances he would have made camp there for the night, but the most he could do was allow the chestnut an hour's rest before moving on. And even that was time they didn't have. On the other hand, running the animal into the ground would only prove to be his undoing as well, since his own two feet were hardly adequate for the journey ahead. He unsaddled the horse and hand fed him the oats he'd brought along, since the desert scrub couldn't provide any real nourishment for him.

The time passed with agonizing slowness. He checked his pocket watch often, squinting at the dial in the pale glow of the gibbous moon and wondering at times if it had stopped altogether. To distract himself, he took out the beef jerky he'd stowed in his saddle bag and gnawed off a piece. But he found that he had no stomach for food and ended up spitting the dried meat onto the desert floor.

Finally the hour passed. He hoisted the saddle back onto the horse. Surprised to feel the familiar weight again so soon, the animal did a little backward dance. But trusting the man, he quickly accommodated himself to the situation. Drummond promised him a full two days' rest and an apple once their journey was over. The chestnut twitched his ears as if he were listening and seemed to move forward with a lighter step.

With only the moon to light the way, their progress was frustratingly slow and searching for tracks pointless. The marshal had no choice but to rely on gut instinct coupled with his years of experience crisscrossing the desert landscape. Trask most likely had a crude lair tucked away in the lee of a sandstone cliff or in a natural cave. A man kidnapped a little girl for only one of two reasons—to collect ransom or to satisfy some perverted pleasure. Since the Jensens were not people of great means, ransom wasn't likely to be Trask's purpose any more than it had been with the other girls he'd killed. As Drummond rode, he ran his hand over the vest pocket that now held the gingham fabric as well as his watch. It seemed like a talisman. He *was* going the right way. He *was* going to find her.

Weary as he was, he remained alert for movement of any kind, rattlers and scorpions being fellow travelers of the night. If the chestnut were bitten by either one, their trip would be over.

The first rays of dawn were peeking beneath the

curtain of night when Drummond saw another piece of blue and white gingham sticking out from behind a good-sized boulder. Perhaps luck was with him after all. Had he passed this way any earlier, he would never have been able to distinguish the cloth from the other features of the desert. With a burst of renewed energy, he jumped down and ran over to it. What he saw when he came around the boulder caused him to sink to his knees. The breath left his body as if he'd been trampled by a herd of cattle.

Before him Betsy Jensen's small body lay broken and battered. Drummond drew the child into his arms, cradling her, a cry of outrage caught deep in his throat.

Chapter 9

After Zeke's vanishing act, Rory stormed through the house, trying to whittle her own anger down to a manageable size. "How on earth is this insane arrangement ever going to work?" she muttered, circling through the first floor as if she were doing laps at a track meet. What could Mac have been thinking?

When she wasn't feeling any calmer by her fourth pass through the entry, she grabbed the keys from her purse and stormed out of the house to vent her frustration outside. Having forgotten that the roads in the area formed a maze of sorts, she didn't make it back to the house for forty-five minutes. By then she was winded and thirsty and feeling less self-righteous. At some point in her impromptu marathon, she'd started to realize that Zeke had not been entirely at fault. She'd pushed him too far under the guise of trying to be helpful, condemned him for overreacting when she had no way of knowing the true depth or nature of the pain he so clearly carried. She knew nothing about him beyond the brief words in Mac's letter, and yet she'd fooled herself into thinking that she could judge him.

Once she was back inside, she called out to him in what she deemed a friendly, white-flag kind of tone. When there was no response, she tried again. Still no sign of him, no indication that he had even heard her. She wanted to apologize for her part in the argument, but she wasn't going to apologize to an empty room.

She drank a cold glass of water without coming up for air. Then she heated a frozen mini pizza in the toaster oven and ate it standing over the sink, too unsettled to sit down. She followed that with half a pint of Chunky Monkey ice cream straight from the container, which somehow always tasted better that way. Her resolution to adopt a heart-healthy diet was failing miserably.

She tried calling Zeke's name again later that evening as she clicked through all the channels that cable television had to offer—a couple hundred of them and not a single thing worth watching. At midnight she gave up on the television and on him. If he wanted to ignore her and stew in his anger, she couldn't stop him. Unfortunately he had a distinct advantage over her. He could be watching her at any given moment, while she had no idea where he was or what he was doing. Like a suspect in an interrogation room, she felt as if she were on the wrong side of a giant one-way mirror. Well, she was not going to let him wage psychological warfare against her. It had been a long day and she was tired. She was going to bed. He could go about his haunting in whatever way he pleased.

Since she'd always slept in the guest room when she'd stayed overnight with Mac, she'd already decided to use that room until her new mattress arrived. She kicked off her shoes and slid between the covers without undressing. Zeke had promised to abide by her rules, but that had been before their argument. She couldn't deal with that issue now. It would have to wait till morning. Right now all she wanted was the luxury of sleep. She closed her eyes and settled into the familiar comfort of the bed. But even as her muscles relaxed, her imagination kicked into overdrive and she couldn't stop thinking about how far she was from the front door. She didn't actually believe that Zeke would harm her, but lying there in the dark, the creative side of her brain was conjuring up one disturbing scenario after another.

At three a.m. she trudged down the stairs with her pillow tucked under her arm to try her luck on the living room couch. Although it wasn't as comfortable as the bed in the guest room, it had the distinct advantage of being closer to the door. Only now she found herself constantly checking to make sure that Zeke hadn't returned to occupy the chair across from her. She was on the verge of giving up and turning the television back on when exhaustion finally claimed her and pulled her into a deep but dream-tossed sleep.

As her eyes blinked open to the daylight, she made a mental note to buy some room-darkening shades in case she spent any more nights on the couch. She took a quick shower and changed her clothes. If the marshal was spying on her, he'd have himself a dandy show. She hoped it brought him a bushel of frustration.

Rory was ready for work two hours early, which was

fine since she'd been wanting to take a look at the evidence in Gail Oberlin's file at a time when she was less likely to be disturbed or questioned about her interest in it. That morning seemed like the perfect opportunity. Not only would she be glad to focus on something other than her enigmatic housemate, but she also knew that Jeremy was waiting anxiously for news about his sister's death.

When she reached police headquarters, she bypassed the main building with its long, deep-set windows that had once seemed avant-garde and now just reminded her of an enormous accordion. She drove on until she reached the property unit where evidence from closed and inactive police files was stored. It was a large, featureless building with the charm of a concrete box. Due to the earliness of the hour and the fact that the repository wasn't open to the public, the only car in the parking lot was a white and blue police cruiser. She pulled into the spot next to it and went inside.

The officer behind the desk was drinking coffee from a 7-Eleven cup and leafing through the newspaper. Since Rory didn't know him, she produced her ID and badge. Once he'd checked them and she'd signed in, he buzzed her through the inner door.

She'd been there only a few times before, but it was as depressing as she remembered. Metal shelves reached from floor to ceiling on either side of the narrow aisles that stretched to the back wall of the repository. These were intersected by other aisles so that the layout was like a grid. Scarred wooden tables with mismatched chairs were situated at several of the intersections. Although the materials stored there were called files, what actually filled the shelves were storage boxes, each holding the evidence related to a single case. The paperwork that went with each closed case was stored in another facility out in West Hampton. To request a copy of those records required the filling out of paperwork as mandated by the Freedom of Information Act, followed by the inevitable wait associated with any bureaucratic transaction. Thankfully Mac had taken care of that before he'd passed away. A copy of the police report on Gail Oberlin was in the file that Rory already had. What she was interested in today was the evidence.

Since the boxes were arranged chronologically, with the oldest at the rear of the facility, Rory had no trouble finding the aisle marked "2008." As she scanned the shelves for Gail's name, it struck her that the place resembled a huge cemetery crypt with cardboard boxes instead of coffins, and names written in indelible marker instead of being etched in stone. In spite of the bright fluorescent lighting, the silence and stillness of the room only served to reinforce that perception, and she found herself thinking again about the murder of Marshal Ezekiel Drummond and wondering what had become of the evidence in that case. The odds were that it no longer existed; otherwise Mac would have found it. She shook her head as if that could dislodge the marshal from her mind. *He* was not the reason she was there.

She found the box marked "Oberlin, Gail" and carried it to one of the tables. When she lifted the lid, she thought the box was empty. Then she saw the ragged two-inch piece of plastic wrap curled in one corner. Although Mac's notes had mentioned only this one item, she'd somehow expected to find more in the box.

With recent advances in forensic detection, it was hard to believe that nothing else had been discovered.

She picked up the thin scrap of plastic. It wasn't as soft and flexible as the kind of wrap sold by the role in grocery stores and used in homes all over the country to store leftovers. It seemed thicker, less flexible, like the outer wrapping on a manufactured product. Rory was sure that she'd handled something similar to it in the past, but she couldn't remember what it might have been. There were so many products covered in so many forms of plastic wrap these days, that without more information it would be impossible to find a match.

She turned it over in her hand, looking for the fine black line described in the report. She found it on the very edge of the plastic. It had probably been part of a label or a UPC code, but there wasn't any way to know for sure. Either Gail had fallen as the ME concluded, or her killer had executed the perfect murder. Even though it was unlikely that the CSI team had missed anything of importance, Rory felt that she had to get back into the house and take a closer look. And she had to do it when she wasn't being watched or escorted. Since she'd already crossed breaking and entering off her list, she'd have to come up with another plan.

She put the piece of plastic wrap back in the box and returned the box to its final resting place on the shelf. Then she went to the front desk to sign out. The officer on duty swallowed the last of his coffee and crushed the cup before tossing it into the wastebasket beside him. He told Rory to have a good day

Once she was back in her car, she drove out of the complex to the nearest Starbucks. If she didn't have a decent cup of coffee herself, she was never going to make it through her workday and perhaps more important, the appointment she'd made to see David Oberlin that evening.

Chapter 10

At six fifty-seven Rory turned onto Oak Tree Lane. The road was narrow, winding and entirely too close to the edge of the heavily treed cliff for her liking. From time to time the wind would stir the branches of the massive old oaks for which the street was named, affording her a glimpse of the Long Island Sound glinting like a puddle of liquid pewter far below. But she couldn't take her eyes off the road for more than a second for fear that she'd be viewing the Sound up close and personal through the windshield of her plummeting car. How on earth had the Oberlins ever managed to leave their house in the winter? Not even a snowplow and sanding truck on twenty-four-hour retainer would be able to make that road safe enough to travel during the blizzards and ice storms that were standards of a Long Island winter. Of course, for all she knew, they had an elaborate sled and a dozen Alaskan huskies just straining in their traces for some Iditarod action. In any case, Rory was grateful that it was summer.

She'd also been surprisingly lucky as far as David Oberlin was concerned. When she'd called him to request a meeting, she'd expected it to be a hard sell. She couldn't identify herself as a police officer, and being a private eye didn't actually entitle you to harass people, in spite of what passed for realism in the world of television. Given that Oberlin had already dealt with the police and with Mac, she knew she was pressing her luck by contacting him.

"My wife's death is a closed case, Ms. McCain," Oberlin had said stiffly after Rory identified herself, "and I'd prefer not to keep reliving it."

"I understand completely," Rory replied in the lilting, slightly addled tone she usually reserved for babies and puppies. "You have every right to refuse to see me, Mr. Oberlin, but I was hoping maybe you'd be willing to help me out." As much as she hated to play the damsel in distress, in this situation she needed to sound as nonthreatening as possible. If she'd thought she could pull off a southern belle drawl, she would gladly have used it.

"And how on earth can I be of help?" Oberlin asked, sounding perplexed but less wary.

"Well, you see, my uncle died recently and I've been trying to close down his private detective agency and send all of his files back to the people who hired him. Unfortunately my uncle had the absolute worst handwriting, so I've been typing up the notes in each file. I can't begin to tell you how hard that's been." She produced a small, self-conscious hiccup of a laugh.

"I'm afraid I still don't understand how I can help," Oberlin repeated impatiently, but at least he hadn't hung up on her.

"If I could just stop by and ask you a couple of questions—it might be enough to help me decipher the notes. It's been a huge help with some of his other case files," she added to assure him that he wasn't being singled out. "I promise I won't take up much of your time."

"I assume these notes you're typing are for Jeremy?"

"Well, yes, is that a problem?" she asked, throwing a little naiveté into the mix.

There was a long pause before Oberlin answered, and for a moment Rory thought she'd lost him after all. "No, I suppose not. You can come by Tuesday evening."

"Oh, that's so gracious of you. Thank you so much. Are you still at the Forest Hills address?"

"No, I'm at five Oak Tree Lane in Cold Spring Harbor."

Apparently the grieving widower had already moved back into the house that Gail had thrown him out of when she'd discovered that he was cheating on her. Rory was careful to keep any surprise out of her voice. "Would seven be okay?"

Now here she was, four minutes past the appointed hour, wondering how much farther the Oberlin home could possibly be. She rounded yet another curve and finally saw a brick driveway parting the trees on her left, the number five written in black script on a huge boulder that stood to one side. She turned into the driveway and followed it around to a large, white clapboard house, which, from her prospective, seemed to be hugging the edge of the cliff.

Carrying her pocketbook and the leather folio she'd bought for the occasion, she locked the car and walked up to the front door. She rang the bell—show time.

The door was opened by a man in his forties, whose cheeks had begun the downward slide into jowls, even as his creeping paunch threatened to overlap his belt.

"Mr. Oberlin," she said holding out her hand, "I'm Rory McCain."

Oberlin gave her hand a perfunctory shake and stepped back so that she could enter. "We'll talk in the living room, if that's all right."

Although his words formed a question, there was no room for debate in his tone. She followed him through an oversized doorway to the left of the entry hall. The living room was large and softly lit by the lowering sun and a wash of pink light from a Tiffany lamp. A highly polished white baby grand piano occupied the far corner of the room. The walls, rugs and fabrics were all in shades of white and cream, the neutral tones providing the perfect backdrop for the stunning collection of artwork and antiques that Gail and her almost ex had amassed.

"Have a seat," David Oberlin said, gesturing to the two white silk sofas that faced each other in the center of the room. Rory chose the one that faced away from the windows so that the sun wouldn't be in her eyes. She wanted to be able to read his expressions. She set her purse on the floor beside her and dug into the leather folio for her notes and a pen. In keeping with the story she'd told him, she'd rewritten Mac's somewhat legible notes into a form that no one else could possibly read. Since it was doubtful that Oberlin had paid attention to

Mac's handwriting during their only meeting, she didn't anticipate any problems.

"Okay, Ms. McCain, I'm listening," Oberlin said. He'd taken a seat across from her and seemed completely at ease, not at all like a man with something to hide. Of course, the odds were that he actually *had* nothing to hide. The only reason Rory was even bothering to interview him herself was that Mac had taught her if you wanted to find a needle in a haystack, you had to sift through every last straw of hay. At the time of Mac's death, most of this particular haystack was still very much intact.

"Hmm," Rory murmured, frowning at her phony notes for a minute. "Oh yes." She looked up with an apologetic smile. "My uncle's notes seem to indicate that you and your wife were estranged."

"Yes, for several months."

"And she'd started divorce proceedings?"

"Not yet, but we'd both agreed that was the next logical step."

"Right," Rory said, taking pains to make her new notes larger and easier to read, so that even from his seat Oberlin would see the difference. "Okay," she said, biting her lower lip to underscore the difficulty of deciphering Mac's writing.

"Please bear with me; I can't make out much of this next paragraph." She let another few moments pass as she pretended to study the words before her. "I think this says something about changing your wills or beneficiaries?"

"Actually there wasn't time to do any of that before Gail died," he acknowledged.

According to the police report he had been the number one "person of interest" until the coroner deemed Gail's death an accident. At that point the investigation into David Oberlin had been shut down, along with the rest of the case. When Rory first read the report, she'd been struck by the size of the fortune he'd stood to lose once the divorce was final. Over a hundred million dollars made for a dandy motive.

"*That* was lucky," she said, hoping the artless comment would catch him off guard.

Oberlin's eyes narrowed; his jaw tightened.

For a moment Rory thought she'd pushed him too far. If he had killed his wife, he would certainly have no compunction about killing her. And if he made a move against her, she wouldn't even have time to retrieve the .380 Walther that she'd tucked into the folio. What's more, no one knew where she was, because she hadn't wanted anyone to know, and the closest neighbors were acres away through dense, sound-baffling stands of oaks. She'd have to play out this scene that she'd set in motion and hope that he was guilty of nothing more than good luck.

"Oh my goodness," she said sheepishly, hand to her mouth in feigned embarrassment. "I didn't mean that the way it sounded."

"Sure you did," Oberlin said. But then his face relaxed into an unexpected smile. "Truth is you're right. I didn't think I'd see any of that money. I guess sometimes there's justice in this crazy world."

Rory smiled and bobbed her head in agreement. One thing was clear, if he *was* guilty, being acquitted by the coroner's report had made him feel untouchable.

"I promise I won't waste much more of your time," she said, squinting at Mac's notes again. "There seems to be something here about a Cathy?"

"Casey. Casey Landis," he said soberly. He leaned forward and looked straight into Rory's eyes. "Listen, Ms. McCain, my wife was married to her career. It was all she cared about. I was pretty much superfluous." He shook his head with a sigh of disgust. "I think she was actually relieved when I met Casey and gave up trying to make our marriage work."

Rory was struck by the honesty in his face and in his voice. Either he was telling the truth, or he was doing a better job of acting than she was.

"Okay. I guess what this says is that you were with Casey Landis the night your wife died."

Before Oberlin could answer, an attractive blonde in her forties strode into the room. She moved with the poise of a woman who knew herself well and was confident in her abilities.

"Yes, he was with me," she said defiantly, taking a seat beside Oberlin. "I'm Casey Landis." She planted a hand possessively on Oberlin's thigh. Rory noted the long tapered fingernails and the emerald-cut diamond on her left hand that had to weigh in at four carats minimum.

From where Rory was seated, she had a view of the entry hall and she hadn't seen anyone come through the front door, so Casey had either come down the stairs or from a room at the rear of the house, possibly the kitchen.

"Nice to meet you." She nodded in Casey's direction, since she was no longer in hand-shaking range. At least

Oberlin hadn't gone for a girl half his age. That raised
him a notch or two in Rory's esteem. But she'd been
planning to call on Casey at another time and preferably when she was alone. Interviewing a suspect with
another suspect present was almost always a bad idea.

David Oberlin seemed as disgruntled as she was,
although no doubt for a very different reason. It didn't take
a supersleuth to deduce that he had stationed his paramour
close enough to hear their conversation without letting on
that she was there. That way if Rory wanted to speak to
her at a later date, their stories would be sure to mesh.
Even if they weren't guilty, conflicting stories might well
raise some red flags and possibly tempt the police into
reopening the case. And that was a situation even the most
innocent of people wanted to avoid, trial by media pundits
being a proven method of ruining one's life.

Casey seemed oblivious to the effect her entrance
had wrought in Oberlin. She was clearly not a woman
who responded well to taking orders or to staying in the
background.

"Ms. McCain," she said, her blue eyes flashing with
indignation, "the only reason David even agreed to this
meeting is because he's too nice a guy to turn anyone
down."

"I do realize that," Rory said, "and I appreciate his
help. I'm really just trying to put my uncle's affairs in
order." Which was at least partially true.

Casey refused to be placated. "It's no secret that Gail
had plenty of enemies. Hell, I hardly knew her and I was
glad to hear that she was dead. But that doesn't change
the fact that it was an accident. If you need someone to
blame, then you're going to have to round up Fate and
put *her* on trial."

"Take it easy, Case," Oberlin said with an uncomfortable laugh. "I don't think Ms. McCain is looking to put anyone on trial here."

"Of course not," Rory said lightly. She gathered her notes together and slid them into the folio. There was no point in staying there with Casey in guard-dog mode. She thanked Oberlin again and said her good-byes.

"Wow!" she exhaled as she slid into her car. She'd pulled it off! She'd really pulled it off. Of course, it was unfortunate that Casey had interrupted the interview, but some things were simply not under her control. Besides, it had given her a chance to see how the two of them interacted. From the moment she'd laid eyes on Casey, she'd known that the woman was not only trying to protect her man, but she was also trying to protect the great wealth he'd just inherited. Wealth that would soon become hers as well. Rory was willing to take bets that the engagement ring on Casey's perfectly manicured finger would soon be joined by an equally impressive wedding band. In her opinion David Oberlin was about to jump from the frying pan directly into the fire.

She pulled out of the driveway and started the winding descent down the hillside, her mind still racing as if she'd just downed a double espresso. She was beginning to understand Jeremy's certainty that his sister had been murdered. She'd just begun to scratch the surface of the case and she already had two people with motive and opportunity and, according to the police report, only each other as alibis.

Rory had taken on the investigation as a goodwill gesture to Jeremy, but she had to admit that she'd found tonight's little caper exhilarating. She hadn't felt this challenged by her work in a long time. No, that wasn't fair. She'd actually *never* felt this challenged by her work.

By the time she pulled into her own driveway, the last of the sun's rays had been all but gobbled up by the horizon. The house loomed in front of her, dressed in murky shadows, compliments of a broken street lamp. Damn—she'd forgotten to leave a light on when she'd rushed off to work that morning. She certainly didn't relish the thought of walking into that darkness, knowing that a sullen, moody ghost was waiting inside for her.

Chapter 11

Zeke was sitting on the staircase, third step from the bottom, like a parent awaiting the return of an overdue child, or a spouse the return of a loved one after a quarrel. But his expression was neither worried nor apologetic.

"You keep even worse hours than your uncle did," he observed. Either he'd forgotten about his tantrum the previous evening, or he was pretending that it hadn't happened. Not that it mattered to Rory. She'd had a long day on very little sleep, and now that the adrenalin rush from her meeting with Oberlin was ebbing away, all she wanted was some peace and quiet. She certainly had no desire to engage in verbal fisticuffs with the marshal.

"I didn't know I was expected to punch a time clock," she said as she walked past him.

She dropped her jacket, purse and folio onto the small upholstered bench that Mac had placed in the entry to facilitate the changing of footwear in bad weather. Then she kicked off her heels and padded barefoot down the hall to the kitchen.

She grabbed a peach from the refrigerator, eating it as she headed back to the staircase. On the way, she stopped to pull her notes out of the folio. Zeke was nowhere in sight. Just as well. Upstairs she turned into the study and booted up the computer. She wanted to write out her impressions from the interview for Jeremy while they were still fresh in her mind. When the monitor flashed to life, Mac's icons covered half the screen. She found a strange comfort in seeing them there exactly as they'd been when she last visited Mac. Before she could start to wallow in melancholy, she opened the word processing program, pulled up a new page and started typing. Twenty minutes later she was about to read through her notes to see if she'd omitted anything important when a sharp whistle made her jump in her seat.

She swung her chair around in a one-eighty, trying to locate the source of the noise. Puzzled, she turned back to face the computer and found Zeke perched on the edge of the desk.

"How's that for a warning signal?" he asked her. His expression was perfectly sober, but she could swear there was a touch of amusement in his voice.

"I appreciate the effort," she said, trying to keep her own voice businesslike, "but a signal that's supposed to avoid startling me shouldn't actually make me levitate out of my chair."

"You sure do startle easy." Zeke laughed. It was a deep raspy sound, as if he was a little rusty in the laughter department. He was looking at Rory as if he expected her to start laughing along with him.

Rory tried to keep a straight face, determined to keep him from reducing her rules to a joke, but his laugh was infectious, and the circumstances were certainly absurd enough to be funny. Her lips twitched with the tug of a smile, and she was quickly overpowered by the laughter bubbling up inside her. She'd forgotten how remarkably good it felt.

"There you go," Zeke said. "I was pretty darned sure you had at least one good laugh in you. You're Mac's niece after all and he had a mighty fine sense of humor."

"He did." Rory sighed, trying to regain her composure. "Look, I'm not trying to be difficult, but that whistle really won't do."

"I could see about tonin' it down some or maybe find a different way to announce myself."

"I'd appreciate that." She turned back to the computer screen. It was all well and good to have a little fun, but the only way this strange living arrangement was going to work was if she remained the alpha dog.

She did her best to focus on the notes she'd written, which wasn't all that easy with Zeke still sitting there, watching her.

"I don't understand what's so all fired fascinatin' about that contraption," he grumbled after several minutes.

Rory looked up at him. "I'm sure there were things in your time that I wouldn't have understood."

"I suppose as how that might be," he said, vanishing from the front of the desk to stand beside her. "Mac tried to explain how it all works, but I can't rightly say that I get it."

"I use the damned thing and I hardly get it," she said.

Zeke hunkered down to read the screen better. "Well now, I see you're writin' there about that Oberlin lady who fell down the stairs and cracked her skull open. So you've gone and taken on Mac's old cases."

"Just this one. Her brother's convinced that she was murdered."

"Interestin' case," Zeke said, straightening to his full height again. "Mac used to talk to me about the interestin' ones. And I believe I was of some genuine help to him."

"You were. He said so in his letter."

Zeke smiled, clearly pleased by this revelation. He returned to his seat on the front edge of the desk. "I'd be glad to help you out same as I did for him."

Rory wasn't sure how he could help her, or for that matter how he'd been able to help Mac, given that modern investigative techniques were so far superior to what they were in Zeke's day. But she had to admit that the idea of bouncing her thoughts off someone else had a certain appeal. In spite of how tired she was, she wound up giving him a detailed account of her meeting with David Oberlin and his fiancée, Casey Landis.

"I expect you're gonna have to wait a good while before tryin' to talk to Miss Casey again."

"My thoughts exactly. If I wait long enough, she might think they're off the hook, maybe slip and say something incriminating."

"Of course, that's assumin' one or both of them is guilty. What's your gut tellin' you?"

"That's the funny part." Rory sighed, leaning back in the chair. "All that money is a great motive, and David probably knew she was working alone at that house, so they had opportunity, but somehow my gut isn't convinced they did it."

"If there's one thing I learned in our kind of work, gut instinct counts for a lot more than folks these days are willin' to allow. Back in my day we didn't have all the bells and whistles. Hell, I don't think I ever heard the word 'forensic' till I started workin' with Mac. What with all the new-fangled testin': DNA, toxicology, fingerprintin' . . ."

"Wait a minute," Rory said. "You must have had fingerprinting."

"I do recall some talk about a fella over in Europe who claimed that no two people had the same fingerprints. But I don't see how you can be sure of that till you've gone and checked every single person's prints."

Rory smiled. "You have a point there."

"Everybody's so focused on the little picture these days that they go missin' some of the important stuff. You gotta learn to trust your gut. We had instincts long before we had tests."

"One of the things bothering me," Rory said, warming to their dialogue, "is that David and Casey don't have decent alibis. These are two bright, savvy people. If they were guilty they would have made sure they had foolproof ones."

"Or they were countin' on investigators thinkin' just that."

"Which would bring me back to square one." Rory sighed again.

"For the time bein'. But as I recall, Mac was considerin' some other suspects. You talk to any of them?"

"Not yet. What I really want to do is get back into the house where Gail died. But breaking in at night is out of the question, and I can't accomplish anything with a real estate agent toddling around after me."

"Well," Zeke said, 'if you can't be there alone, the next best thing is to be there in a crowd. If the agent's busy showin' other folks around the house, that oughta get you some time on your own."

Rory thought about that for a moment. "I guess I could check the newspapers for the next open house and hang out there in my car until I see other people go in."

"Or you could put together a crowd of your own."

She shook her head. "I don't want to get anyone else involved in this." Her friends at work would probably be glad to help, but the more people who knew what she was up to, the riskier it was that someone would slip and say something that might compromise her job. As for her other friends, they were busy juggling jobs, husbands and babies. They hardly even had time to meet for coffee these days.

"It's your call." Zeke shrugged. "I'd help you out if I could."

Rory wasn't quite sure what he meant by that, but she almost dissolved into laughter again as she pictured him in his homespun cowboy duds winking in and out as he made his way through the million-dollar house alongside a horrified real estate agent.

"Thanks for the suggestion," she said. "I'll keep it in mind. But right now I need some sleep." She saved what she'd written, logged off the computer and pushed back from the desk.

"I'll be leavin' you to your privacy then," Zeke said reluctantly.

Rory didn't wait for him to vanish. He could watch her regardless of whether or not she could see him anyway. She said good night and went into the guest room where the sheets were still tangled in the center of the bed from the previous night's insomnia. She made a halfhearted attempt to straighten them out before falling onto the bed without bothering to undress or brush her teeth. It felt like a week since she'd last slept. Her eyes were closed before her head came to rest on the pillow. But just before her thoughts unraveled into the disjointed fabric of dreams, she realized who could populate her makeshift crowd.

Chapter 12

The next morning Rory awakened more rested than she'd felt in weeks. If she'd dreamed, she wasn't aware of it. The epiphany she'd had before falling asleep popped into her mind as her feet hit the floor. She jotted a memo to herself on a sticky note and stuck it on her computer screen. It was too early to call anyone.

She showered and dressed, ate a multigrain cereal bar that promised to give her half a day's worth of fiber and energy and went off to work without seeing Zeke. Except for the fact that she kept expecting him to appear after every little noise she heard, life seemed almost normal. The next time she saw him, they'd have to work out exactly what signal he intended to use. She couldn't be looking over her shoulder every time a bird chirped, a dog barked or the beams and joists in the old house groaned.

At work, the day plodded along as if everything were

happening in slow motion. She arranged a lineup for a witness to a robbery, helped a young mother go through mug shots to see if she could pick out the man who'd tried to lure her little boy away at the playground, then tried to catch up on the inevitable pile of paperwork. If computers were supposed to help cut down on the use of paper, they sure weren't holding up their half of the bargain.

As the day wore on, Rory had a hard time concentrating. Apparently her subconscious found the circumstances surrounding Gail's death more interesting than the work she was being paid to do, and it took every opportunity to hijack her attention.

"No, no, no! That's not what I said!" The middle-aged man who was seated beside her was losing his patience. He was the only witness to a hit-and-run that had sent a woman to the hospital in critical condition. "The guy had a little goatee; he wasn't friggin' Santa Claus."

"You said he had a beard. I'm sorry if I misinterpreted that," Rory replied tightly as she corrected the picture.

"Fine, let's just get on with it. I gotta get back to work; no one else is gonna finish up my deliveries."

Five minutes later he declared the computerized sketch to be a reasonable likeness of the suspect and Rory thanked him for his help.

"Yeah, sure," he muttered as he hauled himself out of the chair. "No good deed goes unpunished."

"You okay there?" Leah Russell asked a moment later as she sank into the empty chair beside Rory. "You usually don't let the assholes get to you."

Rory shrugged and produced a smile that fell somewhere short of genuine. "I guess I've just had a lot on my mind lately."

She could tell from the way Leah's left eyebrow arched that she didn't entirely buy the excuse. For a moment Rory considered telling her about the investigation she'd taken on. She was pretty sure that her friend wouldn't betray the confidence, but it didn't seem fair to make her a party to the rule bending. For that matter she would have loved to tell someone, anyone, about Zeke. But there were no words that didn't sound ten shades of crazy, even to her.

When the workday finally ended, Rory slid gratefully into her car, feeling a bit like a bird whose cage had been left open. Although she had a few stops to make before heading home, she felt glad just to be away from her desk. The first stop was an Italian provisions store fifteen minutes north of the expressway on local streets. She was in the mood for fresh pasta and theirs was the best she'd ever had. She'd pair it up with a container of their homemade pomodoro sauce and a loaf of crusty semolina bread. Mac would approve, she thought. And the thought was accompanied by a twinge of guilt. How many times had she thought of him today? Not more than once or twice. Life was already beginning to seal him off from her. The open wound caused by his death was beginning to heal. She knew this was normal, even imperative, if people were to survive loss and carry on. But it seemed fickle and disloyal just the same.

The provisions store was in a strip mall coming up on her right. Although she signaled well before the entrance, when she slowed to turn into the lot, there was an ugly squeal of brakes from somewhere behind her. She glanced into the rearview mirror. The silver Ford two cars back had stopped inches from the car in front of it. Given how little attention people paid to their driving these days, Rory considered it something of a miracle that there weren't more accidents.

Inside the store, she waited behind half a dozen other customers who had also stopped to pick up dinner. The men behind the counter were used to the rush-hour madness and had her on her way less than ten minutes later. She followed Route 454 down to the Northern State Parkway where the traffic was heavy but moving. At one point when she glanced in the rearview mirror, she saw a silver Ford a couple of cars behind her again. Of course there were probably dozens, if not hundreds, of silver Fords on the road at rush hour, and a good percentage of them would be heading west with her. Between the intervening car, the tinted windows and the glare of the lowering sun, she couldn't see more than a shadowy form behind the wheel. In any case, since she hadn't seen the driver of the squealing brakes, she wouldn't have had any means for comparison. And since the car wasn't directly behind her, she still couldn't see the license plate.

"Come on now, Rory," she scolded herself, "get a grip." When had she become so paranoid? Maybe it was the result of conducting a murder investigation and living with a ghost. She hit the button for the CD changer and found her favorite album by Brule. Although her musical taste ran the gamut from Led Zeppelin to Jeff Buckley, Dar Williams and more contemporary artists like Audioslave and Foo Fighters, she'd found that the Native American music of Brule worked best to calm her when she was tense. But it didn't stand a chance of relaxing her today. Every time she checked her rearview mirror, the silver Ford was still there.

When she exited the parkway at Huntington, the

Ford exited three cars behind her. When she reached Jericho Turnpike, she moved into the left-turn lane and waited for the light to change. The Ford was now two cars back, also in the turn lane.

What were the odds that she and the driver of the silver Ford had identical rounds to make? Well, she was going to find out right now. She pulled into the parking lot at her dry cleaners. The silver Ford didn't follow her. She was breathing a sigh of relief and beginning to feel a bit silly when she saw it pull into the entrance of the adjacent lot. The driver parked but never got out of the car. There was only one explanation that fit the circumstances: he had no reason to be there. He was following her.

She decided to act as if she had no idea he was there. She went into the cleaners, picked up her blazer and got back into her car. When she left the lot, she noted that he waited for two other cars to follow her out before falling in line behind them. As soon as Rory found an opening, she gunned the engine and started weaving around the slower traffic until she had a good lead on the silver Ford. As she rounded a wide curve and could no longer see him in her rearview mirror, she took a sharp right onto a side street, then a quick right off of that. Thank goodness she was in an area where she knew her way around. She looked behind her. No silver Ford.

She made a third right turn and came back up to Jericho Turnpike. The Ford was somewhere up ahead. The hunter was about to become the hunted. After a minute she caught sight of him in the right lane. He was braking to look down each cross street he came to. The cars behind him were honking and swinging into the center lane to get away from him.

Rory reached under her seat for the portable siren

she'd been given when she joined the police force. She'd never used it before and had been certain she never would. So much for the certainties of life. She plugged the magnetized unit into the cigarette lighter, reached out of the window and set it on the roof of the car. With the siren wailing and the light flashing, traffic around her quickly gave way and in seconds she was behind the Ford. When it slowed to get out of her way, Rory matched its speed, signaling to the driver to pull onto the shoulder of the road.

She unsnapped the holster at her waist as she emerged from her car. She'd never conducted a traffic stop before, and since this was not an "Excuse me, sir, but your left turn signal doesn't seem to be working" kind of encounter, she thought it would be prudent to be ready for any eventuality. Like a pitcher shaking off the catcher's signal, she shook off the little voice in her head that was demanding to know what the hell she thought she was doing. It was too late now for second thoughts.

She was halfway to the Ford and still working on what she was going to say to the driver when he hit the accelerator and shot back onto the road, spewing dirt and pebbles in his wake.

Rory stood there for a moment, surprised and angry, and feeling a little foolish. At least she'd memorized the license plate. She got back into her car and called headquarters. Leah was still there. Rory told her that she thought the silver Ford might have been following her and gave her the plate number. When Leah pressed her for details, she admitted that her attempt to pull the driver over had been a fiasco. Although she tried to play up the humor in the incident, she could tell that Leah wasn't amused.

When she reached the house on Brandywine Lane, she found that she wasn't hungry after all. So she put the angel hair pasta and pomodoro sauce in the refrigerator and took out a cold Corona and a wedge of lime. College chums, police colleagues, even Mac had all tried to get her to ditch the lime and take her beer straight. But Rory wouldn't budge. For her, it was all about the lime. When the bottle was empty, she felt calm enough to call her parents.

Her father answered the phone, but he sounded distracted. Rory could hear what sounded like an old Clark Gable movie playing in the background, so she asked to speak to her mother instead.

"You mean we'd be helping you with an investigation?" Arlene asked after Rory had explained that she wanted them to be part of her "crowd."

"Well, yes, I suppose you could say that."

"How exciting! You just tell me the time and place and we'll be there. Oh, can Helene come along?"

"I was counting on it." Rory had already planned to include her aunt Helene, who during the past decade of her spinsterhood had become a perpetual third wheel to her parents' marriage. The three formed a strange symbiotic union. If Arlene wanted to go shopping or antiquing or to a movie with more dialogue than action, she had her sister to accompany her, and Dan would be left in peace to enjoy whatever ballgame or movie was being televised. For Rory's purposes, Helene was hands down the best qualified of the three to keep the real estate agent occupied with endless questions and comments.

"Just make sure she knows not to mention anything about the murder or the fact that I'm investigating it."

"Not to worry. I'll make sure she understands."

They said their good-byes and Rory was about to return the phone to its base when it rang again in her hand. She glanced at the number on the screen. It was Leah's line at headquarters.

"I hope you're not still there because of me," she said by way of "hello."

"I had some paperwork to finish up anyway. But listen, Rory, that car you thought was following you? It was reported stolen five minutes ago."

Chapter 13

"Okay," Rory said, inching forward on the edge of the couch as if that would bring her the news more quickly. "What do you have?"

"Unfortunately, not much. The owner parked her car at the mall to do some shopping and when she came out two hours later, it was gone." Leah paused for a moment. When Rory didn't comment, she went on. "Can you think of anyone who would risk a felony conviction in order to follow you around?"

Rory had been pondering that possibility since she'd called in the plate. As a sketch artist she was generally below the radar when it came to aggrieved criminals seeking revenge. So either she had a garden variety stalker on her hands, which she doubted, or she'd stirred up a hornet's nest by reopening the investigation into Gail Oberlin's death.

"Not off the top of my head," she said, hoping she

sounded more innocent than she felt. If they'd been having this conversation in person, she wouldn't have stood a chance of fooling Leah; the woman had an uncanny knack for spotting a "tell" when someone was dancing a little sidestep around the truth.

There was a long pause before Leah said,"I've known you long enough, my friend, to know there's something you're not telling me and I'm dead serious when I say that you cannot do the Lone Ranger bit. You're a sketch artist; you have zero street experience."

"Understood, Mom."

"Cut the 'Mom' crap," Leah grumbled. "Hell, I'm not even old enough to be your mother."

"And yet sometimes you can be irritatingly maternal," Rory said wryly, hoping to tease her into a lighter mood. She knew that everything Leah said was true, but she couldn't have someone watching over her 24/7. That would be the end of her investigation. And she had a feeling that the conversation was heading precisely in that direction.

Leah refused to be derailed from her crusade. "I'd like to assign a detail to keep an eye on you until we sort this thing out."

"No. No way."

"Is there anything I can do to change your mind?"

"Sure. You can get me a date with George Clooney." Rory laughed.

"If I could arrange a date with Clooney, what makes you think I'd be willing to share?"

"Then I guess we're at an impasse."

Leah sighed. "At least promise me that you won't take any more chances like you did today."

"Yes, ma'am," Rory replied. "Now you get out of

there and go on home before your husband puts your picture on a milk carton."

After Rory clicked off the phone, she remained on the couch for a while longer trying to objectively assess the danger she was courting by continuing the investigation. In the end she found that she wasn't any more successful in talking herself out of it than Leah had been. By way of a compromise, she vowed to be more vigilant. "Caution" would become her watch word.

Having settled that question, Rory realized she was finally hungry. The fresh angel hair needed only a few minutes in boiling water, while the sauce heated in the microwave. She cut a thick chunk off the Italian bread, grabbed the Romano cheese from the refrigerator and was settled at the sleek glass and chrome kitchen table in under ten minutes.

She was still savoring her first mouthful when the overhead lights flickered. Strange, she thought, there was no wind to tug at the wires and the temperature wasn't hot enough to cause a brownout. Of course, there might be a short in the wiring.

Just as Rory was deciding that it would be prudent to have an electrician check things out, Zeke materialized in the chair across the table from her.

"How's that?" he asked, leaning back in the chair and hefting his boots onto the edge of the table. "Attention getting, yet quiet." Beneath the heavy fringe of his moustache, his mouth was curved up in a self-satisfied smile.

How on earth had she managed to forget the Zeke factor?

"Not bad," she said, reminding herself that Zeke's

dirty old boots weren't actually on the table, any more than his physical body was actually in that chair. "I think I can live with that."

"What've you got there?" Zeke asked. He set his feet back on the floor and leaned forward for a better look. "That's that Italian stuff Mac liked so much."

Rory smiled. "It's just pasta with tomato sauce. Mac and I could pretty much eat Italian every night. Didn't you like it?"

Zeke shook his head. "Can't rightly say as how I've ever tasted it."

"I don't suppose you could try it in your present state."

He laughed. "That would be like tryin' to feed it to one of your fancy 'lectrical lights."

Rory laughed along with him. Who would ever believe that she was sitting at the kitchen table having dinner conversation with a ghost? It was a moot point, of course. If she told anyone, she'd wind up in a straitjacket with a standing appointment for electroshock therapy.

She broke off a piece of the bread and chewed it thoughtfully. "Do you ever miss things like eating?"

"In the beginnin' I did. Eatin', among *other things*." Zeke grinned and a roguish twinkle danced in his brown eyes. Then as if a switch had been flipped somewhere inside him, he fell silent. His smile faded and deep shadows hollowed the plains beneath his cheekbones. When he spoke again, his tone was matter-of-fact.

"But that was mostly 'cause I hadn't owned up to bein' dead and all."

Rory was immediately sorry that she'd broached the subject. She was definitely more comfortable around an amiable Zeke than a morose or angry one. She should stick to things of a less personal nature, like her investigation.

Zeke perked up with interest as she filled him in about the silver Ford.

"Sounds like you rattled someone's cage," he said. "But I'm thinkin' they just wanted to scare you off. If they'd really intended to harm you, they would've."

"Let's hope you're right, because I have no intentions of giving up. If anything, they've made me more determined than ever to find out what happened to Gail."

"Now hold on there," Zeke said. "Just 'cause they didn't intend you harm today don't mean they won't try to kill you tomorrow."

Why was everyone so sure that she couldn't take care of herself?

"I'll tell you what," she said. "You can be my sidekick. That way you can come along and scare off the bad guys if things get rough." Although Rory intended the remark to be funny, Zeke didn't laugh. He was busy studying the fraying cuff of his right sleeve.

"I can't leave the house," he said when he finally looked up at her.

"You mean you don't want to leave, or you can't?" Rory asked with surprise. She'd had no idea that ghosts had such boundaries.

"Can't's what I said and can't's what I meant," Zeke snapped. "I may not have as much schoolin' as you, but I know the difference between 'want' and 'can't.'"

Before Rory could say anything more he vanished from his seat. She turned to look for him and found that he'd relocated to the granite-topped workstation in the middle of the room. He stood there, arms folded, glowering at her.

"I'm sorry." Rory said. "I didn't mean to imply . . ."

Zeke's expression softened. "Okay, I'm gonna cut you some slack, seein' as how you've had a whole lot thrown at you lately."

Rory caught herself before she could tell him what she thought of his magnanimous gesture. Instead, she turned back to the table to finish her dinner.

A couple of minutes later Zeke reappeared in the chair across from her. "I was serious when I told you that you need to be careful," he said, as if nothing had happened to interrupt their conversation.

"I'm sure you were," Rory replied, making an effort to keep her voice neutral. "But I've made a commitment to pursue this investigation and I won't go back on my word."

"I ain't askin' you to. But you might consider goin' about it a bit differently."

Rory stood up and carried her dish to the sink. Mac hadn't mentioned that his pal Zeke could be annoying as hell. She took a minute to wash the tomato sauce off her plate before replying.

"Okay, Marshal, I'm listening," she said, drying her hands on a dish towel as she turned to face him.

Zeke was suddenly standing beside her, so close that she automatically fell back a step, until the edge of the sink was digging into her back. He didn't seem concerned that they'd come close to touching, but Rory was left wondering what that would have been like. Would her hand have passed through him as if he were no more than air? Or would she have felt something like the gooey consistency of the wraiths in the *Ghostbusters* films? In any case, she wasn't eager to find out.

"You oughta hold off on talkin' to the rest of the suspects," he said. "They ain't obliged to talk to you anyway. Wait till you can get back into that house like we discussed. Could be you'll find somethin' those other investigators missed. If you don't, you can always go on with the interviewin'."

"Look, I don't know how long it will be before the real estate agent holds another open house. Why should I waste time doing nothing?"

"Cause it would be a heap smarter and safer to do as much investigatin' as you can that don't involve rufflin' the feathers of someone who might just be a murderer."

"I'll think about it," Rory said. Her neck was starting to hurt from looking up at him at such close range.

"Ain't there someone you can partner up with?" he asked. "It's concernin' me that you're goin' about this alone."

"Oh for Pete's sake," Rory replied. "*You* came all the way back east alone to find a killer." She realized her mistake as the words left her mouth.

"And you can see how well that worked out," Zeke said.

Rory was not going to concede anything. "Women have fought for the right to do anything men can do, and most of the time we do it better," she bristled. "And we've sure as hell earned the right not to be harassed about it."

"After what happened today, do you think your uncle Mac would want you to be workin' this case alone?"

Rory's cheeks flushed with anger. "Don't you ever invoke my uncle's name in order to manipulate me!" She threw the dish towel onto the counter and stormed out of the kitchen. She didn't look back to see if Zeke was still standing there. She didn't care if he stayed rooted to the spot for the next two centuries. Tonight *she* was going to have the last word. And tomorrow she was going ahead with her plans to track down Gail's old boss!

Chapter 14

Elite Interiors still occupied the small, gray clapboard house with blue shutters on the main street in Port Washington where Gail Oberlin had begun her career. So tracking down Gail's old boss, Elaine Stein, had not been difficult. However, getting past the telephone screening of Lyle Beaumont, her pit bull of a secretary, had so far proven impossible. If Rory were to believe him, Elaine was never actually in her office. After half a dozen futile attempts to reach her, Rory asked if she might leave a message. Lyle heaved a grudging sigh and at least pretended to take down the message she dictated.

She identified herself as a freelance journalist writing an article about women like Gail who used and abused people in their mad scramble to the top of the career ladder. Rory had her doubts as to whether Elaine ever saw the message, because she never heard back from the woman. Based on Mac's assessment, she'd expected Elaine to jump at the chance to retaliate against her nemesis, even if posthumously. Frustrated, Rory decided to take matters into her own hands and stage an end run around Lyle.

She arranged to take a personal day. At six a.m., with a Starbucks nonfat latte in hand, she parked diagonally across the street from Elite Interiors to begin her first stakeout. Just before eight thirty she watched a slight young man climb the three steps to the front porch and using a key, let himself into the office. Although he was short of stature, he moved with a bearing of self-assurance that bordered on arrogance. She had little doubt that this was Lyle Beaumont. While his voice had been decidedly masculine, he was clearly more of a peacock than the pit bull she'd imagined.

Two hours later Rory was learning her first lesson of Stakeout 101—never drink a large cup of coffee, or any other liquid for that matter, before a stakeout. She debated leaving to find a bathroom but suspected that she would miss the elusive Ms. Stein if she did. While she was still considering how long she could hold out, a late-model burgundy Mercedes with a woman behind the wheel double-parked in front of Elite Interiors. A moment later, Lyle Beaumont hurried down the steps to the street. The woman emerged from the car with a briefcase, and Lyle slid into the driver's seat. A few words were exchanged between the two, after which he closed the door and drove away. The woman made her way into the office. Apparently Lyle's duties included valet service.

Rory figured she had a window of maybe five minutes before Lyle returned. She locked her car and hurried

across the street; her bladder would have to wait. She
entered the building and found herself alone in a small
reception area with several chairs and a neatly ordered
desk from which Lyle presumably ruled his roost. Down
a short hallway, she could see an open door. She headed
for it. There was no time to waste on social etiquette.
She had to grab Elaine's interest before Lyle could run
interference.

The interior designer was standing beside her desk,
frowning as she rummaged through the briefcase that
she'd set atop it. She was big boned with angular features, not a pretty woman by most standards. But her
hairstyle, makeup and fashion sense went a long way to
making up for any hereditary deficiencies.

When Rory knocked on the open door, Elaine looked
up, both confused and annoyed to see her there.

"Excuse me, Ms. Stein. I know how busy you are,"
Rory said quickly, before she could be remanded to the
reception area, "but I think you'll be interested in what
I have to say."

"And who exactly are you?" Elaine demanded in the
imperious tone of one not accustomed to unexpected
intrusions.

Rory introduced herself as she crossed the room,
repeating the same story she'd told Lyle on the phone.
She'd considered using an alias but had decided to go
with her real name. The less she lied, the less likely she
was to trip herself up.

She extended her hand as she reached the desk.
"From what I've heard," she went on, "you've had an
experience with an employee that would be a perfect fit
for my article."

Elaine shook her hand warily, as if it might contain

something coiled and ready to spring. "I assume you're talking about Gail Oberlin?"

"Yes, I am."

She withdrew her hand. "To be blunt, Ms. McCain, although I can see how I might be helpful to you, I don't see what's in it for me."

"Payback?" Rory suggested. While planning for this interview, she'd considered other possible rejoinders to such a question but had decided that vengeance afforded her the best chance for success.

"Look," the designer said with a brief and humorless laugh, "I'd like nothing better than a bit of good old-fashioned revenge against that bitch, but dead is dead. With any luck she's already doing hard time redecorating Hell. That kind of heat is murder on fabrics. What more could I do to her?"

"I see your point," Rory said, changing tactics. "I guess you're one of the lucky ones in that respect. Not many people get to see justice done in their lifetime."

"I suppose that's true," Elaine said briskly, turning her attention back to her briefcase. "Now I believe we've reached the end of our discussion, Ms. McCain. I have a very busy schedule today, so if you would please see yourself out."

Rory wasn't going anywhere quite yet. She had maybe another minute or so before Lyle returned and either tried to eject her bodily or called the police. She was pretty sure she could take him in a fight, but she couldn't chance the police getting involved. In any case, she was down to the wire and there was no time left for subtleties.

"Of course," she mused as innocently as she could manage, "there are those impatient few who take matters into their own hands, rather than wait for justice to be served."

Elaine looked up from her search again, eyes flashing. "I hope you're not insinuating what I think you are."

"Oh, no, no, not at all," Rory said as if she were equally horrified by that possibility. "I just meant that people like Gail make so many enemies, it wouldn't surprise me if one of them gave her a little help down those stairs."

"Well, maybe you should be talking to them," Elaine snapped, "or to the coroner. It's my understanding that Gail's death was ruled accidental. She tripped, fell and cracked her head open on the marble floor. End of story."

"How intuitive," Rory said. "The ME's report never actually mentioned what type of floor it was."

"Come on now," Elaine replied without hesitation, "a custom home worth two point six million dollars would hardly have had vinyl tile."

Nice save, Rory thought. Even so, she'd swear she heard a slightly higher pitch in the designer's tone. Lying could manifest that way. But before Rory could press her further, Lyle appeared in the doorway.

"Sorry, Ms. Stein," he said in bewilderment, looking from his boss to Rory and back again. "I didn't realize you had any appointments this morning."

"I don't," Elaine said tightly. "So if you would please show Ms. McCain here to the door, I'll be able to get on with my work."

At the mention of Rory's name, Lyle realized what was going on. He went from timid sycophant to bouncer-bodyguard mode in under two seconds. Rory couldn't help but wonder how intimidating he would be if the threat to his boss stood six foot two and weighed in at two hundred pounds. As it was, he didn't even frighten a featherweight like Rory. Unfortunately she couldn't allow things to escalate to the point where he might call 911, so as Lyle marched up to her, she raised her hands in mock surrender and backed away until she'd cleared the doorway.

It wasn't until she was back in her car that she became aware of the drumming of her heart. While she might not want to live with a constant adrenalin rush, it could sure add a bit of zest to the day.

In deference to her bladder, Rory made a brief stop at the local 7-Eleven. Then she headed home, dissecting her conversation with Elaine Stein as she drove. She didn't for a moment believe that the designer had just guessed about the type of floor on which Gail had met her end. Elaine either knew about the marble floor because she was the killer, or because she had visited the murder scene out of curiosity, or perhaps just to gloat. But although gloating might be obnoxious, it wasn't yet a crime in the state of New York. Somehow the more Rory learned about the potential suspects in the case, the further she seemed to get from its resolution.

She parked her car in the driveway and was walking up to her front door when she heard the telephone ringing inside. She managed to unlock the door, turn off the alarm and pick up the extension in the living room before it went to voice mail, all the while thinking how nice it would be if it was the killer, distraught with guilt, who was calling to confess.

"Rory?" a male voice said in response to her "hello."

"Yes?" She was having trouble placing the voice.

"Vince Conti."

"Vince, hi," she said, finding herself pleasantly surprised to be hearing from him. With everything else going on in her life, she'd forgotten about their little repartee at the open house.

"I'm afraid I haven't started playing the lottery yet," she said once the mandatory greetings had been observed. She kicked off her shoes and settled herself on the couch.

"Just as I feared."

Rory could hear the smile in his words. "In my defense, I did warn you that could be a problem."

"I believe you did. But I'm hoping you'll let me work on my sales pitch over dinner."

"I think we could arrange that, as long as you're sure you can handle more disappointment."

Vince assured her that he thrived on it. They spoke for several more minutes and then set the date and time to try a new restaurant in Huntington that had received an impressive review in the *New York Times*.

The doorbell chimed as Rory hung up the phone. She glanced at her watch; it wasn't yet noon and she wasn't expecting anyone. None of her family and friends knew that she'd taken the day off, but even if they did, they would never drop by without calling. They were old-school that way.

Since there were no windows near the door and Mac had never felt the need to have a peephole installed, Rory had no choice but to open the door in order to see who was there. When she did, she found herself looking at her empty front porch and the lawn and street beyond it.

Had she imagined the sound? She looked around once more, then closed and locked the door, wondering who she should call to have a peephole installed and whether she could find such a person in the yellow pages.

As she turned away from the door, she nearly ran smack into Zeke. She jumped back with a little yelp of surprise.

"What the hell happened to making the lights flicker?" she demanded once she'd regained some of her composure.

"I did," he said, winking away to reappear leaning against the newel post of the stairway. "I guess you didn't see it."

Rory realized that he might be right. The living room was so bright with sunlight during the day that she could have missed a flickering light if she wasn't paying attention. And with Vince on the phone, she had definitely not been paying attention to the lights.

"This Vince fella your beau?" Zeke inquired.

For a second Rory worried that the marshal was reading her mind, which would make staying on in the house with him completely untenable. Then she remembered with relief that she'd said Vince's name aloud. But another troubling thought occurred to her.

"You were eavesdropping on me, weren't you?"

"I was waitin' for the right moment to ring the bell. You didn't want me interruptin' your conversation, now did you?"

Rory gave him a withering look, but she didn't say anything. "Vince is a friend," she said evenly. "We were making some dinner plans. Does that meet with your approval?"

"I wouldn't know, seein' as how I never met the man."

"Then I guess you're just going to have to trust my judgment."

"I suppose I will, for now. But I gotta tell you, courtin's a whole lot different these days than it was back in my time. Some of the things I've seen on that television set are hard to abide."

"Was there something else you wanted to talk to me about?" Rory asked, hoping to derail a discussion on morality in the twenty-first century.

"As a matter of fact there is." Zeke spent a minute raking his hand through his hair as if that chore required his immediate attention. Rory was about to point out that he should just change the way he was projecting himself if he wasn't happy with his hair, when he finally started speaking again.

"There's this case I worked on some years ago that I've been wantin' to tell you about."

"The case that brought you out here?" Rory asked, walking past him to take a seat on the bench.

He shook his head. "No, it was in my early days as a marshal."

"Oh, well I'm sure it's very interesting," she said, trying to hide her growing impatience, "but can't it wait until after lunch?" She hadn't had anything to eat since the latte hours earlier, and there was a slice of pizza calling to her from the refrigerator.

"You need to hear about it now." His tone left no room for negotiation, and Rory wondered if he'd forgotten what hunger felt like.

"Back in sixty-nine—1869, 'a course—we had us a couple of murders in the Arizona Territory. First an old hobo by the name of Paco fetched up dead near the train tracks in Yuma. He was in pretty bad shape; looked like he'd taken a nasty tumble from one of the freight trains he rode. Now everyone knew he drank when he had the money, so nobody really questioned his death. We gave him a decent burial, though. Even had a preacher say a few words over him."

Rory shifted her weight, wishing that he'd get to the point, if in fact there was one.

If Zeke noticed her impatience, he didn't let it bother him. "Like I said, we didn't think much more about it," he went on in the same languid drawl. "But 'round about the same time there was a bank robbery up in Phoenix. Three men killed the guard and got away with ten grand—a big haul in those days. And they were wearin' masks so no one could identify them. We had no reason to think that the deaths of Paco and the guard were connected, till Henry stopped in. Henry rode the trains with Paco from time to time, you see. Anyhow, Henry was so scared he couldn' stop stammerin' long enough to get two sensible words out. When I finally got him calmed down, he told me how he and Paco had seen the robbers runnin' out of the bank that day in Phoenix. Seen them pull off their masks. So when Paco turned up dead, poor Henry was sure he was gonna be next. But once we knew that both deaths were connected to the same bank robbery, we were able to catch up with the robbers before they got to Henry." Zeke finished his story with a satisfied nod.

"So you're trying to tell me that you think Mac was murdered?" Rory asked, the pizza all but forgotten.

"I'm just sayin' that sometimes when things don't seem to have any connection, they're connected right down to the core."

"But we know that Mac died of a heart attack," she protested. At least the doctors and her parents were certain that he had, and she had no concrete reason to believe that they were wrong. Still, as she'd said to Jeremy, when someone dies alone there are always questions left unanswered.

"Did they do an autopsy?" Zeke asked.

She shook her head. "His doctor said it was a massive myocardial infarction. My folks didn't see any point in violating his body with an autopsy."

Zeke looked her squarely in the eye. "You listen to me, Rory. If Mac was murdered 'cause he was lookin' into Gail's death, then you could be next. And that car that was followin' you could've been the first step in that direction."

Chapter 15

In spite of Rory's own difficulty in accepting her uncle's sudden death, she was not ready to buy into Zeke Drummond's theory that he'd been murdered. The marshal had altogether too much time on his hands, and it was no doubt easy for him to see murder lurking everywhere, since he himself had been a victim of that crime. Still, she struggled over what if anything she should tell her parents. On one hand, they had a right to know if there was even a slight chance that Mac had been killed. On the other hand, such an investigation would no doubt involve exhuming Mac's body, and she preferred to spare them that trauma if possible. In the end, Rory decided that she owed it to her uncle, as well as to her parents, to find out whether his heart had actually been attacked by something more sinister than saturated fat.

She made an appointment to see Dr. Barrett Browning III, the chief medical examiner for Suffolk County.

She'd met the man on two other occasions and then only briefly. It was common knowledge that he came from a long line of distinguished physicians, and that his family, expecting him to follow in his progenitors' footsteps, had given him a name commensurate with that lineage. Rory could only imagine their horror when Barrett eschewed private practice to become a coroner and chose to go through life known simply as BB. But even though he was the blackest sheep in the Browning family, everywhere else he was well loved.

Rory agreed to meet BB where he worked at the Department of Health Services. With one of his assistants away and another out sick, he was almost literally up to his neck in cadavers. When she reached the door to the autopsy suite, she peered through the panel of glass. BB was hard at work on one of his corpses. With age, the patrician features he'd inherited from a long line of Brownings were melting into the doughy roundness of his face. Rory wondered if he ever worried about his own mortality as he spent his days digging through the remains of his fellow man. But by all accounts, BB was a happy man, clever, upbeat and fun to be around.

As Rory watched, he removed a dark red organ from the body cavity and deposited it in the scale above the table. She took a deep breath to steady herself. Although she'd been at the morgue on several occasions as part of her police academy training, her stomach was never completely at peace there. To her way of thinking, there were some sights and smells that were better left to the imagination. She knocked on the door, glad that she'd skipped lunch.

"*Entrez,*" she heard him say, his jovial voice muted by the door. "*Bienvenido,* come on in."

Rory let herself in but stopped several feet shy of BB and the autopsy table, which was fine since she had no intentions of shaking his gloved and gory hand. For his part, BB greeted her without missing a beat as he went about disemboweling his subject. After assuring one another that they were "quite fine, thank you," Rory explained why she was there.

"I guess what I'm asking, is whether there are drugs that can precipitate a fatal heart attack and make it seem as if it occurred from natural causes."

BB didn't stop working, but his brows bunched together in a frown. "If you were a writer asking me that question, I'd figure you were plotting out a murder mystery. But you're not. You're a cop. An artist cop, but still a cop. So now I'm thinking you have a decedent and very possibly a murder on your hands. Am I getting warm?"

"Toasty," she replied.

"Mac." BB nodded as if he didn't need her confirmation.

"Everyone was so sure his lifestyle killed him that an autopsy seemed like an unnecessary indignity."

"Don't torture yourself, Detective," he said, piling intestines onto the scale like a butcher weighing sausages. "There's a good chance an autopsy wouldn't have found anything anyway. There are drugs that don't stay in the body long enough to be detected. And there are injection sites that the best coroner could miss.

"So there wouldn't be any point in exhuming the body?"

"I don't think there'd be much if anything to gain from it."

"But there might be?"

BB turned to face her. "Do you mind if I ask why you think your uncle was murdered?"

Rory hesitated. She had to be careful about how she worded her reply. She couldn't mention Zeke's name, nor did she want to sound as paranoid as she was beginning to feel.

"His passing was so sudden, it just never seemed right somehow," she said. "And then I found out he was investigating another suspicious death at the time he died." She gave BB a quick rundown of what she knew, ending with the theory that the two deaths might be linked. She made a silent apology to Zeke for stealing his theory.

"I see. *Entendu.* Understood." BB's jowls drooped like a hound dog's as he considered this new information.

"I'd still have to say that in all likelihood his heart just gave out. Hard as it is to bear, it happens more often than you'd think. As for the timing? Probably coincidental. Do you happen to remember who autopsied the Oberlin gal?"

"Blake," Rory said, having seen the name on the autopsy report.

"Tom Blake's a good man, bright man, conscientious. I'd be surprised if anything got past him."

"So, if you were in my position?"

"Well, you still don't have any hard evidence that Oberlin was murdered. If you're able to establish that she was, then I might push for an exhumation and autopsy on Mac. But time is not on your side here, Rory. The fact is, even if you were to exhume his body today, I doubt we'd be able to come up with anything definitive."

"That's pretty much what I was thinking. I guess I just needed to hear it from an expert."

"Always glad to accommodate."

"One more thing," Rory said before he could turn back to his work. "Since this theory is still just a theory . . ."

"Not to worry." BB smiled like a giant Pillsbury Doughboy. "Mum's the word. Silence is golden. My lips are sealed."

At four o'clock Rory left what she now thought of as her paying job and went to Mac's office to continue her pro bono work. She had to be out of there by the end of the month if she didn't want to pay additional rent. It was taking her longer than she'd anticipated to transcribe the notes in Mac's files and send them out to the respective clients. Between her paying job, moving into Mac's house and investigating Gail's death, she was often too tired to put in additional hours on the languishing files. But as the month drew to an end, the prospect of having to pay more rent was proving to be a great motivator.

When she arrived at the office and turned her key in the lock, it met with no resistance, as if the tumblers weren't engaged. Her first thought was, "Great, I'm so preoccupied that now I've even forgotten to lock the door." But as she stepped across the threshold into the reception area, it was clear that her memory was not at issue. She'd had a visitor during her absence. And it wasn't the cleaning lady. The desk drawers that she'd emptied shortly after the funeral had been pulled out and thrown onto the floor.

For a moment she stood frozen in place, her mind trying to process what her eyes were seeing. Then her training kicked in. She set her purse on the floor and drew her gun out of its holster before advancing farther into the room. She knew that once she passed the partitioning wall, she'd be visible to anyone who might still be in the office proper. She waited another minute, holding her breath and listening for sounds of movement inside. She could hear the mechanical click of the wall clock, the muted sounds of traffic on the street below, the ringing of a phone in another part of the building and louder than all of them, the hectic thudding of her heart.

The odds were that the intruder was long gone, but since odds didn't always favor the gambler, she flattened herself against the wall and edged forward. When she reached the doorway to the inner office, she gripped the gun in both hands to steady her aim and swung into the room shouting, "Police! Drop your weapons!"

The room had been thoroughly ransacked, but it appeared to be unoccupied. She checked behind the door and within the narrow coat closet. The only bathroom was out in the building's common hallway. There was nowhere else for anyone to hide. She was alone. She didn't realize that she'd been holding her breath until it exploded out of her lungs with relief.

She looked around her. Nothing was where it belonged. All the furniture had been moved. Desk and filing cabinet drawers hung open, their contents scattered everywhere. The ceramic planters had been thrown to the floor and smashed, out of frustration perhaps when the intruder hadn't found what he was looking for. The ridiculous thought crossed Rory's mind that this was actually a worse mess than Mac had ever made.

Although she couldn't be certain, it was a good bet that the intruder was looking for the file on Gail Oberlin. But that file was back in the house on Brandywine

Lane. Unlike Mac, Rory had no hesitancy about arming the security system at night or whenever she went out. Since the central station hadn't called on her cell phone to report a break in, whoever had trashed the office had not yet tried to gain entry to the house. Of course, if Zeke were right about Mac being murdered, then it was possible that the same intruder had already been in the house at least once. Regarded in that light, the office break-in took on a decidedly more troubling aspect.

As Rory started to clean up the room, it occurred to her that she'd broken her promise to Leah. She should have left the office and called for backup as soon as she realized that there'd been a break-in. But then she might have missed an opportunity to capture the intruder. Okay, okay, she knew she was just rationalizing, and that as rationales went, it wasn't a great one. Still, no one had threatened her or made a move to harm her. If they did, she would have no choice but to let Leah and her captain know. Anything less would reflect a serious lack of judgment on her part. She could hear Leah's voice in her head saying that that ship had already sailed, along with a few of its sisters.

"Hello?" a man's disembodied voice came from the reception area.

Rory jumped up from the floor where she'd been trying to collate the blizzard of papers. In that instant she realized that she'd left the outer door open as an escape route and had forgotten to close it once she'd confirmed that the intruder was gone. For that matter, she'd also left her handbag out there.

"Who is it?" she called, her hand poised on the hilt of her gun. She tried to place the man's voice as she positioned herself once more against the wall that separated the two rooms, this time on the opposite side.

"Rory? It's Jeremy."

Her hand dropped off the gun as she came around the wall into the reception area.

Jeremy was standing just inside the doorway with a stunned expression that she imagined was pretty similar to the one that she'd worn upon her arrival.

His face was flushed, and he was wearing shorts and sneakers and a tee shirt that clung to his chest in dark patches of sweat.

"Was there a burglary?" he asked, crossing the room to her. "Were you here when it happened? Are you all right?" His voice ratcheted up a notch with each question.

"I'm fine. I came in after the fact."

Standing beside her now, Jeremy could see into the inner office. He shook his head as if rendered speechless by the view. "What on earth were they looking for?" he murmured finally.

"I have no idea." Rory bent to pick up her purse and set it on the desk. "I don't think anything's missing. It could be they had the wrong address." Privately she didn't think that was the case, but she didn't want to make Jeremy more agitated than he already seemed to be. She really didn't have time to do any serious hand-holding.

"Do you think they were after the file on Gail?" he asked.

"There's no way to know for sure. But if that's what they were after, they must be disappointed, because I have it at home."

Jeremy bobbed his head and chewed on his lower lip for a moment. "Whoever murdered her might want to know what your investigation's turned up so far."

"Whoa," Rory said. "Let's back up a bit there. I know you're convinced your sister was murdered, but I have yet to find any real evidence of that."

"You haven't discovered anything worthwhile then?"

"I would have told you if I had," she said, a sharpening edge to her tone. She was beginning to feel as if she was being questioned, and she didn't like the experience one bit.

Jeremy's tone became conciliatory. "It's just that I wouldn't want you to get hurt or anything on my account."

"I don't intend to get hurt on anyone's account," Rory assured him. "Was there something you wanted to talk to me about?"

"Oh, uh, no, not really. I just went for a run in Heckshcr Park and figured I'd stop in, see if you were here, say 'hello.'"

"I'm afraid it's not the best time for a visit." She couldn't help thinking that it was awfully coincidental for Jeremy to have chosen this particular day and time to stop by.

"Yeah, sorry."

"I'll give you a call as soon as I actually have some news." She took Jeremy's arm and piloted him to the door.

He stopped at the threshold. "Look, I'm sorry if I came across a little too pushy there. I know you have a ton of other stuff on your plate. And you—"

"That's okay," Rory said, hoping to end the discussion.

"You have no idea how grateful I am that you're even helping me with this investigation."

"I'll call you soon with an update."

"Right. Right, thanks."

Rory closed and locked the door as soon as his feet

had cleared the doorway. She glanced at her watch. It was almost six and Vince Conti was picking her up for dinner at seven. As much as she hated to leave the office in its present state of disorder, the rest of the cleanup was going to have to wait.

Chapter 16

Rory jumped into the shower as soon as she got home. Although she was pressed for time, she took a few minutes to simply stand there and let the warm water cascade over her. She could feel the muscles in her neck and shoulders relax as the tension from the office break-in began to drain out of her. She'd never been more grateful that Mac had renovated the bathroom with every modern amenity, particularly the state-of-the-art shower with multiple heads. As much as she loved historic homes, it was hard to summon up any nostalgia for the old claw-footed tub that had been there when he'd bought the house.

She would have loved to linger there in a semi-hypnotic water trance, but it wouldn't be right to cancel her dinner date with Vince at such a late hour. Unexpectedly, she found that thinking about him seemed to reinvigorate her. If she ever made the mistake of telling her mother about that, she would no doubt receive the overly dramatic "this could be the one" speech. Rory didn't subscribe to the theory that there was necessarily a perfect someone out there for her, but she understood how her mother might feel comforted by the thought.

She quickly washed and loofahed, shampooed and conditioned her hair, and was in the process of shaving her legs when the lights in the bathroom fluttered. Muttering some mild obscenities about "bad timing," she dropped the razor, turned off the water and grabbed the bath towel that she'd left on the heating rack just outside the shower stall. She pulled the door to the stall shut and was still in the process of wrapping the towel around herself when Zeke appeared beside the sink. The frosted glass between them made him look distinctly more wraithlike, as if in his haste he'd left some important molecules behind.

"What do you think you're doing?!" she snapped. "We had a deal." The bedroom and bath were supposed to be her private sanctuary. Of course, as long as he remained invisible, he could violate her trust and she would never be the wiser. That thought led her to wonder just how long he might have been there watching her before he chose to show himself. In the name of sanity, she pushed the thought out of her head.

"Oh, right, sorry."

Rory couldn't see his face too clearly, but she decided that he sounded adequately contrite. It was a first offense after all. And maybe he really had forgotten. She had no idea whether ghosts had good memories or not.

"Okay, okay," she said grudgingly. "Now that you're here, what's so important that it couldn't have waited until I finished my shower?" And shaved my other leg, she added to herself. She'd have to remember to take care of that before Vince arrived.

"I'm worried about you. You're as stubborn a female as I've ever known, and I don't think you're takin' my warnin' to heart. But if you keep pokin' around into Gail's death, you're more than likely gonna wind up like Mac."

"Your concern is touching," Rory said dryly, "but right now I'm more likely to die of haunting than of anything else." Her heart was still beating a ragged tattoo from his unexpected appearance.

Although the towel now covered her more than most bathing suits did, she remained in the shower. If she stepped out, she'd be less than an arm's length away from Zeke. The bathroom might be modern and well appointed, but it was cramped with even one occupant. Mac had considered enlarging it, but that would have meant taking away the one small closet in the master bedroom. Not a reasonable option when the house had such little closet space to begin with.

She drew her arms around herself as the heat from the shower dissipated and the central air blew across her wet skin and hair.

"I don't know you long," Zeke said, either unable to see her discomfort or unmoved by it, "but I think I know you some. You're still baitin' the devil, ain't you?"

"Well, that depends. Which devil would you be referring to?"

"You know darn well what I'm talkin' about. I thought we agreed you'd hold off on interviewin' anymore suspects till you had a chance to check out the crime scene proper."

"That's strange," Rory said, wanting nothing more

than a dry towel and some clothes, "because I don't recall agreeing to any such thing." The minutes were ticking away, and soon one unshaved leg was going to be the least of her problems when Vince arrived.

"Damn it, woman, why do you have to be so all-fired difficult? I'm only tryin' to help you."

Hearing the exasperation in his voice, Rory had to admit that she was enjoying his frustration. After all, why should she be the only who was stressed by their relationship?

"If you really want to help me right now," she said, "get out of here and wait downstairs so I can get dressed."

She was surprised when he winked out of sight without argument. She set the towel aside and turned on the water, running the razor quickly over the unshaven leg. Once she was dry, she pulled on her favorite lavender and white sundress and strappy white sandals. She blew her hair dry in under five minutes, a new personal best, and applied a few strokes of mascara and some pale lip gloss to complete the look. She was on her way downstairs with five minutes to spare.

Zeke was in the living room waiting for her. He was seated in his usual spot in the chair across from the couch, one long leg atop the other at a right angle, tapping his hand on the side of the raised boot. Rory noted the look of surprised approval that crossed his face when she entered the room. She realized that he'd never seen her dressed to go anywhere other than to work or to run errands. While it was always nice to be noticed, she had no intention of letting the unspoken compliment soften her attitude.

"Okay, let's get one thing straight here," she said

without preface, taking a seat on the couch. "I've never given you reason to assume that I'd be willing to follow your suggestions or directives."

"Maybe not, but you've given me every reason to believe that you're as smart as Mac said you were."

"Meaning that I should be smart enough to listen to you, I suppose?"

Zeke shook his head in frustration. "Meanin' that you oughta know when you're puttin' yourself in harm's way. Near as I can recall, Mac never mentioned you had a death wish."

"Oh, come on now," Rory said. "That's a little over-the-top, even for you."

The doorbell chimed before Zeke could respond.

"That'd be your suitor," he said tersely, making no effort to hide his irritation. "You need to tell him you're busy. We haven't finished talkin' about this yet."

"I won't do anything of the kind," Rory sputtered indignantly. "Didn't you hear me say that I don't intend to take orders from you? You're going to have to make peace with that fact, or you're going to be very unhappy."

Zeke's jaw clenched shut, and Rory was sorry that she'd come down so hard on him. He was suffering from his own demons, and she had a feeling she didn't know half of them.

"Look," she went on more kindly, "I need to eat, and to be honest, I could use a break from all of this. It's not as if I'm going to do anything rash over dinner."

Zeke didn't reply. He rose out of the chair, vanishing halfway through the motion and leaving Rory to feel as if he'd metaphorically hung up on her.

"Well, I hope you have a good evening too," she said

to the empty room. But as she went to answer the door, she began to think that maybe Zeke was right. Maybe she should just beg off, say she was coming down with a bug. She'd be doing Vince a favor. She wouldn't be very good company in her current state of mind.

Chapter 17

When Rory opened the door, Vince greeted her with an engaging smile. He was wearing chinos and a white linen shirt that was a perfect foil for his bronzed skin. Rory found herself smiling back, her mind apparently willing enough to take a hiatus from stress.

She invited him into the house and then ran upstairs to get the handbag and sweater she'd forgotten to bring down with her earlier. It was a safe bet that the restaurant's air conditioner would be cranked up to frigid. When she came back down, she found Vince surveying the living room with raised eyebrows.

"Interesting choice," he said, joining her back in the foyer. "I imagine you get a kick out of people's reactions the first time they come in here."

Rory laughed. "It's certainly a conversation starter."

"So I guess it's safe to say that you have eclectic taste?"

"Actually I can't take credit for the décor. My uncle was the one who loved the old and ornate as much as the new and sleek. I've just grown to appreciate it."

"Adaptability's an admirable trait."

"In all honesty, it's not really a trait that runs rampant in my life"

Vince laughed. "Thanks for the heads-up," he said, glancing at his watch. "We should probably head out if we want to make our reservation."

"Just a second." At the keypad beside the door, Rory punched in the numbers that armed the security system. "Okay, I'm right behind you."

Vince opened the door and was just stepping over the threshold when the door flew shut, shoving him out and barring Rory's way. She could hear the muted expletive on the other side of the door.

"Ezekiel Drummond!" she growled under her breath. She didn't have time to deal with the marshal at that moment, but he was going to have to answer for his actions when she got home.

Once she was outside, she produced a sheepish smile for Vince's benefit. He was waiting in the driveway beside the little white Mercedes convertible she remembered from the open house.

"I am so sorry about that," she said as she walked up to him.

"You didn't by any chance forget to mention that you have multiple personalities, did you?"

"No." She laughed, thinking that Zeke was lucky he was already dead.

Vince ushered her around the car and opened the passenger door for her.

Rory slid into the plush leather seat. "I think it has to

do with the way the door is balanced," she said, plucking an explanation out of thin air. "A good breeze from
the kitchen windows sometimes slams it shut like that."
Who was she kidding? The man was a builder for goodness' sakes.

"I'll take a look at it later," Vince said, taking his
seat behind the wheel. If he suspected she was lying, he
didn't show it.

Rory thanked him, hoping that he'd forget about the
door during the course of the evening.

When they arrived at the restaurant, Vince gave the
maître d' his name and they were immediately escorted
past a dozen other people with reservations who were
still waiting to be seated.

"I think we've just made some mortal enemies,"
Rory whispered after they were shown to a table in a
quiet corner. She could still feel the well-honed arrows
of envy and anger being shot in their direction.

Vince shrugged. "I've done some favors for the guy
who owns the place." He started browsing through the
wine list. "I don't ask for special treatment, but I also don't
refuse it when it's offered. How does a Cabernet sound?"

"Cabernet sounds wonderful," Rory said, trying to
feel less guilty about the line cutting and more appre-
ciative that they didn't have to wait. She hadn't realized
how hungry she was until the rich, complex aromas of
the food wafted toward her from the other tables.

The meal was smoothly and meticulously served,
everything from the warm, crusty rolls to the dark chocolate crème brûlée beyond reproach. Lulled into a lovely
state of relaxation by the wine and food, Rory found
that she didn't mind the inevitable game of twenty questions that was part of any new relationship.

He told her about his career in the construction field, where he'd worked his way up from a summer job as a "gofer" when he was sixteen to owning his own firm. Along the way, he'd learned how to do every job involved in building a home and was not averse to rolling up his own sleeves even now and pitching in when a worker was out sick or a job was running late.

He found Rory's job as a sketch artist interesting, especially since he'd never met an artist before. And he laughed appreciatively at the anecdotes she recounted. The only awkward note of the evening came when a man with a grubby beard and baggy jeans approached their table.

"I've been trying to reach you all day, Conti," the man said without preface or greeting.

Vince seemed more annoyed than surprised to see him there. "I would have gotten back to you when I wasn't busy," he answered coolly.

"Yeah, well Petrillo told me you'd be here tonight."

"I'll have to remember to thank him," he replied without humor.

The man leaned down so that his mouth was near Vince's ear. "I wasted two hours waiting for you."

Vince stood up so suddenly that the man blanched and fell back a few steps. "Please excuse me," he said to Rory as he took the man's elbow and maneuvered him into the alcove near the restrooms. A minute later he was back in his seat and the man was making his way past their table and out of the restaurant, his face set in an ugly scowl.

Vince offered Rory an apologetic smile. "You just can't please some people. You do your best for them, but they're never satisfied. They think they have the right to intrude on your time no matter where you are or what you're doing."

Rory nodded in commiseration. Even in her job she'd learned that dealing with the public could be difficult, if not downright impossible. She could only imagine how it was in construction, where millions of dollars were often involved.

The rest of the meal was pleasantly uneventful. After they'd sipped a bit of the anisette that had come to their table, compliments of the maître d', Vince asked for the bill. From what Rory could see, it was well over three hundred dollars. She'd never had a dinner that expensive. Or that wonderful. A girl could really get used to being wined and dined like this. Vince paid in cash, including a generous tip.

"You're a brave soul walking around with that much cash these days. I never have more than twenty bucks on me." She laughed. "And I'm a cop."

"Not to worry, I'm pretty good at taking care of myself. Besides, I have this theory that easy credit is what sank Atlantis."

"I'll try to remember that the next time I'm thinking of buying something with money I don't have," Rory said.

The short drive back home was as enjoyable as the dinner had been. The air was still warm, so they rode with the top down and Rory leaned back against the headrest and picked out the constellations that she remembered from childhood. She hadn't enjoyed herself on a date this much in a long time. A first date no less.

Vince came into the house long enough to take a look at the rebellious door. He inspected the hinges and the way they were attached to the doorjamb. He had Rory make sure the kitchen windows were wide open. The door didn't move an inch on its own. Then he tried swinging the door closed using various degrees of strength. The door operated perfectly every time, no slamming shut, not even the slightest squeal or creak. Rory wasn't surprised.

He turned to her with a shrug. "I've never met a door I couldn't fix, but I can't find anything wrong with this one. And you said it's happened more than once?"

"Yes, but not often," she rushed to point out. "Maybe only once before."

"Well, it seems fine now. Maybe it was just a ghost." He laughed. "A ghost who doesn't like company."

Be careful, Rory warned herself, play it for fun. "Oh great," she said wryly. "That should be good for a few nightmares."

"Not to worry. You can call me anytime you need some ghost busting. I run a full-service company."

If he only knew what he was offering, Rory thought, smiling back at him.

They were both silent for a moment, and Rory debated asking him to stay for coffee. But he took the decision out of her hands, thanking her for a wonderful evening and bending his head to give her a quick but tender kiss good night.

Just enough to leave me wanting more, Rory thought as she locked the door behind him and set the security system for the night. She'd have to watch herself; this guy knew his way around women. He could certainly teach the marshal a thing or twelve.

She looked toward the stairway with longing. She could almost hear her new bed calling to her with its promise of comfort and sleep. The day had started early and been emotionally draining, but she had a bit of business to finish with Zeke first. If she went straight to her room, he would have to break another rule to join her there, and he'd already broken too many. Instead, she went into the living room, kicked off her sandals and tried to make herself comfortable on the couch. She called his name without response. She'd give him twenty minutes. After that she was going up to bed and their conversation could wait until the next day. In any case, over the course of the evening her anger had mellowed into irritation and she was no longer looking for a fight. The marshal could thank Vince for that.

Two hours later, Rory awakened disoriented, thinking that she'd gone up to bed and wondering how she'd come to be on the couch. As soon as she saw Zeke in his chair, she remembered why she was there.

"I flickered the lights," he said as soon as he saw that she was awake.

Rory pulled herself upright, her back against the arm of the couch. "That's fine," she said, rubbing her eyes. She wasn't happy that he'd been sitting there watching her sleep again. It made her feel vulnerable, defenseless. But since she'd never covered this circumstance in her list of rules, she had no recourse.

"What's not fine," she went on, groping her way through the cobwebs of sleep, "is that little prank you pulled with the door this evening."

"But it *was* funny," Zeke said, grinning.

"Not to me. I'm the one who had to come up with a crazy story about the door being unbalanced and the wind blowing it shut like this is Tornado Alley or something."

Zeke started to laugh, a rumbling, infectious laugh, and Rory had a hard time keeping a straight face. It actually *was* a little funny, but she didn't dare let him know that.

"I barely know Vince," she said, "and I don't need him thinking it's me that's unbalanced."

Zeke found that to be equally funny. As Rory waited for his laughter to subside, it occurred to her that he looked a little different, and it wasn't just the difference between a sullen Zeke and an upbeat one. His hair was still long and greatly in need of a styling, but he'd made an attempt to comb it into submission. And his shirt, although wrinkled, was whiter and no longer frayed at the cuffs. Even his thick mustache appeared to have been pruned. Rory didn't know how he'd accomplished the makeover, or why. Had he measured himself against Vince and found himself wanting? She decided not to remark on the changes. It was late; she was tired, and based on their record so far, it was reasonable to assume that even a compliment might trigger a new argument.

"I'm glad I've been able to entertain you," she said, yawning, "but I've really got to get some more sleep."

"Hold on," Zeke said, his expression mutating from amused to deadly serious in less than a second. "What if I swore to you on my oath as a federal marshal that I know for sure and certain that Mac was murdered? Would you take my warnin's more to heart then?" His dark eyes were locked on hers, daring her to dismiss his claim.

"I'd still want some proof," she said, momentarily taken aback by his words, as well as by the sudden change in his demeanor. "And I'd want to know how you can be so sure."

Zeke looked away from her to study the fireplace, as if that fieldstone structure might hold the answers to her questions. "You don't make it easy, do you?" he grumbled.

"I didn't know that was my job." She wished he'd forgo the drama and just get on with it. As she waited for his reply, it struck her that he might be trying to scare her into obedience. She was pretty sure that he would never have tried that tactic with Mac. But then Zeke came from a time when a man wouldn't presume to tell another man what to do. Telling a woman how to run her life was an entirely different matter. Of course, Zeke was probably having his own difficulties dealing with the mores of *her* time, what with women piloting spacecraft, serving in government, wearing skimpy clothing and engaging in premarital and extramarital affairs with impunity. He must've thought he was witnessing a modern version of Sodom and Gomorrah. She'd almost talked herself into some sympathy for his plight, when he turned back to her.

His brows had lowered into dark eaves, beneath which she could see a storm raging in his eyes. "I know Mac was murdered," he said in a harsh whisper, as if the words themselves were caustic, grating against his throat as he uttered them. "I know because I was there."

Rory was stunned into silence, a riot of questions conceived but stillborn as she tried to wrap her mind around this new information. It was one thing to harbor suspicions about a loved one's death, quite another to find out that your intuition was right.

"I don't understand," she said once she was able to sort out her thoughts. "If you were there, why didn't you stop it? Why didn't you help him?"

"Don't you think I wanted to?" Zeke shot back. His image started to waver, fading in and out as if his emotional upheaval were making it difficult for him to appear at all.

"It's like I told you before, I can't always be focused on this place. And I don't always have the energy to appear or to affect things. Hell, even at the best of times, I can't actually touch anything or anyone here." His voice, ebbing and flowing with his image, reminded Rory of her parents' old vinyl records that skipped between the grooves, obliterating syllables and entire words. He was becoming harder to understand by the second.

"All right," she said. "All right, I do remember you saying that." She needed to calm down before her own emotions hijacked all rational thought. Maybe if she relaxed, Zeke would be able to relax as well and they could continue this conversation.

"Please, just tell me what happened," she said evenly.

Zeke seemed to have been doing his own version of deep breathing, because when he replied, his image as well as his speech had stabilized.

"I wasn't strong enough to just pop up in front of them and scare them away, so I used what energy I had to knock the alarm clock off the nightstand. It startled them all right, but then they figured one of them had stepped on the clock's wire and tugged it off. They didn't make a run for it till I managed to set off the security alarm."

"Did you know who they were?"

Zeke shook his head. "I didn't recognize them. Don't think they'd ever been here before."

"Was he . . . was Mac . . . already gone when you found him?" Rory found it difficult to say the words aloud, as if she'd just learned about his death all over again.

"I thought he was. But after they left, he came to and pulled himself up enough to grab the phone and hit a few numbers, but he never got a word out. They must've traced the call, or whatever it is they do, 'cause the law showed up maybe ten minutes later. One of those big ambulance rigs too."

"Why didn't you tell me any of this before?" As surprise mutated into anger, Rory struggled to keep her voice neutral, with only limited success.

Zeke was too beleaguered by his own misery to take notice. "I had my reasons," he said. "Besides, I was afraid you'd get it into your fool head to hunt them down."

"Then why tell me at all?"

"'Cause you're after them now anyway, even if you don't realize it yet." Zeke sighed deeply. "I couldn't save Mac, but maybe I can make it up to him by tryin' to save you."

Rory stood up, too agitated to sit still. "For the last time," she said, her face flushing with emotion, "I do *not* need saving!"

She started pacing around the room. "Even if everything you said is true, I don't know how you can be so sure that there's a connection between Mac's death and Gail's. What if it was just a coincidence? There are coincidences in life, you know." But even as the words left her mouth, she realized that she no longer believed them herself.

"There ain't a soul alive who didn't like your uncle Mac," Zeke said. "You don't have to have my instincts or experience to know for certain that he was killed because he was investigatin' that woman's death."

Rory came to a stop in front of him. "Let's say I agree with you. You can't seriously expect me to stop the investigation, especially now that I could be after Mac's killer too."

"'Course not. Truth be told, I don't think I'd respect you much if you did. I just want you to be more careful. You're not just a peace officer here; you're also likely to be the next victim."

"You've made your point," she said, heading toward the stairs, "and I will try to be as careful as possible. But for now, I could really . . . oh my God." She stopped in her tracks. Why hadn't she thought of it immediately?

"Wait, wait a second," she called to Zeke as she raced up the stairs.

A moment later she came running down, holding a sketch pad and pencil. Zeke was still sitting in the chair, his forehead furrowed with curiosity. Rory turned on the lamp and perched on the edge of the couch, her pencil poised over a blank sheet of paper.

"What's all this?" he asked. "You suddenly get the urge to draw a picture of me?"

"Describe them to me," Rory said, ignoring the question. "Describe the men who killed Mac."

"Oh, I get it," he said. "This here's what you do for the police. Trouble is, I don't know how much I can tell you, bein' it was night and all."

"That's okay, just do the best you can."

"Well, one of the fellas was tall and thin, and the other one was shorter, stockier. I'd guess they were somewhere between thirty and forty."

Half an hour and dozens of questions to help jog his memory later, Rory put down the pencil. She had the basic outlines of their faces but little else in the way of distinguishing characteristics. Zeke had described the taller one as bald with sharp features that reminded him of his old pal, Jake. Rory pointed out that since she'd never met Jake, it wasn't really helpful to know that, after which Zeke kept his answers short and to the point. All he could tell her about the shorter man was that he had an accent of some kind.

"I'm real sorry." He shook his head. "But like I said, it was dark."

"It's not your fault." Rory sighed. For a short while there she'd envisioned having pictures of the two men that she could check against the data bank at work. "I guess I was hoping that ghosts could see better in the dark."

"I think that's vampires," he said with a tentative smile.

The remark was so out of keeping with the seriousness of the moment that Rory couldn't help but laugh. She put the pad down on the glass table and stood up.

"Thanks for trying. And now I really am going to sleep." She started toward the stairs again, but halfway there, she turned back to him.

"Zeke, I want you to know that I believe you, that I believe you would have helped Mac if you could have. You don't owe it to him or to me to stick around and try to keep me safe."

He didn't reply, but when she reached the steps, Zeke was already there blocking her way. "I'm not stayin' around just to do penance on your behalf or Mac's," he said, the laughter gone from his eyes. "There's more to it than that. A heap more. But it doesn't concern you, Aurora, and that's all you need to know about it for now." He vanished while his last word still hung in the air.

Rory continued on up to her bedroom, glad to finally

be left alone with her roiling thoughts. Or what passed for alone in this house. As she undressed and pulled on a nightgown, she wondered what other penance he was doing. Despite his protestations, she couldn't shake the feeling that it would eventually impact her life too.

1878

The Arizona Territory

The white clapboard church sat on a low rise just beyond the busy streets of Tucson. Within its simple walls families and friends had gathered for decades to attend Sunday services, celebrate weddings and baptisms, and mourn the passing of loved ones.

That morning in June, so many horses and wagons filled the churchyard that latecomers were obliged to leave their rigs on the other side of the hard-packed road that led from the town to the church and beyond. The horses huddled together beneath the few mesquite and palo verde trees, even though they provided little shade with their narrow, feathery leaves.

The morning sun burned through the hard blue sky with a heat so scorching that it seemed to warp the air itself. Marshal Zeke Drummond road his horse around the church building to the side that had not yet been claimed by the sun, his saddlebags full to bulging for the miles that lay ahead. There were no trees around which to tether the horse, so he looped the reins around the saddle horn to prevent them from tripping him. He knew that the chestnut wouldn't wander far. In any case, he was only going to be a few minutes.

As he made his way through the brooding heat to the burying ground, he felt as if he were walking across the threshold of Hell itself and straight into perdition. He hadn't wanted to be there. He'd even convinced himself that it would serve no purpose for him to go. Yet there he was, hair washed and slicked back, dressed in the best of his hard-worn clothing.

He stopped when he reached the back corner of the building and removed his hat. There was no need to go farther. From where he stood he could see the mourners gathered around the small pine coffin that rested near the lip of the freshly dug grave. Their heads were bent in prayer as Reverend Hopkins read from the Book of Psalms. His words drifted slowly to the marshal in the windless air.

Drummond wasn't a churchgoing man, and he found the cemetery with its wooden markers particularly unnerving. Like a miniature rendering of Tucson and its structures, the city of the dead seemed to be waiting for the souls who were taking temporary refuge in the city of the living.

Since the service was taking place in a back corner of the cemetery, no one took note of the marshal's arrival, which was fine with him. Emotions were too raw, and although he had no problem facing accusations or shouldering blame when it was his due, little Betsy deserved to be laid to her rest peacefully.

After the last "amen" had been murmured, Frank

Jensen, his wife, Katherine, and their two remaining children, Aaron, fourteen, and Noah, ten, each placed a small bouquet of yellow trumpet flowers on top of the casket. It was Betsy's favorite flower.

The marshal walked back to where his horse was drowsing in the shade and swung up into the saddle. He may not have been able to save Betsy, but he was going to make damned sure that justice was served.

Chapter 18

Rory turned onto Pheasant Lane at eleven forty-five, fifteen minutes before the open house was scheduled to start. Since she was last there, construction had been completed on the rest of the houses on the block, with the exception of one, where the driveway was still only a muddy set of tire tracks and a Dumpster waited at the curb.

She slowed to a crawl as she neared number 16. The "For Sale" sign once again listed the hours for the open house, but there were no cars in the driveway or nearby on the street. Rory drove by and parked farther down the block to wait.

It had been a little over a week since Zeke had suggested bringing her own crowd to the next open house. Her aunt Helene had been the first to spot the ad in the real estate section of the weekend newspaper. She'd immediately called Rory and then her sister and brother-in-law. From the moment she'd been asked to help in the investigation, Helene had been awaiting the opportunity with unbridled enthusiasm, watching every detective and CSI program on television in the interest of being more helpful to her niece.

The plan was simple. Her parents and Helene were to go in first, so that the agent would be busy showing them around when Rory entered, leaving her free to explore unattended. If other people showed up, so much the better. The only variable that worried Rory was the possibility that instead of a real estate agent, Vince might be showing the house again. She'd already told him that she couldn't afford the property, and since she didn't want to admit to moonlighting, she was pretty much out of acceptable reasons for being there again. Of course, Vince had run the last open house only because the agent was ill. That wasn't likely to be the case again.

She turned off the engine and kept watch in the rearview mirror. At two minutes to twelve, an ice blue BMW turned onto the street, and Rory was relieved to see it swing into the driveway at number 16. A man of about forty, wearing chinos and a dress shirt, got out of the car and hurried up the walk. He paused for a minute at the front door, fumbling with a large key ring before letting himself into the house.

Moments later the McCain/Brody car arrived and parked at the curb. Rory had gone over the plan with her family a dozen times, until she was confident that they understood their roles. This was a one-shot deal.

Her troop of performers emerged from their car and started up the walk to the house, making a point of not looking in Rory's direction. As they reached the front door, Rory's father turned back and gave her a quick thumbs-up gesture. Her mother saw him do it and jabbed him in the ribs with her elbow. Rory took a deep breath; this was not beginning well.

After they'd been in the house for a few minutes, Rory circled the block and pulled up to the curb behind their car. She opened the glove compartment and withdrew her latest acquisition, a digital camera that fit in the palm of her hand. Since she wouldn't have time to do a thorough-enough search, she planned to take pictures of every room and then study them more closely later. If anyone questioned what she was doing, she would say that she was taking the photos to e-mail to her husband who was away on a business trip. She tucked the camera into the side pocket of her capris.

When she entered the house, she could hear Helene chattering away in the vicinity of the kitchen; words like "granite" and "center island," "sofits," and "convection" floated down the hallway to her. Evidently Helene had also spent hours learning about houses and stockpiling questions to fire at the agent.

Without hesitating, Rory took the stairs up to the second floor. At best, she had only minutes to check out each room. She started with the room that Vince had called the guest room. Standing in the center of the floor, she turned in a slow circle. Zeke had told her to look for anything that struck her as odd or out of place, even if it didn't seem at all relevant to the case. Rory withdrew the camera from her pocket and snapped photo after photo of the room. Once she returned home, she'd pop the chip into her computer and scan the rooms again at her leisure. She harbored no illusions about finding something that the forensic team had missed. And even if they had managed to overlook a clue, the cleaning service that kept the house immaculate would probably have dusted, vacuumed or washed it away by now.

Rory moved on to the little girl's room, conducting her search in the same manner. Again she came up empty. Nothing seemed to fit Zeke's criteria in this room either. Muted waves of conversation drifted up to her from the first floor. Her little team was doing a fine job after all.

She made her way down the hall to the study, which proved equally unremarkable. When she returned to the hall, she was able to hear the agent's voice more clearly. They were approaching the stairway and Rory still needed time to check out the master suite. Then Helene's voice rose above the others, rattling off questions about the burner and the boiler and requesting a tour of the heating system before they went upstairs. She'd left no stone unturned when it came to preparing for this little adventure. Rory sent her a silent "thank you."

In the master bedroom, with its soaring twelve-foot ceiling, the king-size bed was like a small island adrift on a vast sea of dove gray carpeting. The master bath, which was larger than the room Rory had grown up in, was papered in a subtle flower motif that tied in perfectly with the bed linens. If anything was not as it should be, Rory couldn't find it.

As she was about to exit the bathroom through the double doors that led back into the bedroom, she stopped short. A section of the wall that was behind the door on her left had not been papered. She hadn't noticed it at first because the area was largely hidden by the door. She checked the wall behind the door on her right and found it papered like the rest of the room.

Although this could hardly be classified as a great discovery, in deference to Zeke she would ask the agent about it before she left. There was bound to be a simple, logical explanation. Either the wallpaper hanger hadn't had time to finish working on it, or he'd run out of the paper and was waiting for another shipment to arrive. Rory took photos of the bedroom, bathroom and a walk-in closet that was larger than some studio apartments in Manhattan.

The voices of the family team were once again growing louder. Having finished touring the boiler room, they were on their way back to the stairs. Helene's voice rose several decibels above the others, as if she were trying to warn Rory that they were coming. By now the agent was probably thinking that Helene was deaf as well as annoying.

Rory slipped out of the suite and fled down the back stairs into the kitchen. The architect who'd first thought to build an additional set of stairs deserved an award of some kind.

She completed a circuit of the rooms on the main level without finding anything more of note. When the agent escorted her family back to the entryway, Rory was waiting for them. At this point it didn't really matter if someone slipped and indicated that they knew one another. Still, Arlene gave her husband another discreet jab with her elbow as a reminder to behave. Rory decided it was a good thing she didn't need their help on a regular basis or her father would be black-and-blue.

The agent asked them to sign the guest book before leaving. Then, with an unmistakable look of relief, he turned his attention to Rory.

"Hi, I'm so sorry to have kept you waiting." He

offered his hand and a flash of white teeth. "I'm Don Stuart."

"Susan Porter," Rory said, shaking his hand. She'd thought up the name on the drive there when she realized she probably shouldn't use the same name as her parents.

"Great to meet you, Susan. May I show you around?"

"Thanks, but I already did the grand tour while you were with those other folks."

"Oh," Don said, his smile vanishing. "I didn't hear you come in."

To Rory he sounded more perturbed than the situation warranted. "I didn't mind showing myself around," she assured him.

"That's fine, it's just that I can point out things along the way that you might not notice on your own."

"I have a pretty good eye for detail," she said. The agent seemed so unsettled that she was beginning to feel a little guilty about circumventing his usual routine.

Having signed the guest book, Rory's family headed to the door. Her father risked a little wink in her direction as he passed. Rory pretended not to notice.

Don produced another brilliant smile and thanked them for coming. Then he turned back to Rory. "So, if I can't show you around, can I at least answer any questions you might have?" He seemed to have regained his composure. "I feel like I'm not earning my keep."

"Actually I do have a question," she said. "I noticed that some of the wallpaper in the master bath was missing."

"Someone probably miscalculated. You know how that is." He laughed. "Anything that can go wrong, will. Not to worry, though, we're taking care of it." He paused to consult his watch. "In fact, our wallpaper guy should be here anytime now to figure out how much more to order."

Then a young couple with a little boy came in, and Rory was spared any further conversation. When she walked outside, her parents' car was gone, replaced by a beige SUV that had presumably brought the new arrivals.

As she was about to get into her own car, she spotted her parent's car turning onto the street again. Rory couldn't imagine why they'd returned. Had they left something behind? She watched as they parked close to the corner. This was getting stranger and stranger. Then her father flashed his headlights. Was he signaling her? She started walking toward their car. As she came up alongside it, the back door flew open.

"Get in," her aunt Helene whispered urgently, scooting over to leave room for her.

"What's wrong? What's going on?"

Her father rolled down his window. "It'll be easier if you just get in the car, Rory," he said in the tone of one whose patience was being sorely tested.

"Okay then," she said, sliding into the backseat.

"Close the door. Close the door," Helene ordered as soon as she was inside. "You don't want the real estate agent to see us together, do you?"

Rory pulled the door shut. "He's in the house. Besides, it doesn't really matter anymore."

"Well, it might if you need us in the future," Helene said, looking hopeful. "How did we do?"

"You did fine. You did great. Thank you all. But why did you come back?"

"Debriefing," she said, "although I'm not sure if you

should be debriefing us or we should be debriefing you."
Rory was having a hard time keeping a straight face.
Helene had always been a little out there in a sweet and
loveable sort of way, but this was over-the-top even for
her.

"Your aunt has really gotten into the whole cloak-
and-dagger bit," Rory's mom said from the front passenger seat. Her father just shook his head in silence.

"I think I may have missed my true calling," Helene
announced. "If I were twenty years younger, I'd sign up
at Langley first thing in the morning."

"Well, I'll be sure to keep you in mind the next time
I need someone to run cover for me," Rory promised,
trying to sound sincere.

"If these two are in, you can count me out," her
dad grumbled good-naturedly. "Between James Bond
back there and your mother's pointy elbows, once was
enough."

Rory thanked them again, doing her best not to laugh
until she was back in her own car.

She was driving out of the development when she
passed a white commercial van with blue lettering on its
side that read, "Paper Mates, Your Wallpaper Experts."
Beneath it was a picture of a kangaroo with rolls of
wallpaper sticking out of its pouch. There was a good
chance this was the wallpaper guy the real estate agent
was expecting. If so, he might have a definitive explanation for the missing paper. In deference to Zeke, Rory
decided to stop and see what she could find out, even
though the day was feeling more and more like a wild-
goose chase without the goose.

When she stepped out of the car, she saw that the

side panel of the van was open and a man was leaning inside.

"Hi there," Rory said as she came up behind him. He made a point of carefully stepping back from the van before straightening to his full height, no doubt a reaction to some painful encounters with low ceilings and roofs in the past. He was thin as well as tall, with ears that protruded through fine brown hair, and a prominent Adam's apple, all of which reminded Rory of the cartoon about Ichabod Crane she remembered from childhood.

"G'day," he said with an unmistakably Australian accent. He was wearing jeans and a tee shirt with the same kangaroo logo that was painted on the van.

Rory introduced herself.

"Gordon Weatherbee," he said, offering his hand. "What can I do for you?"

She explained that she'd just been to the open house on Pheasant Lane and was wondering if his company had also done the wallpaper there.

"That we did. In fact, I'm on my way there next. It seems we came up a roll short in the master bath. The order was for eight, but only seven were delivered, don't you know."

"That happened to me," Rory sighed sympathetically, "but the manufacturer swore up and down that they'd sent the right amount. Unfortunately I didn't count the rolls when I signed for them, so I had to eat the cost of ordering another roll."

Gordon was nodding. "More than likely what happened here, except it was the decorator who placed the order, may she rest in peace. I suppose she's past worrying about such things in any case," he added soberly.

"Oh my God, was she the one who fell down the stairs?" Rory gasped as if she'd just made the connection. "I read about that, but I didn't realize that was the house where it happened."

"A terrible thing. Just tragic." Gordon appeared genuinely upset.

Apparently Jeremy wasn't the only one on the planet who had not taken joy in Gail Oberlin's sudden demise.

"May I have your card?" she asked. "You never know when the wallpapering bug will bite, and my one attempt to do it myself convinced me that I shouldn't."

"That's what we count on." Gordon smiled, plucking a business card from the front pocket of his jeans.

Rory thanked him and was about to walk away when another question occurred to her. "Would you happen to know the name of the store where the bathroom paper was purchased? It's so pretty."

"That I do. Gail always worked with Anderson and Shor over in Huntington."

On her drive home, Rory tried to decide if there was any point in pursuing the trail of the missing wallpaper. Either the wrong amount had been ordered, or the wrong amount had been shipped. It seemed more like a job for an accountant than for a private investigator. And even if she did resolve the issue, there was no reason to believe that it had any connection to the case.

Still, with no other, more pressing clues to track down, it was probably worth a phone call or two. For starters she needed to see a copy of the original order form. Although Gail was sure to have had one, it was now the property of her almost ex and his fiancée, along with everything else from Gail's estate. The easier route would be through the store where she'd placed the order.

Chapter 19

The black Jeep was several cars behind Rory on the expressway. It had been behind her since she left the gas station near police headquarters. If she was being followed again, her stalker had chosen a strange vehicle for his mission. Having a higher profile than a car, the Jeep was easier to spot in her rearview mirror. On the other hand, the driver of the SUV had a more elevated seat and could keep tabs on his prey from a greater distance.

"Okay, McCain," she chastised herself out loud. "If that Jeep is following you, maybe the silver Acura on your right flank is too. Or how about the little Smart Car over there? Even a thug might be economy minded or worried about the melting of the polar ice caps." Her mouth tilted up in a crooked little smile. She was letting Zeke mess with her brain. While it was true that she'd probably been followed once before and that

Mac's office had been ransacked, she couldn't reasonably believe that every car on the road and every person she passed in the office building was after her. She simply wasn't that important or that interesting, which was just fine. She had no intentions of crying wolf to her colleagues. In spite of all the crime in the headlines, in reality "wolves" made up a very small segment of the population.

Distraction was what her renegade brain needed. She tugged her thoughts back to the meeting she'd had earlier in the week with Bonnie Anderson of Anderson and Shor Textiles. Rory had presented herself as a family friend of the late Gail Oberlin who was checking out some matters for the heirs of the estate.

"Of course I remember the order," Bonnie had bristled with indignation. "I worked with Gail forever. She was my best customer. I don't think it's even sunk in yet that she's really gone. She was such a presence."

Although Bonnie seemed to be at least superficially saddened by the designer's death, Rory had the impression that "inconvenienced" might be a better description. Words like "best customer" and "a presence" hardly spoke of a fond or intimate relationship.

Rory murmured a few generic words of understanding about how painful the loss of Gail was to family and friends.

Having exhibited what she apparently considered the proper amount of grief, Bonnie quickly slipped back into full business mode.

"I'll pull that order up for you," she said, swiveling her chair so that she was facing the computer on the side of her wraparound desk. Her fingers flew over the keyboard.

"Ah, here it is." She turned the monitor so that Rory could see the screen. "The order was clearly for eight rolls."

"May I have a copy of that for our files?"

"Not a problem." The printer was spitting out the page before she finished speaking. She handed it to Rory, who squinted at it. One of these days she was going to have to suck it up and have her eyes checked before she turned into Mr. Magoo. In any case, the number eight was written boldly in the column marked "quantity." It certainly looked as though the mistake had been made by the manufacturer.

"So," Rory remarked casually as she folded the sheet and slid it into her handbag, "I guess you never had any problems dealing with Gail."

Bonnie turned in her chair so that she was facing Rory again. "Look, I know she had a hell of a temper and she didn't always treat people right, but from my perspective she was a dream customer. She knew exactly what she wanted. After she placed an order, she never called back to change it; she never second-guessed herself. She was efficient, punctual, and she had a fabulous eye for interior design."

At least Gail seemed to have had some successful relationships in her career, with the notable exception of Elaine Stein, her former employer. But for all Rory knew, there were dozens of other disgruntled people in the decorating field whose experiences with Gail were less than wonderful.

The next morning Rory had called the manufacturer in North Carolina, using the phone number that was printed on the top of the order sheet. After being transferred from one department to another and back again, she'd finally spoken to a man who was willing and able to bring the invoice up on his computer. He told her that eight rolls of Flower Fields wallpaper had been shipped as per the original order and he would be more than happy to fax her said invoice.

Rory thanked him but declined the offer. Either someone had tampered with their records to cover up the mistake, or a roll of wallpaper had simply vanished into the ether. Maybe she should ask Zeke to look around for it in whatever dimension it was that he inhabited. In any case, that path of her investigation had run smack into a dead end.

When Rory approached the Deer Park Avenue exit, the black Jeep moved into the right lane as if the driver intended to get off there or was gambling that *she* would. In order to test her theory, Rory stayed on the express-way for another two exits. The Jeep stayed too. A few minutes later, it followed her off at Route 110 North. Coincidence? Leah insisted there were no coincidences in life. Rory hoped she was wrong. But she didn't feel threatened or nervous. It would be light out for hours yet, and the roads were congested with traffic. Had she been on some lonely rural road she might have felt differently. In any event, she wasn't planning to go straight home. It was the last day of the lease on Mac's office, and there was one more carton of files that she had to take home.

The Jeep stayed with her as she made her way north into the town of Huntington, but when she was a block away from the office, it passed her. Curious to see where it would go, Rory pulled over to the curb at a fire hydrant. A few blocks ahead of her, she watched the Jeep take the right fork that led through Cold Spring Harbor to Laurel Hollow and points west.

With a lighter heart, Rory continued around the corner to the office. She spent a few minutes making sure that she hadn't overlooked anything in the desk drawers and filing cabinets, since the furniture had come with the office. With Mac's posters and diplomas gone from the walls, the suite seemed to brood with abandonment. Rory bid it a silent farewell, slung her pocketbook over her shoulder, picked up the remaining carton and headed for the door. She nearly walked straight into Casey Landis, who was coming in.

"Ms. McCain," Casey said, glancing around the reception area. "It looks as if I've come at a bad time. Are you in the process of moving?"

"Just clearing out my uncle's things," Rory said, surprised to see the future Mrs. Oberlin there. She'd expected to have a difficult, if not impossible, time trying to set up an appointment to speak with her again and here she was.

"I have some information for you," Casey said with a cool smile that bordered on smugness, "and I'm sure you're going to want to hear it." She was wearing skin-tight yellow capris that would have shown off every bump and bulge, had there been any to show.

Rory walked the few feet back to the reception desk and set the carton down there along with her purse. "Okay. As long as we're out of here by midnight. Otherwise I have to pay for another month, or I turn into a pumpkin. I never remember which."

Casey ignored the attempt at humor. She was looking at the single chair behind the desk. "Is there someplace we could sit down?"

Rory ushered her into the main office and took a seat behind the desk, leaving Casey to choose between the two

smaller chairs in front of it. She'd briefly considered sitting next to her, but decided she needed whatever advantage being in the catbird seat offered. Casey was already
one up on her, since she knew why she was there.

"My fiancé is a wonderful man," Casey said without
preamble, "but he's as naïve as men come."

How fortunate for you, Rory thought.

"He bought your little story without question. I, on
the other hand, am not so gullible. You're not typing up
notes from your uncle's case files so that you can send
them to his clients. You're investigating Gail Oberlin's
death. And you're doing it for Jeremy."

"And how exactly did you come to that conclusion?"
Rory asked, trying for a bewildered expression.

Casey shook her head, causing her blonde hair to
swing across her shoulders in a way that no doubt hyp-
notized men. "Are you really going to try to keep up that
charade?" she asked wearily.

Rory leaned forward and locked eyes with her. "If
you have something to tell me, Ms. Landis, spit it out.
If not, this meeting is over; I'm way too busy to play
games with you."

Casey pursed her full, coral-coated lips and considered her options. "Well, here it is then," she said, pausing
a moment for dramatic effect. "You need to put Jeremy
right at the top of your list of suspects." She settled back
in her seat with a satisfied little smile and watched for
Rory's reaction.

"That doesn't make any sense. Why would he have
hired Mac to find out who killed his sister if he's the one
who did it? It's not as if he needs to appear innocent. As
far as the police are concerned, the case is closed. He's
not a suspect."

"Now that's where you're wrong."

"Okay," Rory said, intrigued in spite of herself. "You have my attention."

Casey took her time crossing one slender, yellow-clad leg over the other. "To his mother he is still very much a suspect."

Rory waited for her to elaborate, but Casey was not in any hurry. She was thoroughly enjoying the theatrics of the situation.

"And his mother thinks he killed Gail because . . . ?" Rory prompted finally, wondering if she was going to have to coax every sentence out of her.

"Well, there's a bit of a backstory to it."

"Like I said, I have until midnight."

"I don't know if you're aware of it, but Jeremy has a gambling problem, a big one."

"It never came up in conversation."

"I'm not surprised. He probably didn't mention that his family is rich either. I don't mean a condo in Florida and a new Mercedes every other year rich. I mean major real estate holdings in Manhattan rich. I mean Lear Jet and sports franchises rich."

Rory shook her head. It was unsettling to learn how much she didn't know about her "client."

"His father died a few years back, a stroke or something. And now his mother's battling liver cancer. She threatened to write Jeremy out of the will if he didn't clean up his act."

"And he didn't," Rory supplied.

"A few months ago, he owed a couple of hundred grand to some mafia guy, and he asked Gail to bail him out again. She was a hardcore bitch, but she'd always had a soft spot for her baby brother." Casey shrugged. "I

guess even that gets old after a while. When she refused
to help him this time, Jeremy was so desperate that he
even asked David to lend him the money."

"Did he?"

"He couldn't even if he'd wanted to. Don't get me
wrong, David does okay, but he doesn't have that kind
of pocket change."

Which, thought Rory, was why he and Casey were
prominently featured on Mac's list of suspects. She
wondered if this little "tip" of Casey's was actually an
effort to shift suspicion to someone else.

"Anyway," Casey went on, "according to Jeremy, not
only wouldn't Gail help him, but she was going to tell
their mother that he was still gambling. Tough love or
whatever they're calling it these days."

"So Gail winds up dead and now Jeremy has to prove
to his mother that he isn't a killer or a gambler?"

"There you have it," Casey said with a self-satisfied
smile.

Rory leaned back in her chair "I'm not sure why
you're telling me this," she said. "I don't have the sense
that you and David are particularly broken up over
Gail's death. And I doubt that you're such good citizens
that you're determined to see justice served. The fact is,
with Gail out of the way you have clearer sailing to the
altar. And given the timing of her death, you and David
will inherit her very sizeable estate. It's all rather seren-
dipitous, wouldn't you say?"

Casey recoiled as if she'd been slapped. Gone was
the look of composure that bordered on arrogance. "I
didn't have to come here and tell you any of this," she
sputtered, rising from the chair. "I was trying to do the
right thing, that's all."

She turned and stormed out of the office, the snap of her stiletto heals echoing along the hallway.

A few minutes later, Rory picked up the carton and her purse and left the office. She drove home looking forward to a quiet evening and an early bedtime. But when she turned the key in her front door it met no resistance. The door was already unlocked.

Chapter 20

Rory hesitated outside the house, her heart thrumming a ragged tune that reverberated down through her stomach. She'd locked the door when she left in the morning, hadn't she? No, she couldn't be absolutely sure. It was one of those things that she did on autopilot when she was rushing off to work, like turning off the coffeemaker or putting the milk back in the refrigerator. But the coffeemaker could be relied upon to turn itself off after an hour if she failed to do it, and the milk could be replaced for a few dollars. Unfortunately, there was a lot more at stake if she forgot to lock the door.

She drew her gun from its holster, turned the knob and slowly pushed the door open. She stepped inside. The house was strangely still, as if in entering it she'd slipped into the eye of a hurricane. It took her a moment to realize why. There was no tone indicating the alarm system was on. No way in hell had she forgotten to set that too.

She held her breath, straining to hear sounds that would mean an intruder was still on the premises. No ancient floorboards groaned under mortal weight. No door hinges squealed. No whispers penetrated the silence. If anyone else was in the house, they must be frozen in place and holding their breath too.

Still, she forced herself to count to one hundred, Mac's only bit of advice upon her graduation from the academy playing like a mantra in her head: "Never act in haste. Never act in haste."

"Ninety-nine, one hundred." Satisfied that she'd done due diligence in her uncle's memory, she called out to Zeke. There was no response from the marshal, nor any sound that might mean a trespasser was making his way toward her now that she'd given away her position.

"Zeke?!" she tried louder. What good was living in a haunted house if she couldn't even count on the resident ghost to scare intruders away? She'd be better off adopting a dog from the pound.

A moment later one of the high hats in the entryway flickered on, then off again, and Zeke appeared beside the bench. His hair and clothing looked more rumpled than usual, as if he'd just been roused from his bed. Of course, there was no actual bed, and as far as Rory understood it, the image he projected was, within certain parameters, his choice. Perhaps he was just trying to provide her with a picture of his current emotional state.

"You can put the gun away," he said soberly. "They're gone."

"Who's gone?" Rory asked, not ready to loosen her

grip on the pistol. She noticed that Zeke was wearing his gun belt, the one he'd had on the night they'd met. Had he conjured it up again, thinking that it would make him more threatening to intruders? She was pretty sure that a ghost materializing in front of them, armed or not, would have done the trick.

"You've got no need to worry," he said. "I've taken care of it."

"Taken care of what?!" Rory demanded. "What's going on here?!"

"Maybe you oughta have yourself a seat first," Zeke said, clearly taken aback by the fire that flashed in her eyes and the deep flush of color on her cheeks. "You're lookin' a mite feverish."

"I assure you, Marshal," she snapped, "that I am not about to swoon or have a bout of the vapors, whatever they're supposed to be." She regretted her tone immediately. Zeke hadn't done anything wrong, unless she counted concern for her as wrong. She'd just needed to vent her anxiety and frustration, and he was a convenient target.

"Yes, ma'am. You do whatever suits you," Zeke said. "Let me know when you've calmed down some, then we'll talk." He started to fade away.

"Okay. Okay." She took a deep breath and slid her gun back into its holster to prove that she was calming. If she let him go, she might not find out for hours what had happened in her absence, and that was even more unacceptable then being treated like she was made of glass. Besides, she had to remember that back in Zeke's day women played the part of more delicate creatures and men were obliged to take care of them. If he was having a hard time figuring out what was expected of him in any given situation, who could blame him? She could only imagine how hard it would be if their roles were reversed and she had to fit into his world. Zeke was slowly coming back into focus, as though he wasn't at all sure that he wanted to stay.

"I'm sorry, it's been a long, trying day," Rory said, doing her best to relax. "But I'm fine. Really. We can talk now."

"All right then. About an hour ago, two fellas broke in here," he said slowly, studying her face as if he still thought she might break down or faint at any moment.

With sudden clarity, Rory realized what had happened. The black Jeep *had* been following her to the office after all, because the driver wanted to make sure that she wasn't going straight home.

"They came in a black Jeep, didn't they?" she said.

"Well, it was black; that's pretty much all I can tell you about it. But how did you know that?"

"It's not important. What I want to know is whether the alarm went off."

"I didn't hear it, but I figured with all the dandy tools folks have these days, breakin' and enterin', even with alarm systems, has gotta be downright easy."

Rory had too many questions jockeying for position in her head, to waste time explaining that it wasn't quite that simple.

"Do you know what they were looking for?" she asked instead. From what she could see, the living room and dining room were exactly as she'd left them, which didn't surprise her. She already had a pretty good idea of what they'd been after.

"They weren't after cash or jewelry or the usual things. I found them in the study, goin' through the filin' cabinets and the papers on the desk. When I popped up, I scared the bejesus out of them and they ran out empty-handed." Zeke seemed to puff up with pride over his triumph.

Rory had finally reached the limits of her ability to remain passive and calm. "Did they get into my computer files?" she asked as she ran up the stairs.

Zeke was already on the upper landing, waiting for her. "I don't think so. But there's somethin' more you need to know."

She stopped short, two risers below him.

"There's no easy way to say this, so I'm just gonna say it. They were the same two fellas who murdered Mac."

Rory crumpled onto the step as if all of her muscles and bones had suddenly dissolved into gelatin. After having heard all of the marshal's theories, she thought she'd accepted the possibility that Mac's death might be linked to Gail's. Obviously she'd been guilty of what Mac liked to call "the ostrich policy." She'd buried her head deep in the sand, leaving her tail feathers to weather the storm. A ridiculous sketch of herself in that position popped into her head as she sat there, trying to absorb this stunning bit of news.

Zeke sat down on the top step. "They were lookin' for the file on Gail, weren't they?"

Rory nodded, not ready to trust her voice. In some ways nothing had really changed, and yet everything had changed. She was still tracking the same killer, but now her investigation might lead to the identification and arrest of the person or persons responsible for Mac's death as well. Until this moment she'd pretty much relegated that bit of closure to the realm of lost causes.

"Whoever's behind this wants to find out what you know," Zeke murmured, as much to himself as to her.

"Then we'll just have to keep them guessing," Rory said, more determined than ever to see the case through to its resolution. She stood up, feeling a whole lot stronger than she had any right to expect after her little meltdown.

She looked Zeke in the eye. "Are you in or out?"

"If I can't talk you out of this, than count me in," he said, moving out of her way as she marched up the last steps. "Somebody's gotta try to keep you in line." The study looked like a mini version of the office after *it* had been ransacked. Rory stepped over the fountain of papers and folders that had cascaded out of the filing cabinet and onto the floor, and went straight to the bookshelf. Based on nothing more than instinct, she'd been keeping the hard copy of Gail's file behind a world atlas and several other oversized books since the day she'd brought it home. Thanks to Zeke, it appeared undisturbed. The intruders had left before they'd had a chance to look for it there.

She brushed a few papers off the desk chair and sat down in front of the computer. When she touched the mouse, the screen came up on the home page of her filing system, the cursor blinking on the window that asked for her password. With more time and the right skills the intruders might have gained access. For a moment she felt as if she'd won a bout in a boxing match, but in reality what had she won? In spite of their impromptu encounter with Zeke, these were not the type of men who were likely to give up as long as they were being well paid for their time and trouble. But at some point, whoever was footing the bill was going to decide that it was more cost-effective to get rid of her than to keep tabs on her.

Zeke was leaning against the doorjamb, thumbs hooked into his gun belt. "Anythin' gone missin'?"

"No," Rory said, leaning back in her chair with a sigh. "But just thinking about those creeps going through my stuff makes me want to scream. And knowing that they're the ones who killed Mac . . . it's, it's just unbearable."

"I know. Best thing to do is stop thinkin' and get busy. You have those pictures you took at the open house?"

Rory sat up straight. "Yes, but I haven't had a chance to look at them yet." She opened the lower drawer of the desk where she kept the camera and took out the memory card. Either cameras weren't on their shopping list, or the thieves had left before they'd had a chance to search the desk, once again thanks to Zeke. Had the marshal been more than smoke and mirrors, she would have jumped up and given him a great big hug.

She slipped the card into a port on her computer and set it for "slide show." She waved Zeke over to the desk as the first photo came up on the screen. Together they watched the parade of photos without comment. After the last one, Rory turned to him.

"You can see, aside from a little missing wallpaper, there's nothing that even comes close to being unusual, let alone suspicious."

Zeke nodded. "It couldn't hurt to talk to the fella who put the paper up, find out who actually opened the package when it arrived from the manufacturer."

"That's already on my 'to do' list," Rory said. "But it sure feels like we're heading down the wrong road here."

"It's not the wrong road if it's the only road around."

Rory suppressed a little groan. She hoped Zeke wasn't spending too much of his free time trying to come up with other pithy words of wisdom.

"Can you leave it so I can look at those pictures again some time?" he asked.

"Sure," Rory said, trying to figure out the best way to broach a potentially delicate question. In the end she decided to just ask what needed asking and hope that Zeke was in an understanding frame of mind.

"The thing is, if I'm not here, how will you manage to work the mouse, you know, to start the program, pause it, or maybe enlarge a photo if you want to?"

To her relief, Zeke was more pragmatic than emotional about the limits of his current condition.

"I can use energy to move things," he said. "Of course, there's the matter of whittlin' the power down to the right amount for the right job. Too little and it won't work. Too much and . . . well, don't you worry, darlin'. I'll be mighty careful about fine tunin' it."

Rory had an awful image of the computer flying across the room and into the wall at the speed of light. She realized too late that her reaction was probably written all over her face. To redeem herself, and in spite of her better judgment, she showed Zeke what he would need to do with the mouse and keys.

He was eager to start practicing right away, but she quickly put that notion to rest. "There's something more important we have to do first. You saw the men while it was still light out. I need your help to adjust the sketches of them."

"Sure enough."

Rory went downstairs to retrieve her sketch pad from

the kitchen counter where she'd left it. Zeke was sitting at the table as if he'd been waiting there for hours. The transporter on *Star Trek* had nothing on him.

She sat down next to him, flipped to the page with the first sketches of the men and showed it to him. "First, tell me what needs changing."

Zeke studied the drawings. "Okay, the tall guy is younger than I thought. Maybe still in his twenties. And he wasn't really bald; it was like he shaved his head on purpose, 'cause I could see the outline of where his hair would be if he let it grow. And his nose was flattened lookin' in the middle like maybe someone broke it for him."

Rory made the corrections.

"Now the shorter guy, I pegged his age right the first time. He had kind of a pudgy face with mean, little eyes. He was the one givin' orders. And he had a tattoo on his arm that looked like a big old snarlin' bulldog."

Rory showed Zeke the reworked sketches, and he suggested a couple of other changes. They were both so engrossed in what they were doing that they were startled when the kitchen phone rang.

"Thanks, that's a great help," Rory said as she reached for the phone.

Zeke gave her a nod and a quick salute of good-bye and disappeared to do whatever ghosts did when they weren't hobnobbing with mortals.

Rory was pleasantly surprised to find Leah on the other end of the line. They hadn't seen much of each other at work, since Leah had been helping out in a narcotics investigation.

"Do you think maybe we could meet for breakfast tomorrow?" Leah asked. "It feels like forever since we've gotten together outside of work."

Rory agreed. She'd been so caught up in settling Mac's affairs, moving into his house, taking on Jeremy's case, not to mention learning to live with a ghost, that she'd left her friendship with Leah on a back burner. But there was something in her friend's voice that didn't quite match the lighthearted tenor of her words.

"Is everything okay?" she asked. "You don't sound right."

Leah didn't try to make excuses. "Well, I do need to talk to you about something, but I'd rather wait until I see you tomorrow."

"Oh, come on now. Are you really going to make me wait?" Rory complained with a laugh.

Leah wouldn't be swayed, and she wasn't laughing. "It'll keep till then."

"Yes, but will I?"

"I guess we're going to find out."

Chapter 21

The diner was noisy, crowded with Saturday morning families of squirming children and work-weary parents. Leah was ensconced in a booth, drinking coffee when Rory arrived. Although Rory was hungrier for information than she was for food, she managed to wait until they'd given the waitress their order before she demanded satisfaction.

"Okay, what's so important that you couldn't tell me over the phone?"

Leah took another sip of her coffee before setting the cup down. "I got an interesting call right before I left work yesterday."

"And?"

"You tell me. What kind of mischief have you been up to, my friend?"

"Do I get to know who's accusing me of mischief?" Rory forced a laugh even as her pulse shifted into overdrive. It was a good bet that her little foray into private investigation was no longer as private as she'd hoped to keep it. Her goose might be well and truly cooked.

"The caller was a woman, or a man with a convincing falsetto, but she wasn't willing to identify herself. I was hoping you could tell me."

A woman—Rory ran through possible candidates in her mind. "Maybe if you told me what she said it would help narrow down the field a little."

"Well, she said she thought it was against our policy for cops to moonlight."

Rory made sure she didn't look away under Leah's scrutiny. "That was it?"

"No, she told me you were working as a private investigator. And that you were harassing people. She wasn't at all happy about it. In fact, she said that her next phone call would be to the captain. Ring any bells yet?"

There were enough bells peeling to make Rory's head feel like a virtual belfry. The leading contenders were Casey Landis and Elaine Stein, but there was always the possibility that some lesser player was the snitch. The more immediate question, though, was whether she was going to tell Leah the truth, the whole truth and nothing but the truth, or something that would temporarily blind her radar.

The waitress arrived with their breakfast. She set the plates in front of them and refilled their coffee cups. While Leah dug right into her egg white omelet, Rory made a production of pouring just the right amount of maple syrup onto her waffle and adding more sweetener and cream to her coffee. When she couldn't reasonably delay any longer, she put down her spoon and looked her friend in the eye.

"I'm not moonlighting," she said. "I've just been checking into things for someone, as a favor. No money has exchanged hands and none will. I'm not in anyone's employ."

Leah listened and nodded. "Okay, it sounds as if you've covered your ass with regard to the exact letter of your contract, if not the spirit of it. But the problem is that you've apparently been stepping on toes." Leah leaned across the table so that she could emphasize her point without shouting over the general hubbub. "If you're so sure that what you're doing is not out-of-bounds, why haven't you ever mentioned it to me?"

Rory suppressed the urge to squirm in her seat. "Because I didn't want to stick you with the moral dilemma of trying to protect a friend but feeling that you were being disloyal to the job. And I didn't want you to have to answer to the captain for any perceived lapses in my judgment."

Leah drew back and forked another wedge of omelet into her mouth. She chewed it as she thought about Rory's words. "Do any of the parties with injured toes have a legitimate reason to accuse you of harassment?"

"I've made every effort to be courteous and considerate," Rory said, feeling a twinge of guilt. Well she had, at least most of the time.

"Can you put it to rest before you dig yourself into some real deep trouble?"

Rory almost said "yes," purely as a reflex. There was no point in lying outright to Leah, and there was no way she was going to quit now that she knew that Mac had been murdered. But how could she bring her suspicions to her superiors at headquarters when she didn't have enough evidence, any evidence for that matter, other than a ghost's eyewitness account?

"I'm afraid that's not possible, and I'm sure that when I tell you everything, you'll understand why and you'll agree with my decision. For now I need you to trust me. I need you to give me some space and the time to run down some leads. Then I promise you, I swear to you, Leah, I will bring the whole case in and lay it out for you and the captain."

Leah was shaking her head like a mother at a loss about what to do with a rebellious child. "I just wish you wouldn't keep going down this road alone, without backup or anything."

Rory put her hand over Leah's. "I'm not alone. I can't say any more about it than that, but you don't have to worry." If Leah only knew that her backup was a ghost, she'd probably be twice as worried, about her sanity as well as her safety.

When Rory returned home and went upstairs to the study, she found the keys on her computer moving up and down like an old player piano. She stood in the doorway for a few bewildered seconds before she realized that an invisible Zeke was manipulating the keys.

"Pardon, just conservin' energy," he said, materializing as soon as he noticed her there. "Come here, I want to show you somethin'."

Rory walked over to the desk and stood beside him. "What did you find?"

He scrolled backward through the photo array until

he found the picture he wanted. He'd clearly figured out the right amount of force needed to work the computer without destroying it in the process, for which Rory was grateful.

He pointed at the screen. "What do you think?"

She hunkered down to get a better view and instantly recognized the wall in the master bathroom where they'd run out of wallpaper.

"I already told you about that," she said with a shrug.

"No, look closer." He moved the chair to the side so that she could look at the screen head-on.

"I don't see anything," she said, impatient with herself as well as with Zeke. "Why don't you just tell me what it is I'm supposed to be seeing?"

"Look at the two panels of wallpaper to the left of the unfinished section."

"Yeah, so?"

"The flowers don't line up right."

Once he pointed it out, Rory could see what he meant. Something had definitely gone wrong there.

"How on earth did you ever notice that?" she asked in amazement. She'd been there in person and had completely missed it.

"Well, to be honest, I didn't see it myself till the ninth or tenth time I went through the pictures. Now, while it might be interestin' to find out exactly what happened there, I realize it don't necessarily mean it's got anythin' to do with Gail's death or Mac's."

"You're kidding me, right?" Rory said. "First you tell me not to overlook the smallest, most trivial detail, and now you're telling me it probably has no bearing on the case."

"No, darlin', it's like this," Zeke said patiently.

"Much as you need to look at everythin', you ought not assign too much importance to anythin' until you know its worth."

"I don't know," Rory said, trying to throttle down the irritability that was creeping into her voice. "It sounds to me like you're making up the rules as you go along."

"Now that there's the whole point. An investigation's gotta change as it goes, and you've gotta bend and change with it. You've gotta be willin' to throw out some notions and consider adoptin' others or you might as well give up before you start."

Rory was on the verge of asking him why he'd never found the fugitive he was after, if his theory worked so well. She caught herself at the last moment. Though she would have liked to hear his answer, she was pretty sure it would ignite a whole new round of sniping between them. Instead, she graciously thanked him for his help.

They spent the next twenty minutes making a list of the people she still needed to interview, what she had to ask each of them and the order in which she should try to see them. They agreed that Gordon Weatherbee would be the first.

Chapter 22

Rory was at her desk an hour before her shift started on Monday. Fortunately, since the night squad was small, no one shared the desk with her. It had apparently been a quiet night, with two domestic squabbles, a drunk and disorderly, one stolen car, and a raccoon doing a Santa Claus in someone's fireplace. As a result, her early arrival attracted more attention than she'd anticipated. The detectives, who still had an hour before they could leave, couldn't imagine why anyone would choose to come in early.

Rory had responded to their raised eyebrows by saying that since she hadn't been able to sleep anyway, she'd decided to catch up on some paperwork. For the most part, her colleagues were too sleep deprived themselves to badger her with follow-up questions.

She waited until they were over the novelty of her early arrival and back to whatever they'd been doing, before taking out the sketches she'd drawn based on Zeke's description of the intruders. She scanned them into her computer and ran the program that searched the database for matches. None were found for the taller of the two men. Either the sketch wasn't accurate enough, or he'd been lucky enough to escape the system so far. The shorter man was not as lucky. Stuart Sanford, aka William Weber, aka Michael Manning, had not only an apparent fondness for alliteration, but also a record that went back eighteen years. He'd done time for breaking and entering, assault and battery, and grand theft auto, the experience from the latter no doubt coming in handy if he was the one who stole the silver Ford and the black Jeep. Rory wondered if he'd gotten away with murder in the past, or if Mac was his first victim of that crime. She jotted down Sanford's last known address on Downing Street in Patchogue, already anticipating Zeke's admonition to stay away from him.

She was just shutting the program down when Leah walked in. Since Leah had a houseful of children, husband, dog and cat to oversee before coming to work, Rory was generally in before she was anyway, so no excuses were necessary on her part. Instead, she gave her friend a warm and hopefully innocent "hi there, nothing's up with me" kind of smile and found some paperwork that actually did require her attention.

For Rory the day dragged on interminably, both because she'd come in early and because she was eager to get to the appointment she'd made with Gordon Weatherbee after work. At a minute past four, she was up from her desk and on her way out.

"Hey, wait a sec," Leah called, running to catch up with her. "What's going on today? Whenever I glanced over at you, you were looking at the clock. And now you're sprinting out of the building. Hot date tonight?"

"I wish," Rory said, forced to slow her pace as they walked out to the parking lot together. "More like an old-fashioned case of boredom."

Leah shook her head. "You'll get no sympathy from me. Have yourself a couple of kids and you'll be too damned busy to be bored. Or to get into trouble, for that matter," she added pointedly.

Rory laughed as if getting into trouble was the furthest thing from her mind, and quickly spun the conversation in another direction by asking Leah about her youngest boy's T-ball league. When they reached her car a few moments later, she opened the door and slid inside with a lighthearted "see ya" before Leah had a chance to reprise her own line of questions.

Rory had arranged to meet Gordon Weatherbee at Anderson and Shor. It was convenient for both of them, since the store was in Huntington and he had to be there to pick up the rolls of wallpaper he would be hanging the next day.

Rory found him inside chatting with Bonnie Anderson. Once the appropriate greetings had been attended to all around, Bonnie went into the back room to find the order Gordon needed.

"I appreciate your agreeing to see me," Rory said.

"Not at all." He brushed a few wispy brown hairs back from his forehead. "But I have to say, I don't quite get why you're so interested in this little missing wallpaper issue."

Rory shrugged. "It's really just a matter of curiosity,

since I'm thinking of making an offer on the house." She wondered how many white lies it took to lose one's reservation inside the Pearly Gates.

"Good enough then," Gordon said. "I had two of my best men working that job while I finished up another one. When they told me the order was short, I didn't think too much about it, don't you know. I went by to see just how much more we needed. In fact, that was the day I met you."

"Then you're *certain* the shipment was missing a roll?"

"Well, that's where it all starts to get a little hazy." Gordon sighed. "My guys claim they never actually counted the rolls when they started on the room; they just pulled them out of the package as they needed them and in the end they were short one."

Rory nodded.

"Of course, once I went in and saw the bathroom, it was pretty obvious to me what had happened there. The guys had gone and made a mess of hanging it, mismatched edges and the like. Who knows how many panels they had to redo. It's no wonder they ran out of the paper. The worst part was that neither of them would own up to the shoddy workmanship. Each man swore up and down that he wasn't the one who screwed up. Well, someone sure as hell did and it wasn't me or the Easter Bunny. I wound up firing the two of them. I'm a pretty easygoing guy, don't you know, but one thing I won't abide is lying."

"Well, of course not," Rory said, thinking that if she were struck dead right then and there, she'd have no one to blame but herself.

Bonnie returned from the store room at that moment,

carrying two packages, one considerably smaller than the other.

"That extra roll you ordered came in too," she said, setting the packages on her desk. "I'd like you to open both of them before you leave, so there won't be any discrepancies to deal with later. That's my new policy across the board."

Gordon opened the packages with Rory and Bonnie looking on and proclaimed them to be complete. Rory and he said their good-byes and walked out together. As they were crossing the parking lot to their cars, one of the rolls of wallpaper dropped out of the package. Rory bent to retrieve it and as she handed it back to him, she had a sudden epiphany. The plastic wrap covering the wallpaper felt exactly like the piece of plastic wrap that had been tangled in Gail's hair when she was found dead at the base of the stairs.

"Thanks." Gordon smiled, taking it from her. "I sure don't want to play 'where's the missing roll?' again anytime soon."

Rory smiled back and murmured another "thanks for your time" as she turned down the aisle where she was parked. She drove out of the lot and headed home, mulling over everything Gordon had told her. On one hand, the missing roll of wallpaper and the mismatched panels seemed to have reasonable explanations that had nothing to do with Gail's death. But on the other hand, it was very possible that it was wallpaper wrapping that had been found in her hair. Gordon Weatherbee might be satisfied with his theory of what happened, but then he only knew part of the story. Rory had the unshakable feeling that she shouldn't be so quick to dismiss that single piece of evidence, that single, tangible clue.

Between that and the results of her computer search earlier in the day, she had a lot of new information to impart to Zeke when she got home. She wondered what he would make of it all. A dizzying thought struck her and she started to laugh. When on earth had it happened? At what point had a ghost become a normal and acceptable part of her life?

Chapter 23

"Kinda makes you wonder how that scrap of plastic wrappin' came to be in Gail's hair," Zeke said once Rory finished telling him about the day's events. They were sitting at the kitchen table. Although it was not yet dark outside, the room was shrouded in a sickly gray-green light, courtesy of a passing thunderstorm that was also spitting rain at the house like a mad carpenter wielding a nail gun.

Zeke rubbed his hand along his jaw, where a week's worth of stubble had sprouted overnight. Rory was pretty sure he was trying to call her attention to his new look. She'd noticed his five o'clock shadow immediately, but had chosen not to comment on it, since she'd never cared for the style and wanted to avoid a possible argument over it. For now their time would be better spent brainstorming the latest developments in the case.

She stood up and went to the refrigerator to pour

herself a glass of iced tea. The house was still warm from the heat of the day, but she preferred open windows and cold drinks to the artificial cold pumped out by the central air. Zeke never seemed to be affected by the heat, and Rory was pretty sure he wouldn't suffer in silence. "If Weatherbee is right about his workmen screwing up and using the last roll to try to fix things, then there may not be anything insidious about the plastic wrap in her hair," she said after downing half the tea.

"That little scrap's the only clue we have," Zeke said, "so I don't think we can afford to give up on it just yet. But that don't mean we can't go at this case from another angle too."

Rory brought her glass back to the table and took her seat. "That's what I've been thinking. I mean, what if the workmen weren't lying? What if *they* didn't do a lousy job of papering? What if eight rolls were ordered and eight rolls were delivered and *someone else* stole that missing roll to try to cover up evidence of the murder?"

"Whoa there," Zeke said, "that's one heck of a lot of 'what ifs.'"

Rory drank the last of her tea. "Look," she said, "what I'm getting at is that just because Gail's body was found at the bottom of the staircase, it doesn't necessarily mean that's where the initial struggle took place."

"Assumin' she was killed."

"*You're* the one who's been trying all along to convince me that she was," Rory protested. She'd never met anyone who could make her angry with so little effort.

"I just wanna make sure we don't overlook anythin'."

"Fine. But . . ." She caught herself before she said "what if" again and rephrased her thought. "There might have been blood spatter or some other evidence on that wall in the bathroom and the murderer tried to sanitize the scene by repapering it. But then he ran out of paper." Even as Rory spoke, she recognized how unlikely it was that the CSI team had missed anything of such consequence. They were trained to go into an investigation without any preconceived notions of how or where a crime was committed. They'd no doubt scrutinized every inch of the house, inside and out.

"So you're thinkin' Gail was attacked and maybe even killed in that bathroom and then she was thrown down the stairs so it would look like an accident?"

Rory shrugged. "I'm just saying that it's possible."

Zeke's brow wrinkled in thought. "You know, you might just have somethin' there. If Gail's death was staged to look like an accident and Mac's death was staged to look like a heart attack, we may have ourselves an honest-to-goodness *motis operendi* here."

The Latin words were so incongruous coming out of Zeke's mouth in his southwestern drawl that Rory couldn't help but smile. "I wasn't aware that you knew Latin," she said, working hard not to let it erupt into laughter.

Zeke's jaw tightened and he drew himself up ramrod straight in his chair. "I expect there's a heap of stuff you don't know about me. It happens that I studied the law for a time, before I decided it was all talk and no action. Most of the lawyers I knew were too fond of their own voices. I prefer being on this end of the legal system, where I can use my gun instead of runnin' my mouth."

Rory produced what she hoped was a neutral expression. She hadn't forgotten how angry Zeke became when he thought she was insulting his intelligence.

"Maybe I should see if I can talk to the workmen," she said, trying to rescue the conversation before it went off on a tangent.

"'Cept how will you know if they're lyin', unless you've got one of those lie-detector things you can hook 'em up to?"

"There's got to be something I can do. I hate to think this information is worthless."

They sat quietly for a while, considering what her next move should be. Zeke tapped his fingers noiselessly on the tabletop, and Rory made wet circle designs with the condensation from the bottom of her glass.

It was Zeke who finally broke the silence. "Let's say that either the paper on the wall, or that missin' roll of paper, was damaged durin' the crime. How would the killer have gotten rid of it?"

Rory set her glass down. "I guess he or she could burn it or bury it, or maybe even put it through a paper shredder. . . ."

"Or maybe just throw it away like any other trash, because they're so danged sure no one's goin' to be lookin' for it."

She nodded. "I guess that's a possibility, since it's not a gun or a knife we're talking about here, just some fancy paper. Still, it's hard to believe that the killer would have been brazen enough to throw away evidence at the murder site."

"You'd be downright amazed at the arrogance and stupidity of some criminals."

"Wait a second," Rory said with sudden animation, "the Dumpster."

"What's that?"

"It's kind of a large, heavy-duty bin that's trucked

into a construction site for the building debris, and then it's hauled away to a landfill."

"Did you see one of them things around there?"

"Actually there was one left, a few houses down from the murder site. The trouble is, by now they've probably finished off all the work on that block." The excitement ebbed away from her voice. "The Dumpster may not even be there anymore."

"Then what are you waitin' for?"

"You're kidding me, right? I can't exactly go Dumpster diving at night in the middle of a residential area. I'd have every dog in a two-block radius barking his head off. Not to mention that I wouldn't be able to see much."

"Every dog I've known barks durin' the daytime too," Zeke pointed out with a smile.

Rory laughed and shook her head. "During the day folks are rushing off to work or too busy with their kids to pay as much attention to the barking."

"It's also easier to get caught durin' the day."

"I can always say I think the workmen threw away an important paper of mine when they were cleaning up. If I got caught at night, my intentions would seem a lot more suspect."

"Okay then," Zeke said, "bright and early tomorrow mornin' it is."

Chapter 24

Rory was up with the sunrise. It was going to take her at least an hour to get out to Mount Sinai in rush-hour traffic. She pulled on her baggiest jeans, her oldest sneakers and a long-sleeved tee shirt to cover her arms. If she'd had a hazmat suit, she would have worn it. Although the Dumpster should have nothing but "clean" trash in it, people often took advantage of the bins to throw away other things, including kitchen garbage. She was not looking forward to her little foraging adventure. Today she would have preferred to have Zeke's job as consultant.

She found her sturdy gardening gloves in the shed behind the house. Every spring since Mac bought the house, she'd planted dozens of flowers for him, while he tackled the job of clearing the detritus of winter from the yard. A sharp, bittersweet ache accompanied the memory. She'd finished the planting this year just weeks before Mac died. Her determination to find his killer redoubled, she hurried back inside and threw the gardening gloves into a canvas tote, along with a clean plastic bag in case she was lucky enough to actually find evidence. She also added a change of clothes, since she'd have to go directly to work after her date with the Dumpster. When she turned onto Pheasant Lane, her heart sank. The Dumpster was gone. She was pulling into the closest driveway to make a U-turn when she spotted it on the back of a truck that was turning right at the far corner. If she'd arrived there even a second later, she would have missed it altogether. She whipped her car back onto the road and took off after the truck, tempering the urge to speed with the knowledge that at any moment youngsters who lived on this block might come running out of their houses.

By the time she reached the corner, the truck had turned right and was no longer in view. She made the right and drove slowly past each intersecting road, hoping to catch a glimpse of it. No luck. The truck was probably on its way to the nearest landfill, but she had no idea where that might be. She could really use the help of someone with a computer. Calling Leah was out of the question, and even if Zeke knew how to do more than just scroll through photos online, she couldn't exactly reach him by phone. She was on her own.

She backtracked to the expressway without seeing any sign of the truck and its cargo. Since landfills were few in number and never in the more affluent areas of a town, there was a good chance that the driver had taken the highway, but in which direction? The traffic light she was stopped at turned green, forcing her to make a decision. Reasoning that the land farther east on the

Island was both less populated and less expensive, she turned onto the south service road of the expressway and took it to the first eastbound entrance ramp.

As she merged into the heavy traffic, she scanned the road ahead, straining to see past eighteen-wheelers, vans and SUVs with tinted windows. If she'd chosen the right direction, she should be able to catch up with the slower-moving truck. She made a deal with herself. If she didn't see it in a few more minutes, she'd take the next exit off and try her luck going west instead.

Time was up. Frustrated, she crossed back into the right lane, prepared to take the upcoming exit. A produce truck directly in front of her exited first, and with it out of the way, she finally had a clear view ahead. At the last moment, she swung her car out of the exit lane and back into the right lane. The Dumpster was a quarter mile ahead of her.

Once she caught up to it, she stayed close behind, determined not to lose it again. Two exits later she followed it off the expressway to County Road 21 and from there to Horseblock Road and the Brookhaven Landfill. The truck turned into the landfill, slowed as it came to a small guardhouse and was promptly waved on through by a stoop-shouldered elderly man who was leaning against the side of the wooden kiosk, smoking a cigarette.

Rory drove up to the guard, trying to decide on the best strategy to use on him. The guard dropped his cigarette butt and crushed it beneath his shoe before walking up to her door. He was wearing a white shirt with a name tag that read, "Burt Avery."

Since she hadn't come up with any brilliant plans, Rory tried a variation of the "important paper" routine.

"Sorry, miss," Avery said, "but I can't let you in there. It's an insurance issue. If you were to get injured, well, I'm sure you can understand."

What Rory understood was that she had only one ace to play. As much as she hated to use it, the thought of being turned back this close to finding what could be critical evidence was even more unacceptable. She pulled out her detective's shield and prayed that the guard would be intimidated enough to let her through without asking any questions. If he told her she needed a search warrant, she could just forget about ever locating the trash left by that particular Dumpster. As it was, the truck was already out of sight.

Avery looked from Rory to the shield and back again. Rory frowned and tried for a stern "you don't want to mess with me" expression, which was difficult given the delicate features she had to work with.

He scratched his head, disturbing the few white strands that had been arranged to camouflage his balding pate. "I don't know, Detective, I'm thinking maybe I should call the office and get permission to let you in."

"Listen," Rory said, backing off to a more affable buddy-to-buddy approach, "the police have absolutely no problem with this landfill and no interest in it other than those papers that may have accidentally wound up in the Dumpster that just went through here. I'll be fifteen minutes tops and no one need ever know I was here."

Avery was blinking rapidly, becoming more and more distraught by the decision he had to make. "Well, I guess—"

"Great, thanks," Rory said, afraid to let him finish the sentence. "I owe you one." She drove on past him before he could object. When she looked in her rearview mirror, he was still standing where she'd left him, as if frozen in his indecision.

She'd seen the truck carrying the Dumpster take the road to the left, so she headed in that direction. Looking around her, she realized that the landfill was specifically for construction-related trash. She was spared the terrible odors that came with tons of rotting food and other decaying organic material. She followed the road around the mounds of refuse, driving as fast as she dared. Her job was going to be a lot more unpleasant if the Dumpster had already disgorged its contents.

As she came around a curve, she saw the truck backed up to a relatively flat area. The door at the back of the Dumpster had been opened, and the driver was in the process of raising the truck bed beneath it, so that the trash would tumble out.

Rory sped toward him, honking as she went. She screeched to a stop a few feet away and jumped out of her car. Detective shield in hand, she approached the truck. The driver had stopped what he was doing at the sound of the horn and was stepping down from the cab as she reached him.

"Hey, what's going on?" he asked, hiking his brown work pants up beneath his pendulous belly, where they immediately began their slide down to his hips again.

"I'm Detective McCain," she said. "And you are?"

"Johnson. Norman Johnson. So what can I do for you?"

Trying to sound as authoritative as possible, Rory explained that she needed to search the contents of the Dumpster as part of an ongoing investigation.

The driver wasn't impressed. He consulted his watch and grumbled, "How long is this gonna take?"

"As long as it takes, sir," Rory replied, her tone polite but clipped. She pulled on a pair of the latex gloves that she'd taken out of the car with her, then tugged the gardening gloves over them. The type of debris she'd be going through was likely to have sharp edges.

Norman followed her to the back of the truck, where the Dumpster sat at a forty-five degree angle to the ground. Rory started going through the trash that had already fallen out. Since it was mainly comprised of large pieces of wood, metal and other building materials, she was hopeful that the wallpaper would be easy to spot.

When she was satisfied that she hadn't missed anything on the ground, she asked the driver to slowly increase the angle of the Dumpster.

"Hey," he said as he came up beside her again, "if you tell me what you're looking for, I can maybe give you a hand."

"I appreciate the offer, but I'm afraid it's completely out of the question," Rory said without looking up. "But you can go ahead and raise the Dumpster some more."

Norman walked away, muttering under his breath.

"Hold it," Rory called out a moment later. "Hold it right there." Pastel colors had caught her eye, peeking out from between other, darker debris. She pulled off the gardening gloves and carefully extricated the wallpaper from its burial place. She wanted to shout out her success or do a little end-zone dance, but given the circumstances, she settled for a whispered, "Yes!"

Although the wallpaper was torn in places and generally smudged and dirty, it was mostly intact. There appeared to be close to half a roll unwound from its spool, along with a smaller section that was separate from the rest.

"That's it?" Norman asked with an expression somewhere between disgust and disappointment, as if he'd expected her to dig out a gun or a knife at the very least. "That's what you were looking for?" He'd clearly been hoping for a juicier story to tell his chums, a story that would have compensated him for his time.

"That's it," Rory said. "Thanks for your help."

"Yeah, whatever," Norman mumbled as he climbed back into the cab of his truck.

Back at her car, Rory placed the wallpaper carefully into the plastic bag she'd brought along for that purpose and locked it in the trunk. Then she slid behind the wheel and started the engine. If her watch was right, she should have just enough time to stop at the diner near her office, grab some coffee to go and change her clothes in the ladies' room. During her lunch break she was going to pay BB another visit.

Chapter 25

"Join me, *sitzen*, have a seat." BB grinned when Rory tracked him down to the cafeteria at Health Services. In one hand he was holding what looked like tuna salad on a roll. Disinclined to put it down, he used his other hand to pull out the chair next to him.

Rory took the proferred seat and placed the bag with the wallpaper under the table, to keep it safely away from hurrying feet and spilled beverages.

"I'm sorry to be interrupting your lunch," she said.

BB chewed happily for another moment, then drank a few mouthfuls of soda to clear his palette. "Not at all. It's always a pleasure to see you. Have something; lunch is on me." He waved magnanimously toward the counter where three middle-aged women were selecting their meals.

Rory thanked him but assured him that she'd already eaten. He didn't need to know that what she'd eaten was a cheese danish with her coffee on the way to work that morning. The truth was that she didn't like eating in hospitals and morgues. She couldn't shake the feeling that microscopic bits of disease and decay circulated through the air in those buildings, eventually raining down on everything, including the food. Since BB was obviously enjoying his meal, she didn't see any point in putting him off his lunch. As she watched him take another hungry bite of his sandwich, she realized that nothing short of black mold or the bubonic plague was likely to make him lose his appetite.

"So, what can I do for you, Detective Rory, my dear?" he asked, using his napkin to wipe the residue of mayonnaise from the corners of his mouth.

Rory leaned toward him and lowered her voice, even though none of the tables closest to them were occupied.

"I think I've uncovered some evidence in Gail Oberlin's death."

"Interesting." He popped the last bit of sandwich into his mouth. "I take it you still want to keep this between us, *entre nous*, on the QT?"

"More or less."

BB licked his index finger and used it to pick up the few remaining crumbs on his plate. Then, satisfied that there was nothing left to eat, he sighed wistfully and sat back in his chair.

"Not a problem," he said. "But I'm not quite sure what it is that I can do for you."

"Well, since I don't want to go through headquarters, I was hoping you might know a forensic tech who could discreetly process the evidence for me."

"I imagine I could scare one up. What's the nature of this evidence, if you don't mind my asking?"

"Some discarded sheets of wallpaper from the murder site."

"And what are we hoping to find on it?"

"I have no idea," Rory admitted. "I'm probably tilting at windmills, but like a friend of mine says, 'When there's only one road, it has to be the right one.'" Oh great, now she was quoting Zeke.

"Well, I don't know your friend, but I've always been a big fan of Señor Quixote, myself. So let's see if we can't scrounge up some DNA for you." He chewed thoughtfully on his lower lip as he went through the Rolodex in his head.

"I believe I have just the guy for your little project," he said brightly. "Reggie Douglas. We've been friends since we were roomies at NYU several lifetimes ago. He really knew how to keep life in academia from getting dull," BB added, staring off into space with a nostalgic smile. "Almost got both of us kicked out with his shenanigans, but I wouldn't have had it any other way." He dragged himself back to the present and focused on Rory again

"In my opinion, he's the best in the business. And luckily for you, he's never been a stickler for rules he considers arbitrary, pointless or downright ridiculous."

"I can't thank you enough." Rory was so grateful that she had to restrain herself from planting a big kiss on his plump, pink cheek. The last thing she needed was to draw any attention their way.

"Now don't go getting your hopes up too high," BB cautioned as he pushed his chair back. "As good as Reggie is, sometimes there's just nothing to be found." Holding on to the table for support, he rose with a small groan. "Arthritis in the knees."

Rory nodded sympathetically and retrieved the bag with the wallpaper from under the table. She handed it to him as they walked out of the cafeteria together.

"There's a slip of paper in there with my cell phone and home phone numbers on it," she said.

"I'll give you a call as soon as I hear anything," BB promised as they reached the lobby. "Take care now, adieu, *hasta la vista*." With a wave of his hand, he headed off toward the elevators.

1878

The Arizona Territory

When Drummond left the churchyard, he turned his horse southeast, in the direction of Goose Flats. During the desperate search for Betsy Jensen, her father believed Trask had taken her to the silver mining town that had sprung up there. The town, consisting of dozens of hastily erected tents and several frame buildings that weren't favored to survive a good wind, didn't have an official name yet and couldn't be found on any map. But that didn't stop a steady influx of prospectors with the glint of silver fever in their eyes, along with prostitutes, gamblers, and businessmen of questionable ethics.

Ironically, although the marshal had not agreed with Jensen earlier, when he considered all the places that Trask might have headed *after* killing Betsy, Goose Flats came up the winner. The town's population changed by the hour, and no one cared much about his neighbor, as long as that neighbor had nothing of interest or value.

Aside from the infrequent visits of the territorial marshals, there was no one charged with enforcing the law or keeping the peace, since the town didn't exist as far as the government was concerned. That was likely to change before too long, but while it lasted, Goose Flats was the perfect place for a killer to hide out.

The only question in Drummond's mind was how long Trask could go before the need to abduct another young girl drove him out of the shadows. Betsy had been his third victim, but the intervals between her abduction and the previous two were all different. There was no way to predict when he might strike again. Only one thing was certain: if he was in Goose Flats, he wouldn't stay once the urge hit him. Families with young girls were in short supply there.

Drummond reached the town at dusk on the third day of his journey. He'd stowed his marshal's badge in his pocket ahead of time. The folks in a place like Goose Flats weren't likely to open up to a lawman the same as they might a fellow seeker of fortune.

There were no street lamps, so the only light that spilled onto the dry, rutted road at the edge of the town came from a few oil lamps and candles in the windows of the raw-boned buildings. The saloon was easy to pick out in the center of town. The large, two-story structure was glowing with light, like a sun to the lesser buildings arrayed around it.

A makeshift sign nailed over the doorway read simply, "Palmer's." The noise issuing from inside was as dense as any the marshal had heard in towns twice the size. It was a good bet that most of the population was in attendance. The question was whether or not Trask was among them.

Generally speaking, Drummond didn't much care if he was able to take a suspect alive or if he had no choice but to shoot him. He'd never yet killed a man who gave himself up, but in Trask's case he might make an exception.

He dismounted and tied the horse to the hitching post. He walked in with his hand poised over his gun and took a minute to get the lay of the place and its occupants. Trask wasn't there. Of course, that didn't account for the rooms upstairs. To the right, a bar ran the length of the room with men two deep knocking back shots of whiskey and trading stories, each more raucous than the next. The center of the room was crammed with tables, several of them with card games in play. The clientele was all men. The half dozen women Drummond spotted were clearly working for the establishment. With low-cut bodices and heavily rouged cheeks, they hovered over the customers, sat on laps and flirted with prospective bedmates. They all looked to be on the downhill side of thirty, a few even older, saloon girls past their prime who couldn't find work elsewhere.

One of the women was standing at the bottom of the staircase, leaning against the newel post. Drummond wound his way to her through the maze of tables.

"Hello there," she said once he was close enough to hear her above the din.

"Ma'am." He dipped his head in polite greeting, as if she were a lady he was passing on the streets of a finer town. As far as he knew, manners had never hurt a man, and they were likely to encourage a woman to let her guard down a bit.

"A gentleman," she said with a saucy smile that

told him she didn't entirely buy the act. "There aren't too many of your kind around here." From her smile, Drummond could see that she'd been quite beautiful once, and she still held herself as if she remembered what it felt like to attract the attentions of a man.

"Now that's a downright shame, ma'am."

"Call me Marie, Mr. . . . ?"

"Emmet'll do." He was sorry to give her a phony name, but he couldn't have Trask finding out any sooner than necessary that he was on his trail.

"Pleased to meet you, Emmet," she said with the hint of a curtsey. "What can I do for you tonight?"

He pulled a piece of paper from his shirt pocket and unfolded it. It was a sketch of Trask he'd cut from a wanted poster. The artist had created a fair likeness of the man, from the eyes as black and empty as the bore of a gun barrel, to the chin that melted into a thick stump of a neck. He held it out to her.

"That's my cousin, John Trask. I'm supposed to be meetin' up with him here. Any chance you've seen him?"

Marie appeared surprised by the turn the conversation had taken, but she studied the picture for a moment. "He's been in here all right," she said with obvious distaste. "You might not want to be advertisin' that you're related."

"Why's that?"

"He was rough with a couple of the girls when he couldn't, you know, perform. Said it was their fault. He got into a nasty tussle with Mr. Palmer over it. Palmer's guys threw him out and told him he'd be shot on sight if he so much as stuck his nose in here again."

"When did all this happen?"

"Two nights ago. But like I said, you're well rid of him." Marie smiled and sidled closer to him. "Surely there's something more I can do for a fine gentleman like yourself."

"Yes, ma'am, there surely would be, if I didn't have some serious business that needs tendin' to."

"I imagine whatever that business is, it can wait till mornin', Emmet."

"Not long ago I might have agreed with you. But temptin' as your offer is, it's been my sad experience that mixin' business with pleasure can cost a man too dearly. I found out the hard way, you don't gamble with what ain't yours to lose."

She reached up and touched his stubbled cheek, letting her fingers drift down across his lips. "There's no work to be done tonight," she said softly.

Drummond grabbed her hand and yanked it away a bit more roughly than he'd intended. He saw the surprise and rejection register in her eyes. "Sorry," he murmured. It wasn't her fault. None of this was her fault. "You take care now." He touched the brim of his hat to her and made his way to the door without looking back.

He felt oddly as if he'd found Trask, then lost him again, all in the space of a few minutes. The stone weight he'd carried in his gut for days was heavier, an anchor that could pull him down and drown him on dry land. As weary as he was, he wanted nothing more than to head out before the killer could put more miles between them. Since his horse harbored no such desire and was sorely in need of food and rest, the marshal made a middling peace with waiting until dawn.

Outside, night had settled in, its hem tucked neatly into the horizon. Drummond untied the chestnut and led him back to the stable they'd passed at the edge of town. He'd see to the horse's feed and quarters, and with the proprietor's permission, he'd bunk down there as well.

Chapter 26

Vince came for Rory at exactly six o'clock. It was
the first time their schedules had meshed for a
Saturday night together. But despite juggling a job and
an unsanctioned investigation, she'd made time to see
him twice since their first date. There'd been a hurried
weekday lunch of clams and calamari outdoors at a
little restaurant near the harbor in Port Jefferson, and
a decadent Sunday dinner at one of the gourmet steak
houses that seemed to have cropped up on every other
block in Huntington.

The time they spent together always flew by, and
Vince seemed as amazed by it as Rory was. She'd con-
fided to Leah that she thought this relationship might
really have legs. Leah was thrilled for her, demanding
details and vicariously reliving the romantic, early days
with her husband.

Zeke was somewhat less than thrilled. He seemed to

begrudge her the time she spent away from the house
and him. When she asked him point blank why he was
acting like such a curmudgeon, he disappeared in a huff
and didn't appear again for two days.

Rory resolved to be more diplomatic about what she
said to him in the future. For all she knew, lacking a cor-
poreal body eroded a person's self-confidence. After all,
he was supposed to be in another realm among blithe
spirits, not here interacting with earthbound souls.

On that Saturday afternoon before her date, she and
Zeke were sitting in the living room, strategizing about
her upcoming interview with Grace Logan. The meeting with Gail and Jeremy's mother hadn't been easy to
arrange, since so much of her time was consumed with
doctors' appointments. In fact, the last time Rory had
been scheduled to see her, the aide who attended to her
had called at the last minute to say that her charge wasn't
up to having company. Rory didn't have any choice but
to be understanding and wish her better days soon. Like
the others she'd already interviewed, Grace had no obli-
gation to see her.

Rory was so engrossed in her discussion with Zeke,
that when she remembered to look at her watch, she saw
it was almost five thirty. She excused herself as politely
as possible, but Zeke's demeanor immediately changed.
His smile evaporated, and after he'd halfheartedly
wished her a good time, he disappeared before she could
even thank him. She raced up the stairs to put on some
makeup and change her clothes, feeling a little guilty
about her hurried exit. No, she told herself firmly, she
couldn't be expected to spend her life mollycoddling an
apparition.

Still, it wasn't until she was ensconced in the leather

cushions of Vince's car that she was finally able to exorcise Zeke from her mind and focus on what promised to be a wonderful evening. Vince had scored tickets, third row center, to the production of *West Side Story* being mounted at the summer stock theater in Bellport. Rory was sure they had not come cheaply, since the theater had sold out an hour after reviewers compared the show favorably to the original Broadway production.

Vince had also made reservations for dinner at one of the upscale south shore restaurants that thrived because of their proximity to the theater. Sitting across the table from him, Rory felt wonderfully buoyant yet at ease, as if she were exactly where she was supposed to be. It seemed impossible that she'd known him for barely a month. But from day one it had been so easy to be with him. There'd been no posturing between them, no trying to embroider upon who they were, no vying to sound more intellectual or more accomplished. And by now they'd asked and answered all the most basic questions, and if they still didn't know what flavor ice cream the other preferred, or which baseball team they rooted for, it was fun to make each new discovery. For Rory it was like coloring in the outlines of their relationship.

The evening was delightful, from the crusted rack of lamb to the cassis sorbet for dessert, to the play that surpassed every one of their expectations. It was almost midnight when they drove out of the parking lot. Vince tuned the satellite radio to a classical station and by the time they reached the expressway, they'd fallen into an easy, companionable silence. Because of the hour, the road carried only a small percentage of its usual complement of vehicles, so Rory found it curious when

Vince exited the expressway and made his way to the Northern State Parkway instead.

She thought about asking him why he'd done that, but she was too sleepy to really care. Her eyes were beginning to close when Vince's voice brought her fully awake.

"Rory, is there any reason why someone would be following you?" He was peering into the rearview mirror. Even though it was dark in the car, Rory could see that he was frowning and that his mouth was set in a tight line.

She twisted around in her seat and saw a pair of headlights a few car lengths behind them. "What makes you think we're being followed?" she asked to give herself time to think. Damn, she didn't want to lie to him just when everything was going so well. Unfortunately she'd never mentioned the investigation she'd undertaken, and this hardly seemed like the best time to bring it up.

"There's a black Camry behind us," he said tersely, "and it's been there since we left the parking lot. Whenever I switch lanes, he switches lanes. I switch highways, he switches highways."

"I'm sure it's just a coincidence," she said, no longer the least bit sleepy.

"Well, we're going to find out." They were coming up on the Commack Road exit. At the last moment, Vince swung the car out of the middle lane, across the empty right lane and onto the exit ramp. Rory grabbed for the door armrest to steady herself, but the Mercedes responded without even a screech of complaint.

Vince looked in the mirror again. "The bastard's still with us, whoever he is."

Okay, it was time for confession. "I guess it might have something to do with a little investigative work that I've been doing for a friend," she said, as if it were only a remote and rather crazy possibility.

"You never mentioned anything about that before."

As they passed beneath a streetlight, Rory could see the tension working in his jaw. She didn't have to turn around again to know that the Camry was still there.

"It didn't seem important before. I mean, we were just getting to know one another and all."

"Who are you investigating for this friend—the Mob? Colombian drug lords?" Vince didn't sound as if he were trying to make a joke.

"Hardly." Rory tried for a little laugh, but it came out more like a croak. "If it was someone like that," she went on quickly, "we'd be dodging bullets, not cars. This is nothing but a half-assed effort to scare me off."

"I don't scare that easily," Vince said, "and *no one* gets away with threatening a woman who's with *me*!" He made a sharp left onto Jericho Turnpike just as the traffic light turned red.

Rory heard the squeal of the Camry's tires as it took the turn after them. Things were escalating. Whoever was following her had never before risked being pulled over for a traffic stop. Where was a cop when you needed one? She choked down a nervous giggle that was trying to make its way up her throat.

"Maybe we could lose him in some of the back streets," she suggested.

"Don't you worry about it," Vince said, taking one hand off the wheel to give her hand a reassuring squeeze. "I know just how to handle this."

Under other circumstances, Rory would have pulled

rank along with the gun in her purse, and made it clear that as a Suffolk County detective she would be calling the shots. Mac would have laughed at the pun; he'd always been a great fan of them. Thinking about him brought Rory a sense of calm and clarity. This was not the time to squabble over who took the lead. Later she would let Vince know that she was not a damsel in distress, nor was she looking for a knight to rescue her. For some women, having a man take care of them might be the answer to their fondest prayers, but for her it was a deal breaker. It occurred to her that in some ways men hadn't changed much in the century between Zeke's generation and Vince's.

Vince made a right turn onto Park Avenue, and the Camry stayed close behind them. Rory still hadn't figured out what he was planning to do. She hoped it would be obvious soon, because she just couldn't play the passive woman for much longer.

She was about to demand some information when he made a left turn into the parking lot of the Second Police Precinct. As he slowed to a stop, they both turned around in time to see the Camry start to follow them, suddenly realize where he was about to go, and swing in a wide arc back onto Park Avenue, narrowly missing a light pole and two other cars.

Chapter 27

Vince dropped Rory at her house early Sunday morning, after making her one of his special omelets. One bite and she proclaimed it the best omelet she'd ever had. It took some playful coercion on her part to wrest the secret recipe from him. He finally admitted that it was as simple as using two eggs instead of three, while not cutting down on the amount of vegetables and cheese. The result was an explosion of flavors with the eggs only playing a supporting role.

Although Rory wanted a shower and some fresh clothing when she got home, she first checked to see if she had any e-mail. When the light flickered, she looked up from the screen to find Zeke leaning against the bookcase across from her desk.

"Welcome home," he said in a tone that fell somewhere between sincere and sarcastic. Rory couldn't judge much from his face, since it was as expressionless as a poorly wrought statue.

"Thank you," she said, determined not to go looking for an argument.

"I'm surprised you didn't take a change of clothin' when you left last night."

No ambiguity there. "It was a last minute—" She stopped herself midsentence. Why on earth was she making excuses for staying the night with Vince? She was an adult living in the twenty-first century. It was Zeke's problem, not hers, if he was offended by the realities of life in this era.

"Look," she said, managing to keep her voice pleasant, "I'm not going to discuss this with you, because it's really none of your business."

Zeke seemed momentarily taken aback by the bluntness of her words. She could see in his eyes that he was backpedaling, trying to change course before he made matters worse.

"Did you have a good time?" he asked lamely.

That was more like it. "Yes, I did, at least until we noticed there was a car following us home."

The studied indifference vanished from Zeke's face and his brows drew together, producing a deep furrow between his eyes. "That's the third time, Rory. What happened?"

"I know it's the third time; I can count too." Why was he so damn good at pressing her buttons? She took a deep breath before she went on. "Vince did exactly what the police always tell people to do—he led the other car straight to a police station." She laughed at the memory. "I've never seen anyone make a U-turn that fast."

"Smart guy you have there." The sarcasm again, even closer to the surface. "At least you were in competent hands."

In spite of her vow to remain calm, he'd managed to push her over the edge. "Ezekiel Drummond, are you ever going to get it through that medieval head of yours that my own hands are quite capable enough?! And by the way, he *is* smart. And funny. And he's probably the nicest guy I've ever dated."

Zeke folded his arms across his chest and glared at her. Rory glared back, wondering how long they'd stay locked in that pose before one of them gave in. With over a hundred years of waiting under his belt, she figured Zeke would probably outlast her. She was grateful when the phone rang a few minutes into their little cold war.

"Good news, Rory girl, good news," BB said, his voice bubbling over with excitement. "Reggie has come through for us. He worked on it over the weekend, so there wouldn't be any questions asked."

"That's terrific," Rory said, excitement pushing her frustration with Zeke from her mind. "What did he find?"

"A couple of hairs, the tiniest bit of dried blood and"— he paused for effect—"a partial set of fingerprints." He sounded as enthusiastic as if he were describing a mouth-watering meal. "What he needs now is something with Gail's DNA on it, so he can see if it's a match. He could also use a set of her prints, if that's at all possible. If the prints aren't hers, then there's a good chance they belong to her killer."

Easier said than done, Rory thought. But even if she couldn't come up with a set of Gail's prints, she could at least run the prints Reggie found through the database to see if their owner had a criminal record. A DNA sample was going to be a lot harder to come by. She hadn't actually thought that far ahead, since she'd had fairly low expectations of Reggie's success, in spite of BB's glowing referral. A cheek swab was out of the question, given Gail's present location. But hair should work.

"Hair would be excellent," BB agreed when she asked him. "Her brush or comb would probably be the best source, but it's unlikely that anyone held on to those items. Do you know who has her personal effects?"

"Unfortunately her husband does, since their divorce was still pending when she died. She'd never even gotten around to changing her will."

"I see, *compris*, understood," he murmured, thinking out loud. "Even if he isn't the killer, it's unlikely that he kept anything of hers that wasn't valuable."

"Exactly."

"Not to worry, my dear," BB said, his voice rebounding with optimism. "I have complete faith in your ability to find what is needed. Don't hesitate to call on me if you have any questions. I am at your disposal morning, noon and night."

Rory hung up the phone, wishing she shared BB's faith in her.

"Well now," Zeke said, "I gather from your conversation that we're finally gettin' somewhere."

Rory jumped at the sound of his voice, having completely forgotten that he was there. Since he seemed to be over his sour mood, she was more than happy to put her anger aside as well.

"Any suggestions about where to find her DNA?" she asked.

Zeke shook his head. "I sure as hell liked it better in the old days, before investigations were based on invisible particles and microscopic specks. Back then evidence was somethin' anyone could see just by lookin' at it."

"While that may be true, it's not actually helpful," Rory pointed out.

"No, I don't suppose it is." He thought for a moment. "What about askin' Grace Logan if she has any of her daughter's things? You know, maybe Gail stopped by to see her mother and forgot a piece of clothin' there that might have a hair or two on it."

"That's a good idea," Rory said, perking up. "It's certainly worth a try, since I'm going to see her this week anyway."

"There you go," Zeke said, clearly happy that she liked his suggestion. "I aim to please."

Chapter 28

Rory left work early on Wednesday, ostensibly to visit the dentist about a filling that had fallen out. She was due at Grace Logan's house at three o'clock.

She had no trouble finding the upscale townhouse in Woodbury that had been modeled after the elegant old brownstones in Manhattan. When she rang the bell, the housekeeper came to the door. She was a tall, powerful-looking woman with short, white hair and a freshly scrubbed appearance. She introduced herself as Anna. Her last name was a strange assortment of consonants and vowels that Rory had no idea how to replicate. As she followed Anna up the wide staircase, she noticed that there was an elevator that could be accessed from the main hallway as well.

Grace Logan was resting on a love seat in a small sitting room off the master bedroom, watching a plasma television that was mounted on the wall. She seemed

small and fragile, as if age had whittled away at her too
enthusiastically. But she was meticulously groomed.
Her short blonde hair showed no signs of gray, her nails
were manicured and her eyes had been tastefully made
up. Either Anna was also a talented beautician, or Grace
had someone else on retainer. The daytime aide, who
turned out to be a full-fledged registered nurse, was sitting across the room knitting. She greeted Rory, told
her patient that she'd be back in a little while with her
medication, then left to give them privacy. Rory was
starting to understand just how well off the matriarch of
the Logan family was.

Grace switched off the television and in a voice
that was surprisingly strong for so frail a body, invited
Rory to have a seat in the armchair that was closest to
her.

"Anna," she said, "would you bring us some of that
wonderful peach iced tea you make?"

"It's actually raspberry," Anna reminded her kindly.

Grace seemed perplexed for a moment. Then she
smiled. "Oh, well of course it is. I can't imagine what I
was thinking."

After the housekeeper left, she turned to Rory. "So,
Jeremy tells me that you've taken over the investigation
into my Gail's death."

"Yes, and I want to extend my sincerest condolences
on the loss of your daughter. It must be a terrible thing
to bear."

"It is the very worst thing that can happen to a parent, even one as old and sick as I am. My only solace is
that I'll be joining her soon in a place that is far better
than this one."

Rory nodded, thinking that if all she'd heard about Gail was true, there was a good chance she wouldn't be going to the same place as her mother.

"I'm sure that having Jeremy is a comfort," she said in an effort to redirect the conversation.

Grace's smile was bittersweet. "Jeremy is a darling boy, you know, but he has his demons."

Rory decided to play dumb.

"Gambling," Grace said. "It's a horrible addiction, like drugs or alcohol, but easier to hide. Over the years his father and I tried everything to help him, psychologists, medication, support groups. I've even threatened to write him out of my will."

"How is he doing?"

Grace shrugged her narrow shoulders and sighed. "He claims that he's on the wagon, so to speak, but I can't be sure."

Anna walked in at that moment, carrying two tall glasses of the raspberry iced tea, along with coasters to place them on. When Rory had thanked her and praised the tea, the housekeeper smiled broadly and said that she'd be in the kitchen fixing dinner if she was needed. Rory was beginning to wish she had an Anna living with her too.

She set her glass down on its coaster. "Were he and Gail close?"

"In their way I suppose. She did try to look after him, being the big sister and all. I suspect that she helped him out of some tight financial situations when I refused to. But she told me not long before she died that she didn't want to keep enabling him. That's one of those million-dollar words psychologists like to throw around. They're very good at making sure everyone in the family shares in the guilt. Anyway, she was going to try what they call 'tough love.'"

"Forgive me for asking this," Rory said, as kindly as she could, "but do you think Jeremy might have been desperate enough to retaliate against that tough love?"

Grace laughed; it was a brittle sound devoid of any amusement. "Are you asking me if I think Jeremy could have hurt his sister?"

"I'm sorry. I know it must be a difficult thing to consider. But addictions make people do some terrible things and often to the people they love most." Rory waited for Grace to tear into her for having suggested such a possibility. To her surprise, Grace didn't even seem offended.

"I'm a realist, my dear, so don't think I didn't consider that possibility, as distasteful as it is. If you had asked me that question even five years ago, I would have said 'absolutely not.' But Jeremy has changed in recent years. There are times when I feel as if I don't really know him anymore, and that's a terrible thing for a mother to admit. But when the coroner determined that Gail's death was accidental, Jeremy went right out and hired your uncle to take on the investigation. And when Mr. McCain passed on so tragically, Jeremy asked you to continue it. He would never have done that if he were guilty. He may have an awful addiction, but he's not an idiot."

No, Rory thought, not an idiot at all. If Casey was right, Jeremy might just be the slyest fox of them all.

"Now then, I think we've spent quite enough time

discussing my son's flaws," Grace said firmly. "I want to know how the investigation is going."

"I may have some evidence to support the theory that Gail was murdered. That's why I have to ask the hard questions, regardless of who hired me. And I apologize again if I've come across as rude or insensitive."

"One does what one has to do," Grace said. "Tell me about this new evidence."

"I can't discuss the details yet, because it's still very speculative at this point. But it would be a great help if I could have something that belonged to Gail—a brush, or maybe an article of clothing."

Grace frowned. "I'm afraid I don't have anything like . . . oh, wait. She did borrow a shawl of mine not too long ago. She'd left her jacket at home and the weather was turning cooler."

"Has it been cleaned since she used it?"

"I don't think so. It's not the sort of thing that gets dirty easily. Would you like to see it?"

Rory said that she would. If her luck held, she might just find some DNA for Reggie after all. "There is one other thing we could really use—a set of Gail's fingerprints."

"Oh my. Anna keeps the house so shiny and spotless, I can't imagine you'd even find my fingerprints anywhere."

"Do you remember if Gail's elementary school took part in the child identification program?"

"I'd forgotten all about that; it was so many years ago. But now that you mention it . . . I recall how disturbing it was, the whole concept of having the prints in case your child went missing." Grace was staring off into space, as if she were lost in that other time when she was a young mother.

"Do you think you might still have them? Grace?" Rory asked, trying to draw her back from the past.

Grace took a moment to come around, looking a bit disoriented, like someone who'd just been awakened from a nap. "Have what, dear?"

Rory repeated the question.

"Oh, I guess it's possible," she said, struggling to focus on Rory. "I always hold on to important papers like that. My late husband, rest his soul, used to tease me about some of the things I keep in our safe."

"You mean a bank vault?"

"No, no, it's here in the house. I've never been comfortable leaving important papers in someone else's keeping."

"When you have a chance to look for the prints, would you give me a call?"

"No need. I'll have Anna take a look right now. She knows where the safe is. She knows everything. I would trust her with my life. Listen to me." Grace laughed. "I already do."

She pressed a button on the intercom that was on the end table and asked Anna to bring her the shawl and the papers from the safe. Rory sipped some more of the iced tea while they waited.

When Anna arrived, she was holding a black cashmere stole and a large manila folder overflowing with papers. She set it all down next to Grace, who in turn handed the stole to Rory and then started sorting through the papers.

Rory placed the stole gently on her lap so as not to

dislodge any potential evidence. She was dying to look at it more closely and in better light, but this was neither the time nor the place. Fifteen endless minutes later, the older woman triumphantly waved a yellowed piece of paper in the air.

"This is why I never throw out important documents," she said, as if still trying to convince her doubting husband. She handed the paper to Rory. It was deeply creased, its edges frayed, but the prints themselves seemed to be in fine shape.

"There is one more thing I wanted to ask you, if you don't mind," Rory said.

Grace nodded, but Rory could see that her eyes had become dulled with fatigue. It was clear that their meeting had taken a toll on her.

"Do you know if there was anyone special in Gail's life?" Rory asked. Even if Jeremy was quickly becoming a prime suspect, she had to make sure that she wasn't overlooking anyone.

"As a matter of fact there was," Grace said, sitting up a bit straighter. "She'd been dating a young man for a couple of months, somebody in real estate, or was it investment banking? Oh dear." She shook her head. "I get things mixed up these days. Anyway, for the first time since her marriage blew up, she actually seemed happy again."

"Did you ever meet him?"

"No, but she'd been planning to invite him here for dinner. Then out of the blue, she tells me that she thinks he's cheating on her. She'd overheard him on the phone, and she was sure he was making a date with another woman. Of course he denied it, but she didn't believe

him. After that fiasco of a husband, it was just too much
for her. She paced around the room here, raging against
him, talking about how she was going to catch him with
her."

"Did she catch him?" Rory asked. Whoever this guy
was, no one she'd interviewed had ever mentioned him,
including her brother with whom she was supposed to
be so close. Aside from whatever details she chose to
tell her mother, it appeared that Gail had kept her private life completely private.

"I'm afraid we'll never know," Grace said, her voice
quavering. "That was the night she died."

"Do you know where she was going to find him with
this other woman?"

"She didn't say, and to be honest, over the years I'd
learned not to press her for more than she wanted to
share."

"Do you happen to remember the man's name?"

"Of course I do . . . wait, let me see." Her forehead
furrowed with concentration. "You know, I had it right
on the tip of my tongue not a second ago." She looked
up at Rory. "Getting old is no picnic. I can't for the life
of me understand why they call these the 'golden years.'
Maybe they've just *forgotten* how tarnished they really
are." She giggled like a child, quite pleased with her
little joke.

The nurse knocked on the open door. She had a pill
bottle and a glass of water in her hands and an irritated
expression on her face that made it clear Rory had over-
stayed her welcome.

"I can't thank you enough for taking the time to
speak to me," Rory said as she rose. "But you probably
should get some rest now." She jotted her phone number

on a pad of paper she kept in her purse, tore out the page and set it on the end table. "I'll leave my number here in case you want to reach me."

"I'll call you as soon as that name pops into my head," Grace said. "I know it's rattling around up there somewhere."

Chapter 29

Zeke wasn't around when Rory arrived home. She went straight into the kitchen, which had the best lighting in the house, and pulled on a pair of latex gloves. Then she carefully withdrew the cashmere stole from the bag Anna had placed it in and started examining it. She found a couple of blonde hairs that were likely to be Grace's. Darker hair was harder to see against the dark fabric.

A few minutes later, she shouted a triumphant "yes!" when she found a hair that could very well be Gail's. She was depositing it in a plastic evidence bag for safe-keeping when the lights flickered and Zeke appeared beside her.

"What are we celebratin'?" he asked.

Rory pulled off the latex gloves and held up the little bag. "Thanks to you, we may have proof that the hair on the wallpaper was Gail's."

Zeke grinned so broadly that his moustache nearly reached his sideburns. He winked out of sight and almost simultaneously popped up in one of the kitchen chairs. Then, as if he were too excited to stay in one place, he popped over to another chair, and then another, before he finally wound up standing with his back resting against the wall. Rory was getting a little dizzy watching him.

"So, what do we do next?" he asked, the remnants of his smile still twinkling in his eyes. "I guess we need us a set of her prints," he answered himself before Rory could get a word out.

She picked up the prints that were on the table next to the stole. "Done."

"Hot damn, now we're gettin' somewhere."

Rory quickly claimed a chair and sat down. If Zeke decided to play musical chairs again, she didn't want to wind up with him in her lap.

"I'll drop the hair and prints off for Reggie first thing tomorrow morning," she said. "It shouldn't take long for him to compare the prints to the ones he lifted off the wallpaper. If they're not Gail's, I'll run them through the database and see if I can find a match."

"Then at least we'd know who pulled off the damaged wallpaper," Zeke said more calmly.

"I'm betting it's the same person who killed Gail."

"Could be. Could be. But you don't want to go leap-froggin' over the truth by skippin' some steps along the way."

"Mac used to say that." Rory smiled, realizing that it was becoming easier to think about Mac without her heart aching.

"And just who do you think taught him that, darlin'?"

"I do remember thinking that was a strange thing for

Mac to say. But then a lot of things have been making more sense now that I know about you."

"We made a good team," Zeke said with a touch of melancholy. But he shook it off and when he spoke again, his tone was lighter, "We're not doin' so bad either, you and me."

Before Rory could comment, he vanished and reappeared in the chair next to her.

"You still haven't told me how your meetin' with Grace Logan went," he said.

Rory summarized their conversation for him. "I was surprised at how candid she was about Jeremy's problems and all. I'm definitely going to have a little talk with him as soon as possible."

"Strangest damn case," Zeke said, mulling over all she'd told him.

BB was waiting outside the next morning when Rory drove up to the curb. He came around to her window, and she handed him an envelope with the hair and fingerprints. He told her that Reggie had already e-mailed the wallpaper prints to her office computer, in case she didn't want to waste time while she waited for the other results.

As it happened, Rory didn't have time to waste. She couldn't recall ever being quite so busy at work before. She had only ten minutes to wolf down a slice of pizza for lunch. It seemed like half the population of Suffolk County had been robbed, assaulted or injured in a hit-and-run in the past eight hours. She didn't have a chance to run the prints until the end of her shift.

She was on her way home when BB called. "The hair

and blood on the wallpaper are definitely Gail's, but the prints are not."

"The prints aren't in the system either," she said.

"Well, at least you'll be able to use them as evidence when you find the killer," he pointed out.

Rory sighed. "Don't you mean *if* I find the killer?"

"Not at all. The glass is always half full, winter always surrenders to spring, and the Yankees will beat the Red Sox and take the series this year."

Chapter 30

When Rory called Jeremy to set up a meeting, he suggested the pond in Hecksher Park at six. She arrived first, after stopping off at Starbucks to buy two frappachinos. Since it was the dinner hour, the park was quiet. The last few mothers were shepherding reluctant children out of the playground. Some of the ducks and swans had already settled in for the night, their bills tucked neatly under their wings.

Rory chose a bench in the shade. The day had been hot and humid, but as the afternoon had worn on, a welcome breeze had come through, chasing a flock of billowing clouds toward the horizon. She sat and sipped one of the iced coffee drinks while she waited.

Jeremy was ten minutes late and armed with excuses. There'd been an accident and road work, and he'd had to wait at the railroad crossing for not one, but two commuter trains to go by.

Rory assured him she didn't mind. She didn't want him to start off on the defensive. She handed him the other frappachino, apologizing because the whipped cream had deflated since she'd bought it. Jeremy was thrilled to have it; he'd been on the go all day and hadn't even had time for lunch. They drank and talked about how the investigation was going.

When Rory told him about the wallpaper she'd found in the Dumpster, he seemed interested, not concerned. When she said they'd found Gail's hair and blood on it, he seemed genuinely perplexed.

"On the wallpaper in the bathroom?" he repeated. "But then why did they find her at the bottom of the stairs?"

"We can't be sure at this point, but there are a couple of theories that would fit the facts as we know them. And best of all, we also found a set of fingerprints on the same piece of wallpaper."

"Gail's?" he asked.

"No, we've been able to rule that out. And it's actually good news, because they may very well belong to her killer. I ran them through the system, but unfortunately they didn't match anyone with a record either."

"If the killer doesn't have a record, then there's no way to identify him with those prints."

"Well, not until we arrest someone," Rory said, thinking that Jeremy was pretty knowledgeable about the subject for an English teacher. But then there were so many TV shows these days about crime scene investigators, that the public had become savvier.

Jeremy finished the last of his iced coffee and set the empty container on the bench between them. "Despite all your hard work," he said, sighing, "it doesn't sound as if we're really any closer to finding out who killed my sister." If he was the murderer, he was doing a fine job of appearing disheartened.

"You shouldn't lose hope," Rory said. "Every day I find out something new about the case. It's only a matter of time before all the bits and pieces fall into place. In fact, you may even have some of the bits and pieces we need."

Jeremy shrugged. "I told you everything I know about it."

"You said the last time you saw Gail was a week before her death."

"That's right."

"Are you sure you didn't see her or talk to her after that?"

"Of course I'm sure." Jeremy regarded her suspiciously.

"The evidence report lists all the calls she made and received from her cell phone. You called her three times the day before she died and then again on the afternoon of her death." Rory finally saw something flash in his eyes, but she couldn't tell if it was fear or sheer surprise about where her questions were going.

"That's old news," he said, recovering quickly. "I already told the police we'd been playing telephone tag. She had so many clients and meetings; it was hard to get a hold of her. It happened a lot. What are you getting at?"

"I think you went to find your sister when she didn't return your calls," Rory said, watching him closely.

Jeremy met her gaze and when he spoke, his voice was honed to a sharper edge. "I was worried about her. It never took that long for her to call me back before."

"But you were a little anxious too, weren't you?" Rory pressed him. "You'd racked up another big gambling debt, and she'd refused to help you out this time. I think you wanted a chance to plead your case again."

Jeremy shifted his position as if the bench had suddenly become uncomfortable.

"Okay," he said, "it's no big deal. I figured she'd change her mind if I made it clear how much danger I was in. When she didn't call me back by the end of the day, I called her office and her secretary told me she'd gone out to the house on Pheasant Lane. I found her car in the driveway, but when I rang the bell she didn't answer. I thought maybe she'd gone out to dinner with someone and was planning to come back for the car later. I didn't know she was lying dead inside there." His voice caught and tears welled up in his eyes.

Rory hated doing this to him, but she couldn't allow sympathy to get in the way of finding out what really happened. Too many murders were committed in the heat of the moment. Jeremy's tears could simply be for the loss of his sister, but she couldn't ignore the possibility that they could also be tears of regret and anguish for having killed her.

"You never told the police you went there," she said.

"When I heard she'd been found dead in that house, I was afraid to tell them. I was afraid they'd think *I* killed her."

"At some point you must have felt like killing her," Rory said evenly, so that Jeremy would be reacting to her words and not her tone. "Especially after she threatened to tell your mother you were still gambling."

"That's a lie," he replied hotly. "Who told you

that—the piece of crap Gail married or the shark he's already engaged to?"

"It doesn't matter where I heard it first, because I didn't put much stock in it. At least not until I spoke to your mother."

"You've been questioning my mother?!" Jeremy's face was flushed, his nostrils flared. "She's old and sick, for God's sakes. She has days when she thinks my father's still alive and Reagan is president. Ask Anna or her nurse if you don't believe me. And losing my sister has taken a terrible toll on her. You had no right to bother her."

"She didn't seem particularly bothered. In fact we enjoyed a glass of raspberry iced tea together. And in the course of our conversation, she mentioned that she'd threatened to cut you out of her will if you didn't stop gambling."

Jeremy stood up, too enraged to stay seated. "You think you have all the answers? Then tell me why I hired your uncle to find the killer after the police closed the case. And why in hell did I beg you to continue the investigation?"

"Maybe your mother said she thought the police had it all wrong. Maybe you needed to prove to her that you couldn't possibly have been involved in Gail's death."

"You're off this case," Jeremy sputtered. "You're fired. And I want you to stay the hell away from my mother."

"You know," Rory said, "that's the beauty of not actually working for you. I wasn't getting paid anyway."

Jeremy stormed off before she finished speaking.

Rory waited until he was out of sight. Then she picked up his empty container and placed it in the plastic bag she'd brought along in her purse. She tossed her own container into the trash can she passed on her way out of the park.

Chapter 31

Rory drove home, still amazed by how easy it had been to get Jeremy's prints. His anger had made him vulnerable and careless. She wondered if it occurred to him later that he'd left the empty cup behind. If so, had he rushed back to the park in a panic, hoping to find it still sitting there?

The entire meeting had gone better than she'd had any right to expect, being something of a novice and all. The only problem was that Reggie was away at a conference and wouldn't be back until Friday. She'd drop off the cup in the morning, but it would probably be Monday before she'd learn if the prints matched the ones he'd found on the discarded wallpaper. It was going to be a long four days.

When Zeke went looking for her an hour after she returned home, he found her in the narrow laundry room that had been annexed onto the kitchen when Mac remodeled the house. She was transferring a load of wet towels from the washer to the dryer.

"You're lucky you didn't get that pretty little head of yours blown off," he said grimly after Rory finished telling him about the meeting with Jeremy. "You don't go accusin' a man of murder, unless you have your gun on him and you intend to arrest him right then and there."

Rory set the dials on the dryer and hit the "start" switch without saying a word. She didn't want to argue with him. As far as she was concerned, she'd handled everything just fine. When she left the laundry room, Zeke moved back to give her room to pass.

"You overplayed your hand," he said as she went by him. "You as much as told him you think he's guilty. I'd be surprised if he waits around for the police to come knockin' at his door."

"Look," Rory said, unable to stay silent any longer, "if I keep pussyfooting around, I'll be old and gray by the time I solve this case." She unlocked the back door and yanked it open. Despite her determination to hang on to her good mood, Zeke had managed to drive a wedge of doubt into her mind. What if Jeremy did decide to run? No, he was a gambler in need of money and the money was right here in his mother's hands. And even if he *were* capable of premeditated murder, which she doubted, Grace was never alone. He'd have to go in there with an Uzi and take them all out.

She went outside, letting the screen door slam shut behind her like an exclamation point. She turned on the outdoor faucet and picked up the hose attached to it. After the heat of the day, the petunias and impatiens that bordered the brick patio looked wilted and thirsty.

Zeke watched through the screen door as she made her way around the patio, giving them a good soaking.

"You know, Marshal," she said, raising her voice over the sound of the water, "you talk a good game, but I don't for a minute believe that you were always so careful to tow the line yourself." She didn't add that if he'd followed his own rules, he might not be stuck here haunting her house.

Zeke waited until she was back inside to continue the conversation. "I don't understand why you're so sure that Jeremy is the killer," he said.

Rory was at the sink washing off her hands. "If you had been there, you'd be just as sure. His anger was completely irrational."

"Innocent people get angry too."

"But it all fits." She turned around to face him. "He had a dandy motive and he *admitted* that he went there to see her that day."

"I think that's what's botherin' me," Zeke said. "I don't think a guilty man would've been so quick to admit that. I think a guilty man would have gone and hired himself a lawyer and maybe even charged you with harassment. It's not like you were on official police business, you know."

As much as Rory hated to admit it, what Zeke said made sense. Maybe she *was* guilty of rushing to judgment. "Okay then," she challenged him, "who do you think did it?"

Zeke ran his fingers through his hair. "Well, there are plenty of other suspects," he said, detouring around her question. "Each one of them had a good enough motive, and I doubt the opportunity would have been all that hard to come by."

Rory sank down onto one of the kitchen chairs, her high spirits gone, as if they'd been a soap bubble punctured by Zeke's logic. Monday suddenly seemed even further away.

After Zeke said good night, she consoled herself with the remnants of the rum raisin ice cream she found in the freezer, read the newspaper without absorbing it and climbed into bed, both exhausted and unable to sleep.

Chapter 32

The house on Pheasant Lane was finally under contract. When Vince called early Saturday morning to say that he had a meeting with the buyer and the realtor at five 'clock, Rory assured him she didn't mind if they postponed their date for another day. Vince wouldn't hear of it. He wanted to celebrate. His good mood was so infectious that she agreed to meet him at the house at seven for a dinner reservation in nearby Port Jefferson.

Zeke didn't make an appearance all day, until, with some very suspect timing, he popped up shortly before she was to head out for her date. She didn't bother asking what he'd been up to earlier, since questions about how he spent his time were often answered in vague terms that sounded as if he was making them up as he went along. She had a feeling that he just enjoyed playing with her head.

"When will you be back?" he asked, having immediately noticed that she was dressed to go out.

"When I'm back," Rory replied. Why should she have to account for her time? "As I recall, women were emancipated back in 1920."

"So I've heard," Zeke said wryly, a grin tweaking at the corners of his mouth. "And just look where that insanity got us."

Having braced herself for a debate, she found his remark twice as funny. She started laughing and couldn't stop until her sides ached and tears were running down her cheeks. The only person who'd ever been able to make her laugh like that was Mac. It seemed that he'd rubbed off some on the marshal during their time together.

Zeke laughed along with her, which only made her laugh harder. She was gasping to catch her breath when the phone rang.

"Rory girl?" BB said. "Sounds like you're having fun there. I hope I'm not interrupting anything."

Since Rory couldn't say that she was entertaining a ghost, she said she was watching an old Marx Brothers movie.

"I love those myself. There's nothing like a good laugh to cleanse the system. I promise not to keep you long, but I just had a call from Reggie."

"I didn't think I'd hear anything until Monday. What did he say?" Her heart was beating a drumroll accompaniment to her words.

"He knows how anxious you are to find out, so he went in to take care of it this morning. He's the best kind of friend you could ask for. Do I know how to pick them or what?"

"What did he say?" Rory repeated, trying to remain calm and polite, even though she felt like reaching through the phone and shaking BB to get the answer out of him.

"Unfortunately you're not going to be thrilled with the results," he said finally. "Jeremy's prints don't match the ones on the wallpaper sample. *Lo siento*, Rory girl, I am sorry. *Je suis désolé.*"

Rory thanked him and asked him to give Reggie her thanks as well. If she could ever be of help to either of them, she would be happy to return the favor. When she clicked off the phone, she saw that Zeke was looking at her, waiting to be told the news.

"It seems that you were right once again, Marshal," she said with a sigh. "The prints are not Jeremy's. But it would have been so much easier if they had been."

"Whoever said life was supposed to be easy, darlin'?" If Zeke was gloating, he hid it well.

He was right. So what if the case took a little longer to solve? She'd always enjoyed a good puzzle. Besides, she had no intention of letting the news ruin a lovely evening of gourmet food, fine wine and great company.

She plucked her purse off the bench and headed for the door, wishing Zeke a good night. She'd barely stepped across the threshold when the telephone rang again. She hesitated for a moment, torn between answering it and not wanting to be late. How important could it be? Everyone who mattered had her cell phone number too. She pulled the door closed behind her.

As she backed out of the driveway, the caller was leaving a message: "Hello, Rory, this is Grace Logan. This old brain of mine finally coughed up that name you wanted. The fellow my Gail was dating is Vincent

Conti. Sorry I couldn't come up with the name sooner, dear. You take care now."

Grace's words echoed through the house with only Zeke to hear them. His jaw clenched with an impotent rage, he flung open the front door, splintering the frame and nearly tearing it off its hinges, only to see Rory's car turn the corner and drive out of sight.

R ory arrived on Pheasant Lane twenty-five minutes early. The day had been hot and humid in a way that Long Islanders knew only too well. As a result, it appeared that many of them had decided to stay longer at the beaches, on their boats, or poolside, because the roads were eerily empty.

She pulled into the driveway beside Vince's little Mercedes. The only other car, a Chevy sporting the dents and dings of old age, was parked at the curb. It probably belonged to the buyer, but it seemed strange to Rory that someone who could afford this house, would drive a car like that. Maybe his Ferrari was in the shop. Since there was no third car, she assumed that Vince and the real estate agent had driven there together.

She decided to wait in her car until the buyer came out, since she didn't want to intrude on any last-minute negotiations. A couple of minutes later the front door opened and a young man walked across the lawn to the Chevy. He was dressed in jeans and a tee shirt and had a knapsack slung over his arm.

Rory watched him get into his car, thinking that she'd seen him somewhere before, but she couldn't immediately place him. When she left her own car and went up to the front door, she found that it hadn't been closed

completely. She walked inside, calling out to let Vince
know she was there. There was no response. Maybe he
and the agent were celebrating the sale with a split of
champagne he'd brought along for the occasion. Yes,
that would be a very "Vince" thing to do. Instead of
shouting for him again, she'd go upstairs to the study
and say a more dignified hello to them.

When she reached the second floor, there were no
sounds of conversation. She peered into the study; no
one was there. The desk where Vince usually set his
laptop was empty. As she got closer to the master suite
she heard the flush of a toilet. Well, that explained why
he hadn't heard her. He was probably alone after all.
She walked into the master bedroom and stopped short
at the arched entry to the bathroom. The double doors
were open, but the door to the cubicle that housed the
toilet and bidet was still closed. A black canvas duffle
bag was sitting open on the granite countertop, plastic
bags of various sizes piled around it. It took a moment
for Rory to realize what she was looking at. At the same
instant Vince emerged and saw her there. It was too late
to run.

"Hi," she said cheerfully, pretending that she hadn't
noticed anything amiss. "The front door was open, so
I let myself in. I guess you didn't hear me calling your
name. How did it go?"

She was jabbering like a fool, and she could tell by
Vince's face that he wasn't buying any of it.

"I told you seven o'clock," he said, scowling at her as
if she'd just broken seven of the Ten Commandments.

Rory babbled on for another minute trying to explain
about the weather and the lack of traffic, while she tried

to absorb what was happening. How was it possible that this man, his face contorted by rage, was actually Vince—attentive, romantic, funny Vince?

She'd have to deal with all that later. Right now she had to figure out how she was going to live until later. Her gun was in her purse, but she didn't know if she could get it out before he grabbed her.

"Here I was, actually falling in love with you, and you had to go and ruin it all!" He spat the words at her, his upper lip curling into a snarl. "I thought you were different, but you're just like the others, just like Gail." He started coming toward her.

Just like Gail? So Jeremy was innocent after all. Rory was so stunned that she tripped over her own feet as she backed away from him and barely managed to keep herself from falling. Vince was the man Gail had been dating. She hadn't overheard him making a date with another woman; he'd been arranging a meeting with one of the lowlife goons he supplied. And she hadn't found him with a lover. She'd walked into the middle of a drug deal and Vince had killed her. Then he'd arranged for Mac to be killed when he started investigating Gail's death.

"The stupid bitch thought I was cheating on her," Vince went on, as if he felt the need to explain himself. "But I would never cheat on a woman. I'm a very faithful guy."

If Rory had any hopes of trying to use logic to talk him out of killing her, they were crushed beneath the weight of those incomprehensible words. She was dealing with a lunatic. At least he didn't seem to have a weapon with him. But he was stronger than she was and could probably overtake her if she tried to run.

"Look at what you've done." he was saying. "You've left me with no choice." He stopped before the archway and bent down. Rory didn't know what he was doing, but she used the precious seconds to open the clasp on her purse. Her gun might be her only chance. But would she have time to aim and fire it before he reached her? In a hand-to-hand battle, she was pretty sure he could get it away from her. Then she would be in an even more precarious position.

When Vince stood up again, he was holding a roll of wallpaper. Weatherbee had apparently dropped it off so that one of his men could finish the bathroom.

As Rory moved backward, she fumbled in her purse, trying to get her fingers around the hilt of her pistol. Vince came at her, smacking the heavy double roll of paper against the palm of his other hand, like a batter getting the feel of the bat. She had to distract him from what she was trying to do.

"Is that how you knocked Gail out? You hit her just hard enough to stop her from struggling, but not so hard that it couldn't be explained by a fall down the stairs. Then you carried her to the staircase and pushed her down."

Vince smiled at her. It was a perverse, chilling smile, misshapen by malice. "Bravo, did you figure that out all by yourself?"

The pieces were all falling into place. "It was your own guys following us the other night."

"Nice touch, huh?"

The hilt was snuggly in her grasp. She just needed to put a few more feet between them, so that when she drew the gun on him, he wouldn't be able to knock it out of her hand with the roll of paper. She increased the length of her strides, but she was at a disadvantage walking backward.

"I'm surprised you didn't try to eliminate me as soon as you realized who I was," she said as they continued their strange dance toward the hallway.

Vince's smile gave way to a peculiar sadness. "What kind of monster do you think I am? I would never kill without having a good reason."

"Then you only asked me out to keep tabs on me," Rory murmured, a quiver of disgust snaking through her as the realization took hold.

"I needed to make sure your investigation wasn't getting too close to the truth," he said reasonably, as if anyone in those circumstances would have done the same thing"

Rory felt as if she'd been violated, emotionally as well as physically stripped bare. She had to force herself to stay focused on the moment. There would be plenty of time for self-recriminations later, if she survived. No, *when* she survived!

"It may have started out so I could keep an eye on you," Vince was saying, "but then I found myself falling in love with you." The sadness vanished as quickly as it had appeared.

"So you plan to kill me the same way you killed Gail?"

"Of course not. It would be too hard to explain a second accidental death like that. As it is, I'm going to have to come up with some creative way of disposing of you. First Gail, then McCain and now you. It's not all that easy, you know." He quickened his pace. "But now you really have to stop trying to get away from me. This is just wasting time."

Any distance Rory had managed to put between them was gone. It was now or never. She drew her pistol and was starting to squeeze the trigger when Vince uttered a gasp like a death rattle and froze in his tracks. Zeke was standing between them.

Chapter 33

Rory pulled her shot at the last moment, missing Vince's shoulder by inches. The bullet slammed into the bedroom wall behind him. Vince didn't move, but the roll of wallpaper fell out of his hand and his face went pale and slack.

Rory took a step to her right. If she should need to shoot again, she didn't want the bullet to pass through Zeke first. She doubted it could hurt him, but she didn't know if his energy would deflect the bullet from its path. Once she had Vince cleanly in her sites again, she rummaged in her purse with her free hand for the set of plastic handcuffs she carried for emergencies.

His eyes wild with confusion and some long-buried childhood fear, smooth-talking Vince was reduced to mumbling incoherently as his brain tried to make sense of what he'd just witnessed. Rory took some pleasure in seeing him floundering out of control. She ordered him to lie face down on the floor with his hands behind him. He obeyed without argument.

Zeke moved out of her way and stood watching from the sidelines, looking almost as bewildered. Rory had a few questions herself, but she didn't have the leisure to dwell on them. Sooner or later Vince was going to recover from the shock of seeing his first ghost, and she needed to get the cuffs on him before that happened.

Once she was satisfied that he was no longer a threat, she pulled out her cell phone and dialed 911, grateful that her precinct would not be the one responding. Her captain was going to demand an explanation, and she needed a little more time to come up with the right words, ones that might not lead to losing her job.

When the police arrived, Zeke made a quick exit, further adding to Conti's state of confusion. Rory would have liked to vanish as well, but since she didn't have that particular talent, she had no choice but to remain there and introduce herself to the two detectives. She briefly considered saying that she was an artist, which was true as far as it went, but the average artist didn't walk around with a gun and a set of handcuffs in her pocketbook.

As Rory had anticipated, she was obliged to follow them back to their station house to fill out a report. She kept it as vague as possible, so that she would have some leeway with what she told her captain. If the two reports didn't jibe she could be adding a felony charge to her growing list of troubles. When the lead detective tried to elicit more details, she claimed that she'd been in a state of shock, overwhelmed at having just discovered that the man she was seeing was a drug dealer who'd murdered at least one person and had probably arranged for her uncle to be killed as well. Not to mention that she'd been in a fight for her own survival. She rambled on until the detective realized he wasn't going to get any more useful information out of her. He let her go with a promise that she'd call if she remembered anything else.

When she arrived home, Zeke was waiting for her in the entry, looking a bit pale and faded like a photograph left too long in the sun. Rory figured it was probably a consequence of his recent trip and decided it would be impolite to mention it. "That was a rush," she said, kicking off her high heels and throwing her purse onto the bench. "At least until the paperwork part." The prospect of imminent death certainly made life more exhilarating. She was beginning to understand the daredevils of the world, even though she still had no intention of trying to jump across the Grand Canyon on a motorcycle or sail the seven seas in an inner tube.

"It's only excitin' when you're the one left standin'," Zeke assured her. "Throwin' caution to the wind don't always work out so well." His legs vanished, then reappeared to emphasize his point.

"I get it. Don't worry, I get it." She headed to the refrigerator for a cold beer.

Zeke was there first. He watched as Rory twisted the cap off the bottle and took a long, satisfying drink. She couldn't remember having ever been quite so thirsty before. She didn't even miss the lime.

"Now," she said, "you've got some explaining to do. I believe you said you couldn't leave this house."

"I don't get it either," he said. "I never could before, but one minute I'm listenin' to Grace Logan leavin' a message on your machine and the next thing I know, I'm standin' between you and Conti."

"What did Grace say in her message?"

"That she remembered it was Conti that Gail had gone to see the day she died."

Rory wondered how much she would have believed the message if she'd heard it before the events of that evening. She probably would have dismissed it as the faulty memory of an aging mind. So much for the reliability of her instincts. Even now, some perverse part of her was mourning the loss of what had seemed like such a promising relationship. No way, she chastised herself, no way was she going to waste the energy of a single "if only" on that psychotic bastard.

What mattered now was figuring out how Grace's message might have unlocked the door behind which Zeke had been imprisoned for more than a hundred years. She went over to the counter where the message machine's red light was blinking. When she pressed "play," she heard Grace saying pretty much what Zeke had already told her. Certainly nothing that sounded like a "eureka!" moment.

She looked up at him. "What were you thinking when you heard that?"

"I guess I was thinkin' that if Conti killed Gail and Mac, then you were goin' to be next."

"So you were worried about me?" Could the answer be as easy as that?

"I suppose." Zeke shrugged as if he didn't see why that made any difference.

"Were you ever worried about Mac?"

"A time or two."

"And you're sure you weren't able to leave here to help him?"

"That's not exactly somethin' I would have forgotten."

"No, I guess not," she said. So if her theory was right, Zeke must have assumed that Mac could take care of himself but that she couldn't. She told herself to take the high road and let it go for now. Old beliefs die hard, and Zeke had been lugging his around for decades. Their time would be better spent trying to figure out just how much concern was required to purchase him another "get out of jail free" card. But even that would have to wait until she'd had some sleep.

She rinsed out the beer bottle for the recycle bin, said good night to Zeke and headed for the stairs. He was waiting for her outside her bedroom door.

"By the way, you're welcome," he said.

Rory sighed. Apparently she wasn't going to get that sleep until he'd finished with his personal agenda. "Okay," she said wearily, "exactly what is that supposed to mean?"

"Most folks would at least say 'thank you' if someone saved their lives."

So that was it. She should have seen it coming. "Sorry to rain on your parade, Marshal, but you didn't save my life. I had everything under control. If anyone should be thanking you, it's Conti. My shot probably would have killed him, if you hadn't interrupted things."

"From what I could see, you were backin' away and he was gainin' on you."

"He wouldn't have been gaining on me once I fired that bullet into him," Rory said tartly.

"Killin' a man ain't so easy. I have my doubts about whether you could have followed through."

"The bullet in the bedroom wall says differently."

"I'll tell you what, Aurora," Zeke said, "you go right on believin' that you didn't need my help tonight, if that's what makes you happy."

Rory turned away, on the verge of stalking into her bedroom and slamming the door on his smug face. But she stopped in her tracks. In some important ways it had been a good day, and he had played a part in it, too good a day to let it end with anger.

"Look, I don't want to argue with you," she said, a bit of apology in her tone. "I . . . I mean *we* caught Mac's killer today. Why don't we just say that everything worked out for the best and not muddy it up with egos?"

The arrogant curl of Zeke's lips slowly unfurled into a smile. "Now, darlin', that's a deal I can live with. It sure has been a mighty fine day."

Chapter 34

Rory left police headquarters in Yaphank carrying a cardboard box of her personal effects. She was dry-eyed and calmer than she'd expected to be. Leah walked beside her carrying a second box, her eyes glassy with unshed tears, her jaw clenched against any further demonstration of emotion. She'd done her best to champion Rory's cause, but the captain had been immovable. Rory would have to face a disciplinary hearing. Rather than put herself through such an ordeal, Rory had decided to hand in her resignation. For sometime now her work as a sketch artist hadn't fulfilled her needs either as an artist or as a detective. She'd tried to make Leah understand that there was no point in staying in a job that she no longer wanted. With no choice in the matter, Leah had finally accepted her friend's decision and given up the crusade.

Rory had no regrets. It was a perfect time to leave.

The case against Vincent Conti was being wrapped up with little trouble. When his attorney tried to have the charges against his client reduced in exchange for the identities of the men he'd hired to kill Mac, the district attorney politely declined. Rory had given the police the name and address of Stuart Sanford, the hit man who was already a frequent flyer in the justice system, and he in turn had quickly rolled over on his partner.

Going through mug shots, she'd also been able to identify the man who'd interrupted her first date with Vince, and he had quickly spilled the names of the other dealers Vince had supplied, among them one Matthew Andrews, aka Andy.

Rory would have to testify at Conti's trial with regard to the charge of attempted murder. Anything she could do to put Conti away in prison for the rest of his life or to have him dispatched to a more permanent hell was just fine with her. It was the least she could do for Mac.

When the two women reached Rory's car, they put the boxes in the trunk and hugged one another. There was no need for words. The hug said it all.

Back home, Rory stowed the boxes in the study to go through at another time. Then she went down to the kitchen. The light on the message machine was blinking. Probably her mother or her aunt calling again to offer solace and financial help until she found another job. Rory appreciated their support, but she wasn't as upset about it as they seemed to think she should be. Thanks to Mac and her own cautious spending, she had enough in the bank to meet her needs for a while. She hadn't told anyone yet, but she was toying with the idea of starting her own PI firm. Mac had done it and so could she. In fact, she had the added advantage of being a sketch artist. It had helped her solve this case and she had no doubt that it would help her clear future cases as well. The prospect of being her own boss and taking on only the cases she wanted to pursue appealed to her.

The lights flickered. "Did you hear your messages yet?" Zeke's disembodied voice inquired while he was still in the process of materializing.

Rory was taken aback and a little annoyed that he hadn't first asked how things had gone at headquarters today. He'd been a remarkably good sounding board when she was weighing the pros and cons of her options. Based on that, she expected him to be more interested in how she was doing then in whatever messages were waiting on the machine.

"What's the big hurry? I'm not punching a time clock anymore," she said to remind him. The last thing she needed was a ghost with short-term memory loss.

He ignored the hint. "That phone's been ringin' all day. You need to listen to the messages."

"Yes, sir," she said, feeling a bit resentful, as if a best friend had forgotten her birthday. When she looked at the recorder, she was surprised to see that seven messages were waiting for her. The first was from a man she didn't know. He'd read the article in *Newsday* about how she'd found the killer behind two deaths that had not even been deemed suspicious. When he'd heard on the news that she'd resigned from the police force, he wanted to hire her. The other six messages were all variations on the same theme.

"You're famous," Zeke said, beaming with the pride of a mentor whose protégé has found success.

Rory was relieved that he hadn't started a downward spiral into dementia. He'd just been impatient to share the good news.

"I can't believe it," she said, trying to absorb everything. In a single day she'd lost her job and hit the ground running with a slew of potential clients for a new firm she had yet to establish. As it all sank in, dozen of thoughts were clamoring for her attention at the same time. She'd have to rent an office, buy another computer, a fax machine and a copier. Have a phone line brought in. Find out about liability and malpractice insurance, and the pros and cons of setting up a corporation. She'd call Mac's attorney Lou Friedlander in the morning, once her thoughts weren't quite so scattered.

"You okay, darlin'?" Zeke laughed, enjoying her wide-eyed incredulity.

"I'm better than okay, just a little shell-shocked. I hardly know what to do first."

"You should probably call back the folks who left those messages."

"Yes, I know. But what will I tell them? There's so much to do."

"Those that can't give us a week or so will have to find themselves another investigator. As I see it, we can't handle seven new cases at the same time anyway."

"We?" Rory repeated.

"We're partners, ain't we?" he asked, looking like a kid who's just been told that he can't keep the puppy that followed him home. It was an expression that seemed out of place on his rugged features.

Partners? Rory hadn't really thought about it. She'd assumed that Zeke would be there to continue offering advice and providing another perspective. Even if she hadn't needed his help to arrest Conti, she wasn't fool enough to believe that she would have solved the case so easily without him. So what was she worried about? They were already partners in fact, if not in name.

"Yes," she said. "Yes, of course we're partners." It seemed like the right moment for a handshake, but since that wasn't an option, she just nodded firmly.

Zeke smiled and inclined his head in a little bow of thanks. "Now we just need to talk about how I'm goin' to be compensated."

"You're kidding me, right?" Rory said. "What in this world could possibly be of any use to you?"

"You can take over *my* case." His words were immediate and to the point, as if he'd had them in mind for a while, perhaps ever since he first met her.

"But you told me that Mac never made any progress with it. Why do you think I can turn up anything useful if he couldn't?"

"I ain't askin' you for a guarantee of success," he said evenly. "I'm just askin' you to make the effort."

"Okay," she conceded, unable to come up with any other reason to deny his request. "As long as you understand how difficult, no, make that impossible, it's going to be."

"Yup, I got that," he said, satisfied with her terms. "So what are we goin' call this new outfit of ours?"

"I don't know. We should probably keep it simple,—something like 'McCain Investigations.'"

Zeke was frowning and rubbing his chin. "Don't I get a mention?"

"It's going to be a little awkward if someone asks to meet you," she pointed out.

"You'll tell them I'm a silent partner."

Rory suppressed a groan. If only that were true. They'd been partners for all of two minutes and they were already arguing. Given their relationship up to this point, why was she surprised?

"Fine." She sighed. If this arrangement had any chance of working, she was going to have to pick her battles, and adding his name to the title wasn't a fight worth having.

"McCain and Drummond it is." She tried to sound happier about it than she felt.

"Well now," he said, "seein' as how I'm the one with seniority and experience, I was thinkin' more along the lines of 'Drummond and McCain.' Sounds stronger that way anyhow."

Rory took a deep breath and counted to ten. She should have known that if she gave him an inch, he'd take a yard and consider it his due.

"Haven't you ever heard of compromise?" she demanded, fairly certain that if the monks of Tibet had been haunted by Zeke, not even they could have remained calm and serene.

Zeke's voice rose in counterpoint to hers. "What's the use in compromisin' when I know I'm right?"

"*That* is exactly the problem. You're always sure you're right, even when you're not!"

"No siree. There've been times I've been wrong and I damn well knew it."

"Really!?" Rory said, digging her heels in for a fight. "It must have been a couple of centuries ago, because it hasn't happened since I've known you."

Zeke wagged his head in exasperation. "You surely are one cantankerous female."

"Well, that's just fine," she shot back at him, "because you're the most frustrating, obstinate man I've ever met."

As they stood there glaring at each other, Rory was already second-guessing the wisdom of this enterprise. Time alone would be the final arbiter, but she was fairly sure that no stranger partnership had ever existed. For as long as it lasted, it was going to be one hell of a ride.